MEGALODON
FEEDING FRENZY

JE GURLEY

SEVERED PRESS
HOBART TASMANIA

MEGALODON: FEEDING FRENZY

1

September 14, 2017   Drillship *Global Kulik*, Chukchi Sea, Arctic Ocean–

For good or bad, the world runs on oil. Almost since that fateful day in 1859 when Colonel Edwin Drake sank the first oil well in Titusville, Pennsylvania, countries have fought over it. Men die for it. Intrepid explorers battle jungle insects, endure swamp-borne fevers, brave desert heat, and ply the frozen seas and tundras for crude oil. Until solar, wind, and other alternative power sources become reliable and affordable, oil will remain king. Even then, the world will still need oil.

Just over fifty percent of crude oil is refined into gasoline, diesel, jet fuel, or lubricating oil. The remainder becomes chemicals, plastic, ink, insecticide, dentures, and denture adhesive. The tires on our vehicles and the asphalt upon which they ride come from crude oil. Environmentalists decry the rape and pillage of the earth's resources and global warming through carbon emissions while using resources derived from oil. Greenpeace ships run on oil. Oil is essential in the manufacture of the Zodiac boats they use to blockade whaling ships.

Emotions run high on both sides of the subject of oil—how we get it, where we get it, and who pays the ultimate cost for it. For good or bad, the world runs on oil. Companies comb the ends of the earth in search of the black liquid that lubricates bearings and powers engines. For that reason, Global Standard Petroleum had come to the Chukchi Sea, 230,000 square miles of frigid, mostly frozen water north of the Bering Sea.

* * * *

Asa Iverson snubbed out his cigarette on the icy railing as if trying to brand the steel with a red-hot ember. He focused all his frustration on the butt; then, with grease-stained fingers, he flicked the crushed butt into the sea thirty feet below. The wind grabbed the still-smoking wad and sent it tumbling along the side of the ship until the churning waves snatched it from the air and swallowed it. The same bitter wind bit into his chaffed cheeks and cracked lips. He pulled the hood of his parka over his head and stepped away from the railing.

"God damned cold is killing me," he bitched.

"No one said it would be easy," his companion, engineer Mick Robbins, replied in a deep basso profundo voice muffled by the fur-lined parka hood pulled so tightly together that only his eyes remained visible through the narrow slit.

"Easy enough for you to say," Asa replied. "Two more weeks and you'll be in the South Pacific—sunny days, warm breezes, cold beer, and hot native women, while I'll still be stuck here freezing my nuts off." Asa grabbed his crotch with his gloved right hand to emphasize his point.

Robbins shrugged, a gesture almost lost within the confines of the heavy parka. "Oil is oil. It's no easier to find on the bottom of the Pacific Ocean than it is here in the Chukchi Sea."

Asa cracked a grin and wished he hadn't. It was too cold to smile. "Yeah, but in Micronesia, your dick doesn't freeze off when you piss over the railing."

Robbins' chuckle erupted from deep in his chest, loud and spontaneous, like the man himself. "There is that. Why not contact Global's HR rep again? Maybe the paperwork got lost or fouled up."

"Two months!" Asa growled. He felt as if he was choking on Global red tape. Every e-mail he had sent had elicited a request for further information or returned with another form to fill out. "Two months I've been hammering them for a transfer to the *Global Challenger*, and I've heard nothing. It's beginning to suck big time."

"Look, you're a master mechanic. I'm sure your transfer will come through soon."

"Not soon enough." His body shuddered as another cold chill racked his body. "God, it's cold."

"Come on. I'll buy you a coffee in the galley. You can dunk your nut sack in it until they're nice and toasty."

Asa shook his head. He needed something warm to fight the chill, but in his stomach, not on his balls. "Mmm. Sounds lovely, Mick, but I can't. I've got too much to do. The aft port thruster is acting up. Can't you feel the rig wobble between waves?"

"In a ten-foot swell?" Robbins questioned. "My sea legs aren't that developed. You're the mechanic. Me? I'm just an overpaid paper shuffler."

Asa opened the hatch into the superstructure, relishing the gust of warm air hitting his face. The ship breeze carried the familiar odor of lubricating oil, drilling mud, and sweat. Four months aboard ship had made them a part of everyday life. However, the aroma of baking bread from the ship's galley a deck below cleaved through the less appealing smells like an icebreaker through an ice floe, enticing his nostrils with its heady, yeasty fragrance. His stomach rumbled a complaint. His body had burned off the meager calories from his quick breakfast of coffee and a sweet roll in fighting the intense cold. In spite of his enormous appetite and the excellent quality of food aboard the ship, he had lost seven pounds. For a moment, he reconsidered; then, the ship lurched to port, reminding him the thruster required his attention.

The seven-hundred-fifty-foot-long drillship *Global Kulik* remained in position above the test well site using eight static anchor lines and six thrusters spaced along the keel—two large aft thrusters and four retractable thrusters amidships. The waterjet thrusters used streaming GPS data and onboard computers to compensate for the effects of wind, waves, and current, but sudden swells were more difficult to control. A weak thruster suddenly failing could place undue strain on the flexible riser pipe through which the drill reached the seabed one-hundred-fifty feet below.

"Sorry. Gotta go," he said to Robbins and hurried down the stairs ahead of him.

"Yeah, later," Robbins called after him

Along the maze of corridors, necessary because of the moon pool directly beneath the drilling derrick comprising the center of the ship, he passed the cramped crew's quarters housing the twenty-year-old drillship's sixty-five-man drilling section in four-bunk cabins. As a maintenance mechanic, he shared a tiny cabin with another mechanic, but it beat listening to the snores and smelling the farts of four others. Space aboard ship was at a premium, sometimes requiring hot bunking, when two men shared the same berth on different shifts. With a drilling crew of forty roughnecks, twenty-five drillers and crane operators, twenty scientists and medical personnel, forty technical and supervisory staff, a catering staff of fifteen, and thirty roustabouts, stewards, and cleaning crew, the corridors and passageways were usually as crowded as the inside of a mall at Christmas. A few off-shift personnel sat in the lounge watching television or playing cards. The company tried to provide various modes of entertainment for the crew, but after four long months at sea, boredom had set in.

The drillship now bored its twenty-seventh test hole, running in a straight line from the shallows of Hanna Shoals to the north, to their present position one-hundred-eighty nautical miles north of Point Hope, Alaska, and two-hundred-fifty miles west of Barrow. The twenty-six previous holes had all been dry. A few had been promising, but so far, they had not discovered a pool of oil large enough to be profitable. Number twenty-seven would be different. Asa could feel it in his bones. Seismographic readings indicated a series of fluid-filled caverns less than a thousand feet below the sea bottom. The engineers predicted a rich mixture of oil and natural gas that could supply the world's oil needs for decades. Asa had grown weary of dry holes. Any bit of good news offered hope.

He passed through the mudroom with its six large pumps sending chemical slurry through hoses down into the borehole to prevent a blowback from gas pressure. He waved at the roustabouts dumping fifty-pound bags of chemical into the mixing hoppers, conversation being impossible in the noisy compartment. Each man wore sound-dampening headphones. Asa preferred the more comfortable lightweight inserts he wore in his ears or kept on a cord around his neck. His milieu, the thruster control room, was much quieter than the mudroom pumps or the engine room.

Stu Macklin, the Dynamic Positioning Officer in charge of keeping the ship on station, saw him enter the control room and waved him over to the main panel. As usual, potato chip crumbs littered the top of the panel from an empty bag sitting beside a Styrofoam cup of coffee. Asa cringed. Each time he saw Macklin with an open cup of coffee near the panel, he expected a short circuit that would shut down all the thrusters, sending the *Kulik* into a tailspin, but the Senior DPO didn't seem to mind, and Asa didn't believe in making waves. Macklin pointed to the readings displaying data on the aft port thruster and frowned.

"I know, I know," Asa said. "I'll fix it."

"The output pressure has fallen by thirty percent," Macklin replied; then, wiped a potato chip crumb from his beard. "Maybe it sucked up some trash from the drill rig. You know how those drillers can be." Macklin's frown turned to a grimace. His constant harping to the Tool Pusher about the drill crew tossing trash over the side of the ship had made him no friends among the roughnecks or of the Safety Officer.

"I might as well check it out now, while I have the time. The way the sea's picking up, we can't afford to lose it."

Macklin nodded. "Good idea. Do you need help?" he asked.

Asa grinned and held out his hands. "Hey, I'm the best, right? If I can't fix it, it can't be fixed."

"Yeah, I keep forgetting, although you remind me often enough. Get on it. If this hole doesn't pan out, we might be moving again, maybe even shut down for the winter."

Asa sighed. "So much for lucky hole number twenty-seven."

Asa wanted oil. Every worker on an oil rig did, but if the *Global Kulik* shut down operations for the winter and returned to port, it might improve his chances at a slot on the *Global Challenger*. It looked as if he might be joining Robbins in the Pacific after all.

Every cold-ass cloud has a warm silver lining.

Passing through the port engine room, one of two engine rooms on the ship, he spared the twin 10,000-horsepower Cummins diesel engines a wary glance, feeling like Jack of *Jack and the Beanstalk* fame, sneaking between sleeping giants on his way to steal the Golden Goose. He had helped the other mechanics tune the engines to peak efficiency, but he preferred working on the smaller engines. It allowed him a little privacy and solitude on the crowded ship. The now quiescent engines, in conjunction with the steel-reinforced bow, endowed the ship with the attributes of an icebreaker, capable of plowing through the thinning ice pack during spring break up, allowing the drillship an early jump on good weather and its competitors. However, with winter fast approaching, the pack ice would soon close in around them, growing thicker every day. The drillship could not withstand the relentless pressure of miles of sea ice. The season would be over until spring thaw, and unless number twenty-seven panned out, Global might give up on Chukchi oil altogether.

The thruster sat in its own little compartment one level below the engine room. The forty-one-inch intake for the 1500-horsepower waterjet thruster was located on the ship's keel. A diverter on the water exhaust pipes channeled flow through either the twenty-nine-inch stern nozzle or the port nozzle. Asa detected something amiss as soon as he stepped into the compartment. The steady high-pitched hum of the impeller had taken on the warbling tone of a drunken contralto. The pressure gauges read too low on the exhaust lines, but the intake pressure needle edged into the red danger zone. Before shutting down the engine, he radioed Macklin to compensate with the other thrusters. He then pulled the access panel to check the impeller, expecting to see shards of metal from a worn impeller. Instead, he found a wad of what looked like stringy, pale gray feces–baby poop.

Hoping some wandering walrus had not taken a dump beside the intake; he scraped the stinking muck from the impeller and examined it with his screwdriver and a flashlight; then, took a cautious sniff. The strong, unpleasant odor did not smell like what he thought walrus shit would smell like.

At first, he thought it might be algae. A few years earlier, a ship had encountered a massive algal raft floating in the sea, and it seemed the logical conclusion. However, on closer inspection, he decided the stuff looked more like pulped *Kombu*, but unlike any kelp that he had ever seen in a bowl of *dashi*, one of his favorite Asian dishes. He decided to take a sample to the biology lab. It would give him a good excuse to see Ilsa Thorin, the biologist working on her doctorate aboard the *Kulik*.

On shore, Ilsa's moderate attractiveness would not make her stand out in a crowd, but aboard the *Kulik* with a dearth of women and over one-hundred-eighty males, she reigned as the Queen of Sheba. Her mousy appearance gave lie to the myth that all Swedish women were buxom blondes. She was too skinny for Asa's taste, but of the fifteen women on the drillship, she topped his list.

He replaced the access panel and powered up the thruster, watching the gauges until satisfied it worked properly. The gauges remained steady and the hum of the drive shaft maintained an even note.

"Singing like a soprano," he said aloud. He radioed Macklin. "Port thruster's back on line. You can add it to the mix."

Reluctant to go back outside in the cold to complete the next task on his daily list, replacing a winch motor bearing on the starboard crane amidships, he sat back to enjoy another cigarette where he wouldn't freeze his ass off. Pall Mall Reds that cost him $5.33 per pack in his hometown of New Orleans, cost $9.80 in Anchorage, almost enough to make him quit smoking. At thirty-one, he had smoked two packs a day since sixteen years of age, and his body suffered the consequences. Climbing the eleven flights of stairs from the engine room to the bridge winded him. The last time he had visited the bridge to repair a faulty weather seal on a window, he had stood outside in the corridor for two minutes catching his breath.

The throb of the thruster and the soothing smoke filling his lungs slowly worked their magic on him, easing the tensions of the day. Maybe Robbins was right. He would try HR one more time. If the *Kulik* rolled snake eyes on hole twenty-seven, his chances of transfer to the Pacific were good. After half an hour, he figured he had milked the job for all the leisure time he could and decided to get moving before he fell asleep. He remembered the strange substance he had scraped from the filter, placed it in the cellophane wrapper from his cigarette pack, and took it with him.

The labs and infirmary in the superstructure took up most of deck eight. The black-and-white linoleum tiled floor always looked as if the cleaning crew had just mopped it, and the air smelled of disinfectant and alcohol. He had no idea of the function of most of the hi-tech equipment in the various lab compartments, but since he didn't work on it, it didn't concern him. He found Ilsa sitting behind a microscope in the biology lab, amid a clutter of specimen bottles filled with seawater. She had swept her long, reddish-blonde hair into a tightly braided ponytail that draped over her right shoulder. Her thick glasses, not needed for viewing the slides, lay on the table beside her. When she looked up at his approach, he noticed the twin furrows above her too-thin nose and the intense look of concentration in her jade green eyes. He laid his prize on the desk before her like a cat presenting a dead mouse to its master.

"What's this, Mr. Iverson?" she asked, somewhat irritated at his interruption of her analysis.

Asa shook his head and offered her his best smile. "Asa, please. Mister sounds too formal." So far, their relationship had been no more than an occasional exchange of pleasantries in the cafeteria or a game of chess in the ship's lounge, but he hoped for something more. "I hoped you could tell me. I found it gumming up the works in the port thruster."

She sighed, but took a fresh slide from a box, and with a pair of tweezers, dropped a sample of the substance on the slide, before placing it beneath the lens. After almost two minutes, he began to think she had forgotten about him; then, she glanced up at him with a puzzled expression.

She cocked her head to one side and asked, "Where did you find this?"

"It was clogging the intake on the aft port thruster. What is it?"

She took another glance through the microscope. "I'm not sure."

Her uncertainty surprised him. Ilsa had never been afraid to express her opinion on matters, even at the cost of drawing hard looks from her fellow scientists. "Please tell me it's not walrus shit."

She frowned at him. "No, but it is definitely organic. It looks like kelp, but of a variety that I've never seen before, at least not living. It looks," she paused and frowned, "ancient. If I'm right, this genus of kelp hasn't been around for at least fifteen million years."

Asa swallowed hard to keep from choking. "Fifteen million …"

"Years, yes," she finished, "since the later part of the Middle-Miocene Epoch."

"That's crazy," burst out of his mouth before he could catch himself.

To his surprise, she nodded in agreement. "It would be, except I've been examining seawater samples collected over the last two days."

"And," he prompted when she fell silent.

"I've identified living phytoplankton and crab larvae thought extinct for twenty million years."

"That's …" he almost said crazy again, but caught himself. He stared at her, trying to judge if she was attempting to pull his leg. She had never displayed an active sense of humor, but her remark sounded like the punch line of a joke. Her face betrayed no telltale signs of amusement. In fact, she looked frightened. He did not doubt her findings—she would not have been aboard the drillship if she weren't a competent biologist. Global Petroleum only hired the best. Still, he had to ask. "Are you sure?"

She sighed. "Of course, I'll send samples to the biology department at the Alaska Pacific University for verification, but, yes, I'm fairly confident of my identification."

He had never studied archaeology or kept abreast of marine biology discoveries, but for some reason, the idea of viable twenty-million-year-old crabs frightened him. "Why?" he asked.

"Do you mean why the new, previously believed extinct species? It's possible they came up through the drill hole when the drill struck a cavity. Clark in the chemistry lab took gas bubble samples. He found a mixture of oxygen, nitrogen, carbon dioxide, and methane with traces of hydrogen sulfide. The kelp has a symbiotic relationship with sulfur-eating bacteria. That's how it can survive without sunlight." She smiled. "I think we've discovered an underwater biome, one that has survived since the Cenozoic Era, the Middle-Miocene Epoch, perhaps the Pliocene. This could make my career."

He was glad someone on the *Kulik* was happy, but he hated to burst her bubble. "You'd better work fast. If this hole is dry, we may pack up and go home in a week or less."

Her pale complexion paled even further. "We can't. This is ... this is a tremendous find."

"Maybe so, but it won't pay the bills, Ilsa. Global Petroleum isn't in the noble benefactor business. They want oil."

She rose from her seat. "I must speak to the captain. Maybe he—"

The entire cabin rose and fell like a rollercoaster car, leaving his stomach hanging somewhere halfway up his esophagus. Ilsa staggered into his arms. He grabbed her and held on tight, as both of them slammed into the wall. He turned to take the brunt of the impact. Her chair rolled across the room and crashed into the wall beside them with enough force to crack the wooden paneling. Glassware and laptops slid from her desk and lab tables and crashed to the floor amid a blossoming of glass fragments. Books spilled from shelves, pelting his body. The room danced for several seconds before settling again. Alarm bells began sounding throughout the ship. Ilsa stared at him stricken with horror. His stomach twisted itself into a hard knot.

"That's no thruster malfunction," he said.

"Rogue wave," Ilsa suggested.

He shook his head. "In the Arctic? Not likely."

The room righted itself but continued to shudder. He released Ilsa and stuck his head out the door to peer down the passageway. One of the staff raced down the passageway. Asa yelled at him. "Hey! What's happening?"

The man barely glanced over his shoulder as he disappeared down the stairs. In a voice rife with panic, he yelled back, "We struck an air-filled pocket with the drill. The seafloor is collapsing beneath the ship."

The tight knot in Asa's stomach began to crawl back up his throat, threatening to squeeze the air from his lungs. His heart shuddered and skipped two beats before reasserting itself. A sudden volume of gas bubbles in the water could spell disaster. The 55,000-ton drillship could float on water, but not on air.

He turned to Ilsa. "We have to get to a lifeboat. Grab your coat, anything warm." She stood and stared at him in confusion. "Move!" he yelled to snap her out of her stupor. To his relief, she took her heavy coat, a hat, and gloves from the coat rack. She glanced around the room, almost in tears at the disarray, before joining him. He had left his parka in the thruster control room, too far below decks to go after. He grabbed a voluminous bright red parka from the coat rack.

"That's Anderson's parka," Ilsa said.

That explained the large size. Jason Anderson was one of the biggest men on the ship, most of it his rotund belly. "If we see him, I'll give it back to him."

He grabbed Ilsa's hand and started down the passageway toward the stairs, lurching into the walls as the ship twisted and rolled from side to side. He worried that too much torque could snap the anchor chains. The thrusters alone could not hold the ship steady. He thought about the drill crew. Any roughnecks or drillers on the derrick and not harnessed in would have been flung into the freezing water or onto the steel deck below. If the ship rolled too far onto its side, the weight of the derrick would topple the ship.

On the way down the stairs, the abandon ship signal began to wail, seven long blasts on the air horn. He and Ilsa burst out of the hatch on the deck main level and stepped into chaos. Men bolted from open hatches and from beneath the two-hundred-foot drill tower, racing toward the four lifeboat stations in the bow, where the ships' crew worked to winch them over the side and into the heaving sea. Ninety-foot-long joints of twelve-inch-diameter drill pipe shaken loose from the vertical pipe rack. Asa watched in mute horror as a fifteen-foot-long section of metal bracing from the collapsing derrick fell on top of one hapless worker, crushing him beneath tons of twisted steel. Ilsa screamed and froze.

As the ship shook itself to pieces around them, he dragged her toward the only lifeboat already over the side of the ship, one on the forward starboard side, straight through the hail of falling debris. He trusted to luck. He took a deep breath and didn't look up or slow down in their headlong rush to reach salvation. If they stopped, they would die. If the derrick collapsed, they would have no time to avoid it. It would ensnare them in its miles of steel cable and sweep them into the depths of the sea.

The top-heavy drillship had become more unstable in the roiling sea. Sulfur hydroxide rose from bubbles breaking the surface around the ship, churning the water for five-hundred feet in all directions into a cauldron. A thick, swirling mist reeking of rotten eggs floated just above the surface, as warm water from the underwater caverns mixed with the frigid waters of the Chukchi Sea. Asa also recognized the stench as the sweet odor of dichloromethane, used as a degreaser. It occurred naturally when methane from decaying organic material mixed with chlorine under heat. If Ilsa were right, the cavern contained lots of algae and kelp.

The ship's bow slid sideways several yards, as if yanked by a giant, invisible hand. The deck tilted ten degrees to starboard. The portside lifeboats careened wildly, bright orange-and- white pendulums crashing into their cranes and shattering their fiberglass hulls like cracking an egg. Ilsa fell, pulling Asa down to the deck on top of her, a position that at any other time he would have found pleasant. Now it only slowed them down. They slid across the sloping deck toward the railing, sections of which the crew had removed to lower the lifeboats. The yawning gap loomed directly in front of them. Ilsa screamed as she slid over the side, her eyes wide with fright. Asa made a frantic grab at a steel hawser with his free hand, as the other clung desperately to Ilsa. He managed to grasp the cable but felt it go slack in his hand as he continued to slide. Just as his legs dropped over the side, the cable snapped taut. The pressure on his right arm became unbearable, as Ilsa and his combined weights threatened to pull his arm from his shoulder.

Ilsa dangled below him, staring up at him and pleading with her eyes. His gaze fell to the sea below them, a churning frigid beast waiting to suck the heat from their bodies and devour them whole. Ignoring the wrenching pain in his shoulder, Asa summoned all his strength and slowly pulled Ilsa back up the side of the ship.

"Find a foothold," he yelled down at her over the din of screeching metal and men's screams. "Anywhere to brace your feet."

He felt her scramble until she found purchase on a weld between hull plates. "Okay," she said. Her voice quavered on the verge of tears, but she retained her wits, trusting him to save her. Asa hoped she had not misplaced her faith in him. He was determined to save them both.

"Okay, now climb up my arm." She glanced back down at the sea below her and hesitated. "Hurry," he urged. He didn't know how much longer he could retain his grip in his rapidly numbing left hand.

Using the weld for traction, she climbed up his arm. The ship heaved back to port, aiding their frantic struggle to re-board the ship. As soon as she sprawled safely on the deck, Asa released her, shaking his numb arm to restart the circulation. He pulled himself farther away from the edge. Afraid to stand because of the tremors coursing through the ship like mini-earthquakes, they crawled across the deck toward the lifeboat, his dislocated right arm dragging uselessly behind him.

Despite their heroic efforts, they did not make it. The ship gave up the struggle to remain upright. The flexible riser pipe, stretched beyond its endurance, snapped at the moon pool. The tensioner cables parted with the gunshot crack of a volley from a firing squad. Like a Macy's Thanksgiving balloon that had lost its tether, the drillship floated free, bobbing wildly on the churning water. The massive *Global Kulik* groaned out its death dirge, and like a whale in Sea World showing off for the spectators, rolled over onto its belly, catapulting him and Ilsa through the air like a pair well-tossed jai-alai balls. One dizzying moment they were flying, and then struggling in the frigid water the next. The shock of the near-freezing water numbed the pain produced from striking the surface. He remembered watching the hulk of the ship falling relentlessly toward them, and then the giant wave that separated him from Ilsa as the ship landed less than ten yards away, but little else.

The heavy borrowed coat became a shroud trying to drag him to the bottom. He shed it like a molting lobster, fighting through the folds of cloth to reach the surface. The cold water seared his exposed flesh like a fire, as he frantically searched the heaving sea for Ilsa. He saw a dozen men drifting away from the rapidly sinking ship but no sign of Ilsa. The sea had taken her, as it soon would take him.

He spotted a bright yellow neoprene equipment box floating fifteen yards away, his only hope of survival. With his injured arm, he could not swim, but he kicked his legs to move his body toward it. Using only his good left arm, it took all his strength and willpower to scramble atop the box. It was too small. Every movement threatened to overturn the wobbly makeshift life raft. He curled into fetal position to keep his extremities out of the water and to steady the raft. Surprisingly, he heard no screams, no cries for help. The eerie silence after four months of constant background throbbing frightened him almost as much as the ship's sinking. He checked to make sure his earplugs weren't in and discovered them still dangling around his neck. The silence was real and disconcerting.

Asa held out little hope for rescue. He didn't know if the captain had time to radio a distress call or if any ships were in the immediate vicinity. The regular supply ship would not arrive for another day. He could expect no rescue from his fellow shipmates. None of the four lifeboats had gotten away. All had gone to the bottom with the ship. The few minutes warning would not have been enough for the crew sleeping below decks or the engine room crew to reach topside. If he had not found the kelp and taken it to Ilsa ... In the end, it would not matter. He would die of hypothermia, a slower death than drowning but just as permanent. Already, he could feel his mind shutting down from the extreme cold. He tried to do simple math problems, recall the steps necessary to break down a carburetor, but his mind would not focus. His arms and legs grew numb, as his blood pooled in his body's center to conserve heat.

Twenty minutes after the sinking, his strength almost gone, his body shivering out its last heat from his muscles, Asa saw a gray shape like a submarine's sail break the surface. He tried to wave his good left arm to hail it, but could not move. As the gray silhouette drew nearer, he decided the shape too odd, triangular, rather than oblong, to be a conning tower, and a second, smaller sail seemed to move side to side behind it.

Slowly, the entire bulk of the object surfaced. It was not a submarine or rescue craft of any kind. At first, he thought his failing mind had conjured the unbelievable hallucination, a gray ghost Grim Reaper to take him away. He stared numbly at the largest shark he had ever seen, that he had ever imagined. He estimated its length at over a hundred-eighty feet. The pale gray dorsal fin he had mistaken for the conning tower of a submarine protruded twenty-five feet into the air. The shark glided like a silent nightmare toward several bodies floating on the surface. Asa watched in horror, as the shark swallowed three bodies in one massive gulp. That the creature's eyes were dead, pupil-less white orbs only made the shark appear more ghostly. Sightless, it detected the corpses with its keen sense of smell.

Its meal finished, it turned and began circling him in a leisurely fashion. He willed his heart to stop beating, fearing the shark could hear its frantic hammering through the equipment box. He waited for the creature to eat him, almost welcoming the end to his current frozen misery. At least the entire crew of the *Global Kulik* would be together again.

To his surprise, the shark turned away and disappeared beneath the surface, leaving hardly a ripple. Had he imagined it? A few minutes later, the sound of a helicopter approaching him broke the stillness. He looked up and saw the white underbelly of a U.S. Coast Guard Sikorsky MH-60T *Jayhawk* helicopter hovering twenty feet above him. The *whoosh* of the rotors sounded like a voice speaking to him, but he could not make out the words. He tried to cry out for help with his frozen larynx and only produced a weak squeak. He watched with frozen tears, as a diver dropped from the open door and splashed into the sea beside him. He tried to help the diver fasten a harness around his chest and shoulders, but his arms and hands were too numb to work. He lay like a corpse and allowed the diver to buckle him in. He slid into the water, choking on a mouthful of icy water.

Then, he was flying again, rising in the air towards the helicopter. Helping hands drew him inside, unharnessed him, and laid him on a stretcher. He could not speak to thank them.

"He's barely alive," one of them said.

"Grab a heat pack and put it under his arms," the other replied. "He'll make it."

They hovered while they recovered the diver; then, wrapped both of them in warm blankets.

Asa glanced back down at the sea below him, but saw no sign of the drillship, Ilsa, or the giant shark he might have imagined with his fevered mind. In fact, the sea showed no sign of human involvement, except for the floating yellow equipment box fading out of sight as the helicopter turned southeast toward the Alaskan coast. The Chukchi Sea had erased all traces of man's attempt to subdue it, as easily as wiping a chalkboard.

But he was alive.

2

February 19, 2018   *Prilagat' Usiliya,* Chukchi Sea, Russia–

The sea was a jigsaw puzzle scattered by the hand of a disgruntled giant. The pieces did not fit correctly. For kilometers in every direction, open leads of dark blue water wound between patches of two-meter-thick ice. To an untrained eye, the reflection of clouds on the softly undulating surface of the water produced the mirage of a solid ice pack. Anastasiy Berezhnoy, captain of the *Arktika*-class nuclear-powered Russian icebreaker *Prilagat' Usiliya,* was no rookie. After forty-two years at sea and twenty-one years as a captain in the Arctic Ocean, he knew ice and snow as well as any native Inuit or Chukchi.

He wondered what he was doing in the Chukchi Sea. The Northern Sea Route was open. Ships plied the waters along Russia's Siberian coast between Vankarem and Yanranay unimpeded by treacherous sea ice. The extent of ice in the Arctic was a million square kilometers less than the previous winter. The thermometer hugged the -3 degrees Celsius mark. It was unlikely the water would freeze again before the spring thaw. He would much prefer to be home in Tsilik with his wife and son than wasting time staring at sea ice, but he went where his superiors told him to go. It was a new Russia, but not so new that he could disobey orders. Like the name of his ship, he would endeavor.

The one-hundred-forty-five-meter-long, twenty-four-thousand-ton icebreaker presently made fifteen knots through open water. The twin OK-900A 171-megawatt nuclear engines could push her to a top speed of twenty-one knots, but he was ever wary of ice. The icebreaker's double-hull could handle ice twice as thick as they would likely encounter, but ice was a monster lying in wait with only its eyes showing above the surface, bent on sending the unwary to an icy grave. Anastasiy was responsible for the one-hundred-forty-two lives aboard his ship—comrades and friends all. He turned to his first officer, Evgeni Aleyev, a swarthy native of the Urals. He and Aleyev had sailed together for twelve of his forty-two years as sea. The taciturn Kazakh was closer than was his own brother.

"Evgeni, inform the helmsman to steer ten degrees north of our present position."

Aleyev frowned. "Why the unscheduled change in course? Are we not still headed to the Siberian Sea as our orders read?"

Anastasiy allowed Aleyev a certain degree of familiarity that the rest of the crew did not have. None of them would dare question his command or feel it proper to remind him of his orders. "I wish to investigate the report of a fishing vessel sinking two-hundred kilometers west of Wrangel Island."

"The report is over twenty-four hours old. Surely we can do nothing for it."

"Perhaps not, but I am curious," Anastasiy replied, grinning. "It is only an hour or so out of our way."

Aleyev nodded and turned to the helmsman. "Ten degrees to starboard, Dima."

Anastasiy returned to his position near the bridge wing rail and smiled at the sight of the crew chief, Kalek Guryev, leading the night watch in exercises on the forward deck. The physical exercises were more an effort to reduce boredom than to keep them in good physical condition. Life in the Arctic kept a man hard and ready for anything. Guryev was the exception. Tall and rotund, in his white parka he looked like a polar bear stalking the deck. Anastasiy half-expected someone to shoot him with a tranquilizer dart at any moment, and then tag him with a radio collar.

He felt a slight vibration through the deck, as the rudder swung about to move the ship to starboard on its new heading. He lightly patted the rail with his gloved hand. If a man could love an inanimate object, he loved the *Prilagat' Usiliya*. Lately, he felt more at home aboard his ship than he did with his family. He would hate leaving her, but at fifty-six, retirement loomed before him like an iceberg, the exposed tip beckoning, but the unseen portion below the water frightened him. What would he do? Could he live on land for the remainder of his life without the familiar roll of a steel deck beneath his feet?

He sighed to break the depressive mood that had settled over him of late. He attributed his melancholy to the strange weather and the odd reports of ship sinkings. Since the American drillship had mysteriously gone down with all hands last fall, eleven ships had joined it. Odds like that were unnatural even in the harsh seas of the Arctic Ocean.

He sighed again, aloud this time. "I'm going below for a glass of vodka. Would you join me, Evgeni?"

Aleyev smiled. "If you insist, sir."

"I do not wish to drink alone."

As if sensing his friend's mood, his first mate offered, "Perhaps I could ask Kalek and Alexi to join us for a game of Vint."

Usually, a brisk game of Vint, similar to Whist or Bridge, was an enjoyable way to pass the time; however, today he was not in the mood for as much company, nor could his mind concentrate on the cards.

"Not this morning I think," he replied.

Aleyev looked perplexed but shrugged his shoulders.

The wardroom was empty, which pleased Anastasiy. The steward immediately stepped from the side door with two cups of coffee. Anastasiy waved him away. "Bring my bottle." He removed his hat and laid it on the table beside him. He ran his fingers through his thinning gray hair and stroked his salt-and-pepper beard.

The steward said nothing but returned a moment later with two glasses and a bottle of *Zelyonya Marka* vodka, his favorite brand. He poured two liberal amounts into each glass and left. Anastasiy lifted his glass and said, "*Vashe zdrovie!*"

"Cheers," Aleyev replied in heavily accented English in keeping with his fascination of all things Western.

Anastasiy downed his vodka in one gulp, allowing the familiar burn to trickle down his throat. Aleyev took only a token sip. Anastasiy arched one eyebrow over his sea blue eye and looked at him.

"You're not drinking, Evgeni?"

"I am on duty, and I am not the captain with a captain's privileges."

Anastasiy nodded. "You are right. I will drink enough for both of us. This run is boring. I need ice." He slammed his fist on the table, startling Aleyev and the steward, who peeked around the corner ready to provide the requested ice. Anastasiy shook his head. "No, I need to feel the ship shudder as it rams ice, crushes it out of the way, as a bull through a crowd." He set his empty glass on the table. "What is wrong with me, Evgeni? I was never bored before."

Aleyev's face became serious. "A sailor should be buried at sea, not in the dirt. Do not retire, Anas. They cannot take your ship from you."

"But my wife ..." The excuse sounded trite even to him. Raisa would not care. Even on his two-week furloughs, he restlessly stalked the floors of their home like the deck of a ship after only a week. She understood and encouraged his love of the sea. Perhaps she enjoyed her time alone as much as he did his time at sea.

"Men of the sea, such as you and I, belong here. The sea is our mistress, one we can share without jealousy because she is so big, like a fat, rosy-cheeked, babushka-wearing Ukrainian whore."

The image brought a chuckle to Anastasiy's lips. He splashed a finger of vodka in his glass and raised it in the air. "To fat Ukrainian whores."

This time, Aleyev poured vodka in his glass and joined him in his toast.

The intercom crackled to life. "Captain, sonar has detected an object two kilometers astern. It is closing rapidly with our position."

Anastasiy frowned. A submarine? Ours or American? Or Chinese? The Chinese were growing bolder lately, exerting their dominance on the seas. He exchanged glances with Aleyev and saw his concern mirrored in his first mate's eyes. "I'll be there in a moment. Change our heading five degrees north. See if it follows."

"The Americans?" Aleyev asked.

"Unlikely. They know we constantly monitor these waters. Besides, what of interest would bring them here?" He rose from his seat. "We will soon see."

On the bridge, he went directly to the sonar room. He saw immediately that the object had changed course to follow them. "What is its speed and size?" he asked the sonarman.

"Twenty knots. I estimate the object at just over forty-two meters in length. The image is blurry, difficult to hold a fix on."

"Some kind of stealth technology?"

The sonarman shook his head. "No, sir. It's more likely it is not metal. Organic perhaps."

Anastasiy relaxed. Whales swam the waters of the Arctic this time of year hunting walruses. He was getting jumpy over nothing.

"Continue to keep an eye on it. Report to me if it gets too close. We will send it scurrying away with a sonic blast."

"Yes, sir."

Anastasiy caught Aleyev smiling at him. "What?"

"For a moment there, you looked like the old Anastasiy, eager to do battle. Still bored?"

Anastasiy returned Aleyev's smile. "Perhaps not so much now."

"The sea. The sea is where we belong."

His good mood evaporated like the morning mist when the sonar operator reported, "Two more objects have joined the first, sir, slightly smaller than the first. Their speed has increased to thirty-two knots."

With a frown, he turned to Aleyev. "Reduce speed to ten knots. I must take a look at these jet-propelled whales."

Blue whales reached lengths of over thirty meters and could reach speeds of fifty kilometers per hour for short bursts, but these creatures, if creatures they were, were maintaining a speed of fifty-six kilometers per hour. He could not outrun them. His duty was to observe them and report them to the Navy's Northern Fleet at Murmansk.

As the strangely behaving pod of whales drew nearer, he decided to err on the side of caution. "Mr. Aleyev, please sound general quarters."

Aleyev nodded to the bridge watch supervisor, who keyed the ship's intercom and announced, *"Obshchiye pomeshcheniya! Obshchiye pomeshcheniya!* All hands to their stations!"

Seconds later, eighty men burst from cargo hatches and hatches. Some carried axes and water buckets for fire fighting. Most simply assumed ready positions around the deck, but four men designated as ship's security held either *SKS* 7.62mm carbines or *Bizon* 9mm machineguns, ready to repel borders if necessary. Aleyev went to the bridge arms locker and returned with Anastasiy's old *Nagant* M1895 seven-shot revolver. He wore his *Tokareu* semiautomatic pistol in a holster around his waist. Both were 7.62mm. Aleyev was an excellent marksman, shooting at old wine bottles tossed over the side for practice. Anastasiy had not fired his weapon in over a year. He now regretted being so remiss in his duty. As captain, he should set a better example for his men.

The lookouts scanned the sea with due diligence, but saw no apparent threats. They turned to look up at their captain as he stood on the bridge. He understood their confusion. He felt he owed them an explanation. Taking the intercom microphone, he said, "Gentlemen, we are whale watching, but these are very large whales moving quickly toward us. If they nuzzle our *Usiliya* too closely like a love-sick suitor, we must dissuade them from harming her. Shoot them only if they pose a threat. We do not want the United Nations to accuse us of illegal whale harvesting."

This drew a few chuckles from the crew and lightened the mood on deck.

"The whales are one thousand meters dead astern," the sonarman called out, "closing quickly."

If his duty required him to destroy the whales, he would do so, but he did not take pleasure in the killing of defenseless creatures. With a sinking feeling deep in his stomach, Anastasiy worried that perhaps these creatures were not as defenseless as he imagined. If the mysterious pod were responsible for the sinking of so many ships, they would pose a threat to his. The water-filled double-hull was thick near the bow, but the stern was more vulnerable. A heightened sense of excitement mixed with dread coursed through his body, dispelling the chill of the air. His hands gripped the rail more tightly, as he leaned out for a closer view of the approaching creatures.

As a civilian vessel, the *Usiliya* carried no deck gun or weapons more powerful than the handful of rifles, pistols, and machineguns, but she did possess explosives in her arsenal for use against larger ice floes or icebergs posing a threat to shipping. Because of the danger they posed to the ship, he would use explosives only as a last resort.

"I see them!" one of the lookouts called out.

So did Anastasiy, about three hundred meters away. As soon as the pale gray dorsal fins broke the surface like the sails of a regatta of racing yachts, he knew these were not blue whales or any other kind of whale with which he was familiar after over forty years at sea. Three fins, each over five meters in height, marked the positions of three massive sharks cutting the water just below the surface and closing steadily with his ship. Their sleek form reminded him of Great Whites except for their remarkable size. The longest of the sharks measured over twenty meters from nose to tip of its caudal fin tail. The pair flanking it were slightly smaller, but giants in their own right.

This explains the poor fishing season.

"You men with the *Bizons*," he called down. "Go aft and stand ready." He could not believe even creatures as large as these would attack a ship seven times their size, but his mother did not raise a fool. Better to be safe than sorry.

The trio of sharks continued to close with his ship. As the largest lifted its head from the water, Anastasiy saw that its eyes were the same pale white as the ice. Could it be blind? He knew sharks hunted by smell and vibrations in the water, but how could they locate his ship among the ice floes?

"They're submerging!" the lookout shouted.

Sure enough, all three fins disappeared beneath the water. He tensed, wondering what was to follow. Would they be so bold as to attack his ship, or were they merely curious? His answer came a few moments later, when the deck canted forward, as the stern lifted from the water. The sound of the impact rang the hull like the bells of St. Ambrose Cathedral in Tsilik.

"Report any damage," he yelled; then, waited breathlessly for the damage report.

"Minor damage to outer hull near the engine room," Aleyev reported.

Anastasiy shook his head. What would drive sharks to attack a moving vessel? Where had such monsters come from? He remembered the reports floating about after the American drillship disaster. The solitary survivor had reported an undersea cavern collapsing. He, too, had seen a large gray fin, but later recanted his story. Anastasiy suspected the authorities had silenced him. For all their boasts of freedom, the Americans were as quick to drop a veil of secrecy over something they wished to remain unknown, as was his government.

The barking sound of a *Bizon* drew his attention to the stern. One of the crew was firing into the water. The outline of the shark was visible just below the surface. Anastasiy knew the bullets would not penetrate the water very deeply and would do little damage to a creature so large if they did. They would need something more powerful than the *Bizon* to stop these creatures.

"Evgeni, please bring the package of RAMS."

The remotely activated munitions system, pre-packed one-kilo blocks of C4 plastique equipped with an attached radio-activated detonation device, allowed a person to position the necessary amount of explosives at the weakest point of a small iceberg or ice sheet and detonate it from a safe distance. Under normal circumstances, he would never use a RAM so close to his ship, but something in the determined manner in which the sharks cooperated in the attack overcame his caution.

While Aleyev was gone, the sharks attacked again, this time as a team, slamming the stern from both sides. The ship shuddered, knocking several men to the deck. One crewman toppled from his duty station near the starboard lifeboat into the water. Before anyone could shout 'Man Overboard,' the sharks were upon him. The largest swallowed him completely in one bite.

This time, damage control reported several leaks in the engine room and starboard hold. If the engine room flooded, they would be adrift and at the mercy of the creatures and the sea. If he did nothing, the creatures would shake his ship apart around him and more men would die.

He called Antonov Dreski to the bridge. The native Siberian had hunted seals, walrus, and whales before joining the merchant marines. If anyone could place a harpoon into one of the creatures, it would be he.

"Antonov," he said when the tall, broad-shouldered Yuit-Eskimo stood before him. "Do you think you could hit one of the sharks with the harpoon and *norsaq* adorning the wall of the wardroom?"

The Yuit smiled. "If it is a true harpoon and throwing stick and not some cheap trade trinket sold as trade goods."

"It is real, given to me by a Chukchi chief. I have need of your skill."

Aleyev arrived with the neoprene case containing the explosives. Anastasiy showed Dreski one of the RAMs. "How far can you throw the harpoon with one of these attached?"

Dreski picked up one of the RAMs and hefted it in his hand. The one-kilo RAM weighed as much as the harpoon. He nodded his confidence. "Easily twenty meters."

The stern lifted again as the sharks rammed the keel. He wondered how they knew the steel was thinner there. The damage alarm sounded.

The damage crew chief reported, "Engineering reports a substantial breach in one of the welds. We can slow the flow of water, but we cannot sustain many such hits."

"Helmsman, tell the engine room to be ready for flank speed at my command."

"Yes, sir."

Aleyev looked at him and nodded his approval. They could not outrun the sharks, but a bloody corpse in the water might draw their attention from the ship long enough for them to get away.

"Come, Antonov. It is time to test your skill. Aleyev, remain on the bridge. As soon as Antonov kills one of the creatures, you will order full speed."

"*Da*, Captain."

The three sharks circled a short distance off the ship's starboard beam, churning the water in a frenzied dance, as if they could sense the breech in the hull; tasted the spoor of man in the water and anticipated a forthcoming feast. The largest animal remained too far away for a harpoon strike, but the two smaller creatures brushed the ship as if familiarizing themselves with it.

After taping the RAM to the harpoon a short distance from the iron tip, Dreski shed his heavy coat and stripped to his long-sleeved shirt. Paying no attention to the bitter cold, he placed the deadly harpoon into the wooden *norsaq* and cocked his arm for throwing, waiting silent and motionless. Like a part of the ship, he stood watching the sharks. One of the sharks surfaced less than ten meters from the ship moving away from the ship presenting its broad back. Dreski took several running steps, and using the full weight of his body to propel the harpoon, released it. The harpoon arced high into the air, wobbling in its flight. Anastasiy feared the harpoon would fall short, but it found its mark in the shark's body two meters behind the dorsal fin.

Anastasiy pressed the button on the detonator, and the RAM exploded. It produced no bright flash, just a muffled thud, as the shaped charge sent its full force into the shark's body. A geyser of flesh and blood spewed into the air amid cheers from the crew.

Anastasiy pumped his fist into the air. "Yes!" He slapped Dreski on the back. "I will double your vodka ration for this feat, Antonov."

Dreski smiled. "Too bad I cannot mount a trophy."

Anastasiy took his cell phone from his pocket and snapped several photos of the dead shark floating in the water. "Perhaps this will do," he said.

The large shark attacked the dead animal, removing chunks of flesh the size of small motor launch. Blood filled the water. The remaining smaller shark warily circled the larger, trying to snatch morsels of the prize.

He waved at Aleyev. "Full speed, Evengi!"

The ship shuddered as the engines churned up the water behind them. As the icebreaker pulled away from the scene of the slaughter, Anastasiy knew they had been lucky. He had lost one crewman and his ship had suffered damage in the bizarre encounter between machine and monster, but they could make port. If more of the creatures swam the waters of the Arctic Ocean, shipping could come to a standstill.

Aleyev was right. The thrill of the hunt still burned deep within him. He felt more alive than he had in many years. He could not retire as long as creatures such as these remained at large. Raisa would understand. She had married a sailor, a Russian sailor.

3

October 15, 2018   *Fools Luck,* Bering Sea, Alaska–

Daryl Ottman scanned the horizon, searching for the bright orange buoys marking his string of crab pots. The crab pots would mean financial life or death for his crew. The low-lying sun cast a ruddy blush across the gently undulating water, making spotting the buoys more difficult than usual. The last two strings had produced less than five-hundred pounds of red king crab, *Paralithodes camtschaticus.* The short four-week crabbing season would soon end. If this last string proved as disappointing as had the others, they would all go home broke; not what he wanted for his first season as captain of his own boat.

Technically, the aptly named *Fool's Luck,* a seventy-eight-foot, one-hundred-thirty-ton steel-hulled multiuse boat out of Homer, Alaska, had belonged to his father Horace Ottman, but an accident the previous salmon season had left his father crippled, barely able to walk with a walker. Now, the boat and the bank lien were Daryl's, and he had hoped to carry on his father's tradition of leading the fleet in king crab tonnage each season. Unfortunately, there seemed little chance of that.

He was not alone in his crabbing woes. From chatter over the radio, *Straight Shooter, Cutty Sark, Demon Rum,* and *Sundowner* were having no better luck. No one had heard from *Casey's Chariot* in a couple of days. Either she had given up already and gone back to port, or her radio was dead. That did not make him feel any better. He had a family to feed, new wife and child, and a mortgage on a house. His crew worked on a percentage basis. They expected him to take them to the mother lode of crabs, as his father always had, and make them rich. He would be lucky to pay for fuel.

In the 80s, the crab fleet harvest was two-hundred-million pounds. Last season, it had been less than twenty-million pounds. This year, half as many boats were in the water as the previous season. He had barely broken even on the opilio tanner snow crab catch a month earlier. *Chirinoecetis opilio* had been his mainstay, as steady as any marine creature could be. The North Pacific Fishery Management Council imposed a short season and strictly enforced restrictions on crab size, but the plan was not working. If things did not improve, the crabbing fleet would go the way of the tuna fleet.

The only thing going right was the weather. The sun shone down on a gentle sea. No dark storm clouds marred the perfect powder blue of the sky. The burnished copper glow of the sunset beckoned them toward the horizon with the promise of a better haul from the next string of pots. The unnaturally warm mid-October weather teased them into forgetting just how treacherous the Bering Sea could be. Ships that disregarded the weather reports or played too close to the edge in pursuit of crabs often paid a heavy price for their folly, like his father.

"How much farther?"

Daryl turned to see deckhand Jonas Long standing at the open bridge door with a cup of coffee in his hand. He had known Long for years, since high school. They had toiled together under his father heaving heavy six-hundred-pound pots baited with shad over the side, and then winching them in again two days later, usually filled to overflowing with red or blue king crab or opilio snow crab.

He glanced at the GPS screen. "Another couple of miles." He saw Long staring ahead of the boat. "Too far away to see yet."

Long smiled. "You caught me. I hope it's a good haul this time."

Daryl frowned. "Me and you both." He looked at Long's drawn face and guessed what he was thinking. "Go ahead. You can say it."

Long shook his head. "It's not your fault. No one is having any luck."

"Maybe so, but I'm the captain now." He paused afraid to ask. "What do the others think?"

Long shrugged. "There's some grumbling, but no calls for a mutiny yet."

"Maybe an armed insurrection would enliven things a bit." He craned his neck to stretch aching muscles.

Seeing his discomfort, Long asked, "Want me to take over for a while?"

Daryl shook his head. "Naw, I'm okay. You go below and get the others ready. We'll be there in a ten or fifteen minutes."

"Okay." Long turned to leave; then, paused and squinted out the window. "What's that?"

Daryl followed Long's gaze toward a speck in the distance. "Too big for a buoy." He checked the radar and saw a small blip on the screen, appearing and disappearing between troughs in the waves. "It's showing up on radar. Must be some debris from a passing cargo ship."

Two minutes later, as they drew near enough to see it more closely, Daryl recognized the rudder and keel of a ship upside down in the water. The tension in his aching shoulders pulled at his spine with a dread of impending doom.

"It's a boat," Long noted. His voice showed equal concern.

Daryl slowed the engine and let *Fool's Luck* drift closer. As he circled the capsized boat, he read the upside down name on the stern. "It's the *Casey's Chariot*."

"This is bad, real bad," Long replied.

"Go alert the others. We'll search for survivors." He didn't have much hope of finding anyone alive in the water. Twenty minutes in the frigid 34-degree water was enough to kill a person. The *Chariot* had been incommunicado for forty-eight hours. It could have capsized anytime during those two days. He wondered what could have caused it to roll over on its belly. The weather had been as perfect as it got in the Bering Sea. He had heard no SOS, no distress call, no plea for help. He picked up the radio and dialed Coast Guard Channel 16.

"Mayday. Mayday. Mayday. This *Fool's Luck* position 125 miles east of St. George, 145 miles NNE of Unimak. Mayday.

Encountered capsized vessel *Casey's Chariot.* Searching for survivors. Over."

"*Fool's Luck*, this is Coast Guard Cutter *Trinity.* Is your vessel all right?"

"Affirmative, *Trinity*. We are in no danger. I'll send GPS coordinates."

"Appreciated, *Fools Luck*. Standby."

After relaying the coordinates, he replaced the mic. By then, the entire crew had crowded into the small bridge cabin. By their distraught expressions, he knew they too held out little hope of survivors. Crabbing in the Bering Sea was one of the most dangerous professions on the planet. Every season or two, a boat sank. Each season produced its share of injuries or casualties. On a crab boat, you spun the Wheel of Fortune and took your chances. *Casey's Chariot* had landed on Bankrupt.

"We'll run an expanding spiral around the *Chariot* until the Coast Guard cutter arrives. Anders, you climb atop of the bridge and keep a sharp lookout. Give a shout if you see anything."

Chris Anders, a skinny eighteen-year-old college student from Portland on his first trip to sea, nodded and left, eager for a change in the brutal routine of dropping and hauling in crab pots. To one so young, who seldom dwelt on death, the fate of the crew of the *Chariot* did not affect him as it did the more experienced hands that saw the Grim reaper's visage in very storm. They knew it could have very well been them.

"First, we'll pull, alongside and pound on the hull. If anyone's alive inside, they'll hear and respond. Chachi, Steadman, get out the medical kit and some blankets, just in case."

"What about the string?" Kelly Kacek, a native Homer boy on his third season with the *Fool's Luck* asked.

Daryl frowned. "The crab can wait. People come first."

Kacek looked as if he wanted to say more, but nodded and left. The others followed suit, all except for Long.

"This is a waste of time," he said.

Daryl nodded. "Probably, but they'd search for us if we sank."

Long lowered his head and spoke softly. "Yeah. You're right. Too bad. I knew the captain, Hassel Mays. A real bastard, but a good captain."

Daryl knew Mays, too, as well three of the crew of *Casey's Chariot*. At sea, they were competitors, but on shore, they were friends and drinking companions. "Don't speak ill of the dead," he warned. "It's bad luck."

Long looked up. "Bad luck. Well, we've had our share, I suppose."

"Look, chances are slim that they're still alive. If we don't find anything, my last spiral will take us to close to our string. It'll be dark by then anyway. We'll pull the pots before we come back at daybreak to resume the search. The Coast Guard will be here soon. Maybe they'll find something."

"Makes sense." Long grinned, pulled a well-worn rabbit's foot from his pocket, and rubbed it. "For luck. Maybe this one is the one."

Daryl said nothing. The rabbit's foot hadn't been lucky for the rabbit. Their luck wasn't running much better. He wondered idly if the *Chariot's* holding tanks were full or empty when she sank. It would have been a bitter twist of fate to sink with a full hold. He nudged *Fool's Luck* gently against *Casey's Chariot's* hull. As Long prepared to leap across the open gap to the ship's exposed keel, *Casey's Chariot* heeled over onto its port side, revealing a gaping ten-foot-wide rent in the starboard section of the bow.

"My God," Daryl exclaimed, incredulous at the amount of damage to the *Chariot*. "What did she collide with to cause that?"

Long leaned over the side and plucked something from the edge of the rip in the hull, and then showed it to Daryl. It took a moment for Daryl's confused mind to comprehend what he was looking at. Its curved triangular shape was unmistakably a tooth, but it was at least eleven inches long, the biggest tooth he had ever seen.

"It's a damned shark's tooth," Long said, as incredulous as Daryl.

"Impossible!" Daryl responded, refusing to believe what he was seeing. "If it is, the shark would have to be fifty or sixty feet long. No toothed shark grows that large."

"It's something's tooth," Long challenged. "What else could it be but a shark?" He touched the cutting edge of the tooth with the tip of his finger, yelped in pain, and drew it back. Blood dripped from his lanced finger. He jammed the finger in his mouth, and then examined the laceration. "It's as sharp as my knife."

Daryl studied the rent in the hull more closely, now noticing the regular jagged pattern; exactly what a row of teeth the size the one Long held would leave. It was unbelievable, akin to claiming to have seen a sea monster, but the tooth was proof. It was difficult to grasp that a creature so large roamed the Bering Sea, had killed the crew of *Casey's Choice*.

The stricken ship rolled slightly, revealing part of the drowned interior of the cabin. The upper torso of a body floated out. Though the corpse had been in the water overnight and nibbled on by fish, Daryl recognized Captain Mays. His gaunt face still bore the look of horror it had worn as the shark had bitten off the lower half of his body. Daryl hoped he had died quickly.

His voice cracked as he said, "Bring him aboard, and wrap him in a blanket. Put him in the freezer."

Long and Kacek used a boathook to snag May's coat and pulled him onto the deck of *Fool's Luck*. Kacek took one look at the mutilated body, and his face turned a sickly pale. He heaved his guts over the side of the ship; retching until no more came up. Daryl didn't blame him. His own stomach felt like a disturbed nest of vipers. He covered Mays' face reverently with a corner of the blanket.

"Let's go," he said. In spite of the tragedy that had befallen *Casey's Choice*, they still had crabs to catch.

* * * *

Their spiral search pattern produced no results—no lifejackets, no more bodies, or no debris. Just after 9:00 p.m., they pulled alongside their first buoy, hooked it, and began winching in the pots. Daryl could tell by the sound of the winch that the pots were empty. When the first one broke the surface bearing only two king crabs, a peculiar silence fell over the usually boisterous crew, a gloom that had begun with the discovery of *Casey's Choice* and now reached into the bridge and clamped icy fingers around Daryl's heart. He stared at their faces in the ghostly glow of the work lights and saw their bitter disappointment. They dutifully placed the pair in the holding tank, as if hoping they would mate and miraculously fill the tank with offspring before they reached port.

The second pot produced similar results, not enough for a good dinner for the crew. The third pot looked as if someone had attacked it with a sledgehammer and bolt cutters. The door dangled from the misshapen pot by a single bent hinge. Most of one end of the pot was missing, ripped away. Daryl immediately thought of the fate of *Casey's Choice.* His instincts told him to leave, but economics demanded they recover their string of pots, empty or not. They were too valuable to leave behind.

When the hoist winch began groaning as they raised the fourth pot, the mood on the deck lightened. Maybe their luck had changed after all. The cable suddenly snapped taught, placing a strain on the winch. Shadows danced on deck, as the work lights bounced on their stand. The motor whined out its agony. Daryl eased off on the ship's engine; then, cut it altogether, as the davit arm continued to bend under the strain. With a loud snap, the line hauler tore away from the davit. Long shoved Kacek aside just in time to prevent the errant cable from decapitating him. They rolled across the deck, as the line hauler pounded the hull, and then went slack.

At first, Daryl thought they had lost the pot. They would have to grapple it to recover it, a time-consuming process. Then, the cable snapped taut in the water and beat a staccato tempo against the gunwales.

One bit of luck in an otherwise dismal day.

Long quickly rose from the deck. "Restring the cable through the port winch pulley."

The crew scurried to comply. Long manned the second winch and began hauling the errant pot aboard ship. When the ship listed to starboard, Daryl thought the pot had snagged something on the bottom, a piece of wreckage or a rocky spire. Just as he started to tell them to cut it free, the pot broke the surface, followed by a living nightmarish creature plucked from Neptune's watery hell.

The pot held not a load of red king crabs, but a single monstrous crustacean clinging to its side. The pale white creature looked like no crab with which he was familiar, certainly nothing in Alaskan waters. Its pasty carapace measured six feet across.

Spikes protruded from the edges of the shell like some dystopian armored vehicle. As soon as the pot broke surface, the giant crab leaped from it onto the deck, spreading its thirteen-foot-wide legs and scuttling along the deck. Two sightless waved atop its eyestalks. Blind, the creature swiveled to follow every sound.

Faced with an armored monster, the crew scattered, but not quickly enough. The crab reached out one massive clawed chelipad and grasped Kacek around his shoulders, as his booted feet slapped the first rung of the ladder. The serrated claw dug deeply into his flesh. The sickening crunch of breaking bones was audible over the groans of the still straining winch and Kacek's screams. Long had the presence of mind to attack the crab with the boathook, pounding at the claw that held Kacek in its grip, but the crab ignored his pitiful efforts, plucked Kacek's head from his body, and brought it to his mouth. With a cry of anger, Long jabbed the tip of the boathook into the crab's blind eye. Wounded, it reared in pain and dropped Kacek's limp body to the deck.

Daryl fumbled in the desk drawer for the Very pistol. Loading it, he took careful aim at the giant creature stalking the deck of his ship. He took a deep breath, released it slowly, and squeezed the trigger. The flare struck the creature squarely in the mouth. The crab danced in a circle, trying to extricate the burning object from its mouth, knocking over the work lights, plunging the deck into darkness. It stumbled against a stack of empty crab pots in the stern. The pots toppled over the crab, trapping it beneath tons of steel cages, but before anyone could get close enough to kill it, the creature began flinging pots away from its body. One flying six-hundred-pound pot caught young Chris Anders in the chest, crushing him against the gunwale and killing him instantly.

Long and Chachi Cuthbert raced to the open door and dove open down the steps to the cabin. The crab, now free of its entanglements, followed them. Using the only weapon available, Daryl stepped from the bridge holding a fire extinguisher. He sprayed the creature in its remaining eye with the freezing foam. The crab screeched in pain and backed away, clawing at its damaged eye, until falling over the side of the ship. Dropping the empty extinguisher, he slid down the ladder to the deck, grabbed a fire ax from the wall, and freed the stringer cable from the winch.

Then, racing back up to the bridge, he shoved the throttles forward. The propeller, powered by the *Luck's* GMC 725-horsepower engine, dug into the water. The bow rose from the water, as the *Fool's Luck* shot forward away from the grisly scene of death. He had lost two crewmen, his string of crab pots, and, when he failed to pay his bank loan, probably his boat as well, but he was alive, and for now, that was enough.

Then, from the darkness, illuminated by the fallen work lights, he saw the thirty-foot-tall fin rise from the water paralleling the ship, and his heart hammered in his chest. The shark, if one could call such a monstrous creature a shark, raced ahead of the *Fool's Luck* and rose to the surface. He stared at the pale gray flesh, the dead white eyes watching his approach, and felt a deeper fear than he had ever felt in his life. He could not outrun the creature. His only choice was to crash into it head on, use the *Luck's* powerful engines and momentum of the ship as a battering ram.

He crossed himself, something he had not done since his days as an altar boy at Saint Andrews. He braced himself for impact, the image of Captain Mays of *Casey's Choice* running through his kind, the amputated torso, waterlogged and fish nibbled. The ship struck the shark like ramming the dock. The ship stopped, but he did not. His body flew across the bridge and through the forward window. The pain of glass slicing into his flesh was momentary, compared to the impact with the bow deck. *Fool's Luck* rolled to port, tossing him into the freezing water.

His ship, his father's ship, slowly sank beneath the waves, the bow staved in. The giant shark, a *megalodon*, if his few biology classes in school were right, was unharmed. It circled the sinking ship, like Moby Dick circling Ahab's *Pequod,* creating a whirlpool that spun him in a circle. Then, the megalodon came for him. Its open mouth looked cavernous, the fourteen-inch teeth, pearly white razor-sharp stalactites and stalagmites that closed slowly to meet around his body. He felt no pain, just an instant of shock, and then nothing more.

4

December 24, 2018   Semi-submersible *Drillship Vanguard*, Beaufort Sea, Arctic–

Asa Iverson avoided his crewmates on the *Vanguard* as much as possible, earning him a reputation as a lone wolf. He didn't mind that they thought him aloof and laconic. Since the *Global Kulik* incident, he had no love for his fellow oilmen, many of whom had seemed determined to blame him for the *Global Kulik's* sinking and the deaths of friends or people they had known. That his own friends, people he had worked with for years, had died did not seem to matter to them. Someone was to blame, and he was a handy target.

His story to the Coast Guard when they rescued him had not helped. They assumed it the ravings of a half-frozen survivor. The more he repeated it to various agencies, the less they believed him. He saw in their eyes and in the manner in which they perfunctorily nodded their head in agreement that they considered his unbelievable story a desperate concoction designed to conceal some blame he might have had in the ship's demise. He soon learned to keep his mouth shut, especially when the U.S. Navy eventually became involved. The military squelched his story before it reached the newspapers and threatened him with prosecution under some obscure national security law if he spoke about it publically.

Global Oil dropped him like last week's newspaper, citing unspecified emotional turmoil due to stress, another name for bat-shit crazy. He had spent seven months ashore, living off his savings account, replaying every moment of the sinking in his mind in a desperate attempt to persuade himself he had imagined the entire episode. No one returned his phone calls or asked for a meeting when he left his resumes. Word spread. He had become persona non grata, a pariah.

Finally resorting to calling in old favors and practically begging, he got a job aboard the Shell Oil *Vanguard*. Even that would have been impossible but for the fact that he worked through a contract labor firm. They paid less than his old job on the *Global Kulik*, but at least he was working. He did his job, took his pay, and avoided any conversation that dealt with that dark time in his life. A few fellow workers recognized his name as the lone survivor of the ill-fated drillship. He could see in their faces that they wanted to know what had happened, but were afraid to broach his carefully constructed façade of indifference. At times, he did not know which was worse, their antipathy or their sympathy. He wallowed in his self-imposed solitude and called it penitence, atonement for the sin of surviving.

Unlike the self-propelled *Global Kulik,* the *Vanguard* was a towed semi-submersible drillship. Delivered to her destination, her tow ship left her on station and returned to port. Like the *Kulik*, it remained on station with eight thrusters and anchored mooring lines. As second mechanic, Asa maintained the winches, generators, HVAC systems, and anything else with moving parts not maintained by the roughnecks or drillers. It kept him busy, allowing him less time for brooding.

At least he did not have to deal with his fellow workers while perched sixty feet above the frozen waters of the Beaufort Sea. He knelt beside the frozen sewage discharge pump carrying wastewater from the crews' quarters to the waste holding tank where it was biodegraded before shipment to a treatment facility on land. Literally, he was up to his elbows in shit. At least the 40-mph wind gusts kept the smell to a minimum. His hands, numbed by the minus-twelve-degree temperature, had trouble tightening the last bolt to seal the pump cover. He cursed his lack of coordination and his luck at his reduction to the status of second mechanic, two pay grades below his usual title of master mechanic.

He finally managed to seal the pump housing, stood, and stretched his aching back before gathering his tools. The pump was working. The fecal slurry was making its merry way to the waste tank, and the added insulation would help keep it from refreezing—another tedious job well done. The crew could safely take a dump again. *Where's the applause?*

The *Vanguard* was smaller than the *Global Kulik*, with a crew of only fifty-six. She was essentially a drilling platform perched atop four eighty-feet-long vertical hollow pylons attached to two horizontal pontoons. On station, water pumped into the pontoons lowered the platform into the sea helped stabilize it. She presently sat at 75⁰20'20''N, 148⁰50'35"W, some 215 miles NNE of Barrow, Alaska, just off the continental shelf in twenty-five-hundred feet of water. Normally, in December, the Beaufort Sea would be a frozen wasteland of pressure ridges and crevasses, and the Vanguard would have returned to her homeport. The surface water temperature was 38-degrees, but warmer, deeper currents were keeping channels in the ice open.

Asa found a spot out of the wind to smoke a Pall Mall and watched as a Sikorsky S-92 supply helicopter landed on the helipad. A stiff crosswind blew the red, white, and blue, thirteen-ton craft back and forth above the pad like a yo-yo on a string, as the pilot fought the controls to set her down. Watching the flapping windsock for a lull in the wind, he placed the chopper in a sideways dive across the deck, hit the pad with one skid, and immediately powered down the twin GE CT7-8A turboshaft engines. The chopper settled down firmly if not gracefully. It was a rough ride for the passengers, but they had made it. Fifteen passengers spilled out of the door, got their bearings, and headed for the stairs, swaying like drunken sailors from their harrowing ride.

More rookies.

He tossed the stub of his cigarette to the wind and sauntered toward the main building for a closer look. He enjoyed watching the stunned faces of newbies getting their first glimpse of an offshore drilling platform. The maze of cables and pipes that looked like a prey animal's guts strewn about by a wild beast; the bitter, biting wind slicing exposed skin like invisible razors; the dull roar like someone jackhammering your eardrum—all were mysterious and unnerving to first-time offshore visitors. A few looked frightened, as if ready to turn around and climb back aboard the helicopter. One or two looked eager, ready for the challenge. Most of them simply appeared confused.

A woman from human resources wearing ridiculous high heels and a spotless blue hardhat met them at the foot of the steps and ushered them into the building to fill out their paperwork. They looked relieved that they would not have to wander the platform on their own. Asa wondered if he had looked as green the first time he went offshore some twelve years ago. Two years at inshore facilities had not prepared him for the major differences between drilling on land and ocean drilling. The main distinction: On land, if something went wrong, you could run as far away as necessary or hop in a vehicle and drive. On the *Vanguard* in the middle of the ocean, in an emergency, you rushed for one of the four freefall lifeboats suspended nose-first in the canted racks on the side of the platform, hoping you made it in time and praying the lifeboat survived the sixty-foot plunge into the water. On a drill platform at sea, if the shit hit the fan, you were in the shit.

An involuntary shudder racked his body as he remembered the *Global Kulik*. No one had time to reach the lifeboats then. Given the monstrous shark that he saw circling the drillship afterwards, he doubted it would have mattered. *Why did I live?* He had asked himself that question every morning since the incident after waking up bleary-eyed and exhausted from a troubled sleep wracked by nightmares. He still did not know the answer.

He followed the new hires into the building, but broke away from the group to go downstairs to the cafeteria for an early lunch. The one thing oil platforms provided was food—lots of it. A bad chef risked being chucked over the side. The quality and quantity of food aboard the *Vanguard* was excellent. Unlike most rigs her size, the culinary staff included a pastry chef. Freshly baked bread, croissants, and an assortment of pastries accompanied every meal.

The cafeteria was less than half full, mostly supervisors and administrative staff getting their fill before the Roughnecks plowed through the serving line like a head of grazing caribou. Silver and gold garlands draped from the ceiling reminded him it was Christmas Eve. A live Douglas fir tree stood in the corner, festooned with little twinkling lights, ornaments, and candy canes.

Soft Christmas carols drifted from the overhead speakers filling the room with holiday cheer. Trays of sausages, peppers, and onions resting in a spicy tomato sauce, baked salmon in a butter cream sauce, herb roasted chicken smothered with roasted root vegetables, potatoes, and pan *au jus* were the main entrees. A carving station held a fat roasted turkey with a gravy boat holding thick giblet gravy beside it. The catering staff had done all it could to bring the Christmas spirit to an oil rig in the middle of the Beaufort Sea, but he felt no lifting of his spirits or abundance of joy.

Stir-fry vegetables, bright yellow turmeric rice with peas, French fried potatoes, mashed potatoes, brown gravy, grilled asparagus, and sautéed polenta cakes were the sides. Various soups, breads, sandwiches, cheeses, and fruits finished off the thirty-foot-long serving line. His months sitting at home had not been good for his waistline, so he chose black coffee, a turkey and Swiss croissant, a bowl of clam chowder, and an apple for later.

A couple of people glanced up as he chose a table in the corner. One man wore a bright red Santa cap over his head. He nodded a perfunctory greeting at Asa, but most continued their conversations or ignored him completely. He saw no looks of disdain or open sneers, which was a welcome relief. He wondered if any of them knew who he was or anything about his checkered past. It was a small rig, and gossip was as good as news from home and more abundant. He took a few bites from his meal, but the food seemed tasteless and unappetizing. He laid his fork on his plate and sighed.

The faces around him seemed to stare at him even when they weren't, and the quiet whispers were veiled accusations. His psychologist at the hospital had called his condition survivor's guilt. He didn't know about the survivor part. That had been pure luck. Except for the frostbitten tip of the little toe on his right foot and a dislocated shoulder, he had escaped unscathed. *Physically*, he reminded himself. *Inside, I'm a mass of scar tissue.* His guilt irritated the mental scars and exacerbated his anguish. *Why did I alone survive?* He had played no part in the destruction of the *Global Kulik*, but months of deep, often liquor-induced retrospection brought up the dire specter of his inadequacies.

Could he have helped save more people? Could he have saved Ilsa?

It was becoming more difficult to tell fact from fantasy. Large slices of the frantic flight from the lab to the lifeboat station had vanished, as if sliced away by a surgeon's scalpel. The doctor had called it self-induced retrograde amnesia, a trick employed by his brain to reduce the shock of the event, a mental safety valve. Were the snippets he did recall real or simply false images his imagination supplied for the sake of continuity? Did a giant shark exist? Certainly no one else thought so. The psychologist, Doctor Merkel, suggested the giant shark represented the trauma of the sinking, a boogey man. He was no longer sure, his mind thankfully disguising the truth in a fog of uncertainty. In a way, he no longer cared.

The problem was that forgetting was easy. The difficult part was getting his subconscious mind to forget. It remembered every little detail and fed them back to him in his nightmares or in sudden sounds or smells, a kind of non-combat PTSD.

"What's the matter? You don't like my cooking?"

Asa glanced up and saw Simon, the ship's chef, staring down at him, his beefy arms crossed over his barrel chest. His face bore a glum expression. The sudden shift from his dismal thoughts to Simon confused him. The chef was the only man who went out of his way to speak to him. He wasn't sure why Simon singled him out, but the attention made him a little uncomfortable.

"No, er, it all smells great. I'm just, er, not too hungry," Asa stammered out in explanation.

Simon relaxed, uncrossed his arms, and grinned. "Just screwing with you. I've seen you wolf it down before." He narrowed his eyes and stared at Asa. "Something on your mind?"

"Not much. I'm a mechanic. They hired me for my hands not my mind." His attempt at levity sounded lame even to him.

"We should talk sometime. You play chess?"

Simon's offer of companionship bewildered him. Before he could form a polite refusal, Simon continued, "Meet me in the lounge at seven tonight, and we'll start a game. I need a challenge. Most of the roughnecks play chess like they drill, straight ahead and full bore. No finesse."

"Uh, yeah, okay, uh, maybe," he stammered. "Seven sounds fine."

"Good. See you then."

Simon walked back around behind the serving line and began examining chafing dishes on the hot line, leaving Asa confused, wondering if he had just been hustled. Maybe he did need something to take his mind off his problems. He hadn't played a game of chess since … Ilsa had been the last person with whom he had played chess.

"Iverson."

He looked up and saw Ellis Brock, the chief mechanic, walking across the cafeteria with one of the new hires in tow. The pair stopped beside his table.

"Iverson, this is Marcus Settlemires. He's a new apprentice mechanic. Show him the ropes this afternoon when you repair the stabilizer pump in pillar three."

Asa didn't know if Brock was trying to goad him because the chief mechanic didn't like him, or if he thought he would be the best teacher for the apprentice. Either way, he couldn't refuse. He nodded.

"Good. Pick him up in the shack when you finish eating."

Asa sighed. *No reason to put off the inevitable.* "I'm ready now."

"Good." Brock turned to Settlemires. "Watch him closely. He's pretty closed mouth, but he knows his shit."

It was as close to a compliment as Brock had ever given him. Asa stared at Settlemires, who glanced away nervously at his scrutiny. He didn't want an apprentice, especially one he didn't know. He had grown used to his solitude. First a chess game with the chef, and now an apprentice to deal with—it was too much too soon.

He nodded his chin in non-committal greeting and asked, "How much on-hands experience do you have?"

"A year as a pumper's helper and six months at vocational school."

Asa let a quick smile play on his lips. Maybe it wouldn't be too bad. "A pumper's helper, huh? At least you're not a virgin. So I guess you at least know which way to turn a valve."

Settlemires' eyes flashed his anger at Asa's barbed comment. "Yes, I do."

"Good. I'll let you handle this next job replacing gaskets on one of the stabilizer pumps while I supervise. You might as well get your hands dirty right off."

"Do you dislike everyone, or is there something in particular about me that annoys you?"

The question surprised Asa, but he answered as truthfully as he dared. "I got nothing against you, kid. I just prefer working alone."

"I thought maybe ..." His voice trailed off.

Asa sighed. He could see in the kid's eyes that he knew something about him. "What did you hear about me?"

Settlemires hesitated, and then blurted, "That you claim you saw a sea monster."

Asa chuckled. "So you're afraid I'm crazy. Well, it ain't catching, so don't worry."

"Did you?"

Asa shook his head in dismay. The kid wasn't going to let it lie. "Jeez, kid. Maybe I was hallucinating from shock and hypothermia like they said, or maybe I lied to cover up some part I played in sinking the *Global Kulik,* as some blowhards claim." He stared hard at the young apprentice, but to his credit, Settlemires did not flinch. "Or maybe I really saw something, something so fucking horrible I still piss my pants when I think about it. It doesn't matter. You show me you got some talent, and I'll teach you what I know. Just don't get too chummy with me, or you'll find yourself ostracized, and lonely is a bad place to be on an oil rig."

Settlemires took a deep breath and nodded.

"Okay, let's go." He had been crosser with the young man than he had intended, but a particularly bad round of nightmares had left him miserable and short tempered. *At least he won't try to buddy up with me.*

* * * *

Chef Simon had run some of the finest restaurants in San Francisco. As the head chef, he had paid particular attention to detail in his kitchens. All ingredients that went into each dish, each garnish, and every plate that left his kitchen passed his personal inspection. His meals aroused first the diner's sense of smell; then, sight, texture, and taste, in that exact order. His name, his reputation demanded no less. Cooking aboard an oil rig in the middle of the Beaufort Sea presented its own distinctive set of challenges.

He still demanded excellence from his staff. The rig workers expected both quality and quantity, and he strived to provide a varying menu that satisfied as well as provoked taste buds too used to mediocrity. He wished to make each meal something to which they looked forward instead of merely a means to fill their bellies and store calories to stave off the cold. He fought boredom with a knife and a spatula as others fought it with books, cards, television, and video games. He liked to think he was winning.

Lunch shift over and the kitchen staff well along in preparations for the evening meal, Simon returned to his quarters on Level 3 for a short rest. Space aboard the *Vanguard* was extravagant compared to some drill rigs. Most quarters were doubles, but as head chef, he enjoyed a single-bunk room. This allowed him the privacy to unwind between shifts. While posters of semi-naked women, photos of tropical locales, or of family decorated most cabin walls, Simon's wall bore a single item, a wrinkled, well-worn map of the Arctic Ocean, including the Bering, Chukchi, and Beaufort Seas. At first glance, the numerous red X's dotting the map could be mistaken for oil rigs, but closer examination of the scribbled notes beside each X described the dates, circumstances, and locations of mysterious ship sinkings and odd sightings. So far, he had pinpointed forty-two separate events—twenty-six ship sinkings and sixteen reports of strange sea creatures. The largest X and the earliest date on his map marked the sinking of the *Global Kulik* in the Chukchi Sea, the epicenter of a pattern of events spreading south into the Bering Sea and eastward into the Beaufort.

The sinking of the *Kulik* had changed his life forever. His sister had been a marine biologist on the drillship. She had died with all the others, all except Asa Iverson. Now, fate at placed Iverson on the *Vanguard*, and he intended to learn all he could from him about what really happened to the *Global Kulik*. He had read the initial reports and had dismissed them, as had so many, as the ravings of a madman, but the continued sinking of vessels and sightings in the area had eventually convinced him factors other than simple fate were at work.

Pushed by his desire for answers, Simon had quit his job in San Francisco, and to the bewilderment of friends and acquaintances, accepted the job as head chef for an offshore catering company. The job paid far less than his previous salary, but traveling the polar oil rig circuit allowed him the anonymity to continue his investigation without arousing undue suspicion. He did not actually think the military or Homeland Security would break down his door, but they made it quite clear that they frowned upon questions concerning the *Global Kulik* and similar disasters at sea. He wanted answers, not more red tape.

He sat at his small desk staring at the map for a long moment. His wooden chair, strained by his bulk, creaked with each movement. His vision misted, remembering his younger sister's face. He turned away with a tear in his eye. "Ilsa."

He had watched Asa Iverson carefully since he had arrived on the *Vanguard*. Though quiet and abrasive, he did not seem unhinged. He hoped to gain Iverson's trust. Other than a much-disputed report from a Russian icebreaker, Iverson was the only survivor of any sinking under unusual circumstances. Iverson might have answers, and Simon desperately needed answers.

At seven p.m., after assuring the staff got the evening meal on the serving line for the hungry crew, he changed into casual clothes, in this case jeans and a colorful Hawaiian T-shirt, ran a comb through his blond hair, and went to the recreation lounge to wait for Iverson. To his surprise, Iverson showed up.

"I hoped you'd make it," he said.

Asa looked uncomfortable, glancing at the few faces watching a soccer game on the television, but he took a seat across from Simon with the chessboard acting as a barrier between them. "I thought a game of chess might help me unwind."

"Tough day?"

A quick grin flickered on Asa's lips. "New apprentice."

"Is he or she any good?" Simon knew little about anything mechanical except gas ranges, ovens, and deep fryers. His mechanical ability was another reason wanted to gain Asa's trust. He needed to get Asa to relax. Idle chitchat seemed a good way.

"He's got good hands and a grasp of the fundamentals, but he's a little ill at ease on a rig."

"He'll get over it," Simon replied. "Rigs are intimidating." He glanced at Asa as he set up carved black and white chess pieces on the chessboard. He clutched the white queen in his hand, thinking of Ilsa. "Have you worked on many rigs?"

The grimace that crossed Asa's face meant he had touched a raw nerve. Simon decided to pull back slightly.

"This is my fourth," he said. "*Vanguard* seems like a tightly run ship. I've got a good kitchen staff to work with." He finished setting up the board, placing the white queen on her square, and leaned back in his seat. "You move first."

An hour later and after two beers each, Asa conceded defeat, knocking over his king when Simon's bishop and queen prevented any hope of escape. Asa's cigarette, now only a long column of ash, sat untouched in the ashtray, forgotten in his concentration on the game. Simon had adjusted his game, playing less aggressively, but Asa had not exploited the numerous openings Simon had intentionally left for him. His mind seemed on things other than the game, but he had eventually relaxed. Most, but not all, of the tension had left his face.

Asa sat back in his seat and smiled. "Good game. It's been too long. I played defense all night." He cocked his head to one side and stared at Simon with a mischievous grin. "I think you took it easy on me. Why?"

Simon spread his hands. "Kicking someone's ass is not a good way to make new friends."

Asa cleared his throat. "You might not want to invest too much time in me as a friend. You might make a few enemies instead."

"Because of the *Global Kulik*?"

Asa's eyes flashed, and his face instantly went cold. Simon thought he would stand up and walk away, but after a few seconds, Asa's expression softened. "So you're just curious."

"More than curious." He paused. "Come with me to my room. I want to show you something."

Asa stared at Simon, refusal on his lips. Simon thought he had lost him, pushed too hard, but to his surprise, he nodded. As soon as they entered Simon's quarters, Asa's gaze fell on the map on the wall. He stiffened, but walked to the map as if drawn by it. He stared at it for over a minute, his finger tracing a line between several of the points on the map. He withdrew his hand and made a fist; then, turned to look at Simon.

"What's your game?" he demanded.

"No game. My sister was on the *Global Kulik*. I wanted to know how she died. The more questions I asked, the harder the Navy pushed back and the more curious I grew. It took me four months and a lot of time spent surfing conspiracy websites to separate the wheat from the chaff and come up with this. You," he nodded his head at Asa, "may be my best hope."

Asa sat on the edge of the bed, his face ashen. "Look, the Navy, the Coast Guard, and fucking Homeland Security shoved their collective noses up my ass and ran me through the ringer the entire time I was in the hospital. They made it abundantly clear either I keep my mouth shut, or I go to jail. Hell, they already set it up so I look like a mental case. Hell!" He slapped the bed with his open palm. "Maybe I am. I don't know anymore."

Simon shook his head. "Over two hundred people have died under mysterious circumstances since the *Global Kulik* disaster. People have reported giant crabs, enormous sharks, and strange-looking fish. The water temperature of the Chukchi Sea has increased three degrees, and the warmer water is spreading outward into the Arctic Ocean and the Bering Sea. Fishing and crabbing catches have dropped sixty percent over the last six months."

He saw he had Asa's attention. "The Navy has sent three nuclear submarines into the area. A small task force of two LHD helicopter carriers, three missile frigates, and almost a dozen attending vessels are cruising the Arctic Ocean between Wrangel Island and Prince Patrick Island. No one knows how many ships the Russians, the Canadians, and the Chinese have in these waters. Tensions are running high. Things are nearing a critical breaking point. One wrong move and we'll have WWIII."

Asa shrugged. "So what am I supposed to do about it?"

"Why did you come back to the Arctic?"

Asa shrugged again. "I needed a job."

Simon shook his head. "You could have gone anywhere. You want to see it for yourself, to make sure you didn't imagine it." Simon went to the map and swirled his hand across it. "The current moves this way. The warmer water has already reached this area. Eventually, those megalodon are going to show up here. That's why I'm here. I think you're here for the same reason."

Asa lowered his head. "I have to know," he said just above a whisper. He raised his head and looked at Simon. "What did you call them?"

"Megalodon, *Carcharodon megalodon*, giant sharks that supposedly went extinct twenty million years ago during the Late Cenozoic Era, toward the end of the Miocene Epoch."

"That's what Ilsa said." He winced as he said her name. He looked up at Simon. "I didn't get the connection until I saw your culinary school photo on the desk—Simon Thorin. I knew your sister. She was my friend." He paused, as if he wanted to say more but stopped. "She mentioned phytoplankton and crab larvae she had found in the water. I found some type of pale gray kelp clogging the thrusters. Then, the *Kulik* drilled into a cavern below the seabed. It collapsed and sank the *Kulik*."

Simon nodded. Now, things made sense to him. No wonder the military wanted to keep it a secret. "And released the megalodon and God knows what else into the Chukchi Sea." He placed his hand on Asa's shoulder. All doubts he had harbored about the mechanic vanished. "It's not your fault. My sister died because of a senseless accident. We came up here searching for oil and found a gateway to the past. Now, we've unleashed creatures so terrible we may have to abandon the oceans to them."

Asa looked up bewildered. "Because of giant sharks?"

"From what I've learned, megalodon were top predators in their time. No one knows exactly how big they really grew. A few scientists made comparisons to modern-day sharks by analyzing teeth, but it looks as if they were wrong. I read reports of megalodon from fifty to eighty feet. One is purported to be two-hundred-feet long."

Asa shook his head. "The shark I saw was big, but not quite that big."

Simon gasped. "You really saw it?" He didn't know if he was relieved that the rumors were true or disappointed. He hesitated asking the question he really wanted answered, the one he had been dreading since he had learned of the monsters.

Asa shuddered at the memory. "I saw it, all right." He clamped his hands over his eyes. "God help me," he sobbed. "I can't get the image out of my mind, like a silent gray ghost rising from the depths."

Simon felt sick to his stomach with the horrifying thought that his sister might have ended up inside the creature. "You need a drink. We both need a drink." He reached into a drawer of his desk and pulled out a dark wooden box with the Roman numerals *XXV* printed in gold leaf on the top. "This is twenty-five-year-old *Bunnahabhain* Scotch. It's a single-malt Scotch—really smooth and fruity. I think you'll like it." He removed the three-quarters-full bottle from the box, found two glasses, and splashed two fingers of Scotch in each glass.

Asa whistled. "*Bunnahabhain.* At $385 a bottle, it's a little out of my price range."

Simon shrugged. "One of the perks of a chef. I use a little in a steak sauce, and the company pays for it." He waited for Asa to take an experimental sip, and then smiled at his reaction.

Asa ran his tongue over his lips. "I taste ginger and chocolate."

"Good taste buds." His estimate of Asa went up slightly. In his opinion, no one with sensitive taste buds could be all bad. "Look, why don't we work together?"

Asa shook his head. "I'm not chasing giant sharks. I just want to get my life back."

Simon sneered. "Bullshit! You're here because the sharks are here. You want to prove to yourself that you're not crazy. Well, you're not."

Asa took another sip, and then sighed. "Maybe we both are."

"Ilsa wasn't."

Asa blinked his eyes several times rapidly and set his glass down on the desk. His hand trembled slightly. "Look, I appreciate the drink and understand what you're doing, but you've got the wrong man. I'm not the man I once was. I'm ..." he winced, "broken."

Simon was not going to let him off so easy. He needed Asa's help. "We're all broken, some more than others. The only way to mend ourselves is to see this thing through."

Asa stared at him looking distraught. For a moment, Simon thought he would leave; then, with a heavy sigh, Asa replied, "We could die."

Simon shrugged. "I owe it to Ilsa to try."

At the mention of his sister's name, Asa swallowed hard and then nodded. "Okay, I'm in."

Simon smiled and held out the bottle. "Another?"

Asa shook his head. "I shouldn't have had that one. I leaned heavily on the bottle for a long time. I don't want to become too familiar with it again."

Simon nodded and set the bottle back down. "Later, I'll show you copies of reports I managed to get from a friend in the Navy Office."

"You've got friends in high places."

"Not everyone agrees with the current policy of secrecy. They're treating this occurrence as if it's a battle to win, not as an ecological disaster."

Asa rubbed his forehead. "Between the Scotch and the information, my head's ready to explode. I think I need to mull things over tonight."

"I understand. We'll get together tomorrow." As Asa headed for the door, Simon said, "Thanks for helping me. I appreciate it."

"Don't thank me yet. I'm not sure what I can bring to this little cabal, except maybe doubt."

"You're an eyewitness. That's enough. There are few around. Tomorrow, then."

Asa said, "Yeah, tomorrow."

Asa shut the door behind him, leaving Simon alone. He faced the photo of his sister and lifted his glass to it. "I have an ally, Ilsa. I'll set things right."

5

December 24, 2018   *USS Sunfish*, Beaufort Sea, Antarctic Ocean –

A day spent fishing beat any day lumbering ashore. At least that's what Captain Wilson 'Will' Cobb used to think. Now, he wasn't as certain. The kind of fishing expected of him defied credibility. His orders were plain enough, although he had read them twice to be certain. His mission, to seek out and destroy any giant sharks he encountered on his way to Barrow, had read like a poorly written science fiction short story, but the Navy hadn't asked his opinion; they simply sent him where they needed him. He had reservations about his mission in spite of the rumors he had heard, but the Navy was not one for jests. The two new depth charge racks on the stern of his Mark VI patrol boat, the *USS Sunfish*, installed just before embarkation from their homeport at San Diego Naval Base, added a lethal credulance to his strange orders. The shipyard had also revamped the pair of MK-38 Mod2 25mm miniguns mounted fore and aft, increasing their rate of fire. Four .50 caliber machineguns added to the *Sunfish's* lethal arsenal.

Giant sharks. What next, sea monsters?

He had read the carefully worded reports of sunken and vanished ships, but ships disappeared without a trace in the Bering Sea and the Arctic Ocean all the time. Still, something strange was occurring in the area. He scanned the horizon with his 7x550 binoculars. Both the radar and sonar, newly refurbished, operated at maximum range, but nothing beat a pair of human eyes scanning the ocean. Will did nothing by halves. Neither did the Navy.

His boat was one of four Mark VI fast attack craft in the area, along with three submarines, four missile frigates, a pair of new Littoral Combat Ships, and numerous support vessels. His eighty-two-foot boat might seem a poor choice for hunting a ninety-foot shark, but the boat's formidable firepower and speed gave him an edge.

Another Christmas Eve at sea. He didn't mind. It was not the first holiday he had been away from home and family. He was single. Some of his crew wasn't. It was rougher on them. The tiny, artificial three-foot tree on the bridge lent a holiday air to the boat, but it could not replace family and friends. His executive officer, Ensign JG Richard 'Rich' Hall, caught him staring at the Christmas tree with a forlorn expression.

"Thinking about family, Will?" he asked.

Hall, who had just returned from the outside deck, wore his woolen watch cap pulled down over his ears and had buttoned his pea coat all the way up. Will, inside the cabin, wore his cap and a light waterproof parka.

Will shook his head. "Just wondering what my present was."

Hall glanced at the oblong box wrapped in shiny red paper tied with a large white bow. "It's from the crew, so it could be anything. My guess is a bottle of rum."

"I wish. No alcohol on a U.S. ship." He removed his cap and rubbed his shaved head. "Maybe it's hair tonic."

"Or shark repellent."

Asa stared at his second. He and Hall had served together for two years, and he could read Hall like a novel. "Not you too, Rich."

"The whole crew's got *Jaws* fever. Are we supposed to believe there is some kind of mutant sharks out there as big as the *Sunfish*?"

"Megalodon, not mutants, and that's what the orders say."

Hall waved his hand in dismissal. "Megalodon, smegalodon. Someone's been hitting the medicinal brandy. Thirty-million-year-old giant sharks my ass."

"Not that old. They've just been around that long, underground."

"Yeah, the *Global Kulik* report. I read it. I still don't believe it. An ocean under this one sealed off for millions of years. It doesn't seem possible, like something you'd hear from a Hollow Earth kook."

Will shrugged. His shoulders ached from leaning against the console for hours. He worked his right shoulder to loosen it. Standing rather than sitting in his command chair allowed him to pace the cabin without looking nervous. "It doesn't matter. We still have our orders. Just think of it as a holiday cruise to Barrow."

"Not the first destination I would pick to spend Christmas. Why Barrow, Alaska?"

"To refuel, refit, pick up a group of civilian scientists and a Navy submersible dive team, and then transport them to their destination, the *USS Utah*, a *Virginia*-Class sub."

"A taxi, that's what we are, a freaking water taxi."

"It pays the same."

Hall smiled. "If there are giant sharks out there, I hope we run into one. I'd love to cut loose with the 25mm miniguns. Shark fin soup sounds good."

"Careful we don't wind up on the menu. Personally, I'd like nothing better than to transport our passengers to the *Utah* without incident and head back home, an uneventful voyage."

It was what he was supposed to say, but deep down inside, he agreed with his second. If giant megalodon roamed the Arctic Ocean, he wanted a chance to test the *Sunfish* and her crew in something other than simulated battle conditions. Make-believe could never replace the thrill of actual combat, where fear and adrenaline washed away everything but the moment, and time stood still.

The paragraph in his orders about a refit bothered him, especially since they had just undergone an extensive refit in San Diego. It's like they expected more of him than simply ferrying passengers. If it meant chasing giant sharks, he was all for it.

Hall checked his watch. "Three hours to Barrow. It'll be dark before we get there." He grinned. "If we open her up, we can be there in two."

Apone, the coxswain, looked up from his control seat and grinned. His hands held the two joysticks controlling the engines, and he wanted to test them out.

"We'll keep the helm steady at thirty knots," Will warned. "It wouldn't do to arrive too early."

He understood the pair's desire for speed. The *Sunfish's* twin diesel engines that powered her water-jet drives were capable of producing a cruising speed of forty-five knots, but the wear and tear on the engines shortened their effective operational lifespan.

"We'll save the extra throttle in case we need it."

Apone grinned. "Whatever you say, Skipper."

When Gunner John Mason, who had drawn mess duty, came in with a tray of cups of coffee and doughnuts, Will gratefully accepted both, the caffeine to stay awake and the doughnut for quick energy. The day had been long with little chance for rest, and the *Sunfish* would be in Barrow for less than three hours for refueling, refitting, and embarking their passengers. He would have little time to rest. The night passage to the sub rendezvous would be dangerous. The unusually warm water had forced most of the ice farther north, but small bergs and floes still lurked in the darkness. Hitting one at thirty knots would be disastrous. He and the crew would be at alert stations all night.

I'll sleep tomorrow, he thought, stifling a yawn.

He turned to Hall. "As soon as we dock, send someone ashore for pizzas, something quick and easy. I like Italian sausage on mine, minced."

"This is Alaska, Will. You'll get caribou and like it."

"As long as it's spicy."

A loud *whumph*, followed quickly by a shudder that rattled the bulkheads, accompanied the boat's rapid deceleration. The helmsman struggled with the joystick in an attempt to keep the boat from veering to port. Will lunged forward, catching himself with his hand against the console. His coffee slid off the console and spilled onto the deck.

"What the hell was that?" he yelled. "Did we hit something?"

"Starboard engine is down," the coxswain replied. "Felt like we sucked something into a water intake."

"Great! We're almost within sight of port, and we're dead in the water. Reverse the thrusters and see if we can blow it out."

The whine of the starboard thruster rose to a crescendo. Will watched the temperature gauge needle climb into the red.

"No good. Shut it down before we burn it out."

Hall sighed. "Looks like someone will have to go over the side and clear it by hand. I'll go."

Will could think of no other option. He did not want to call for assistance and have the *Sunfish* towed into port. It was too undignified. He would never live it down.

"Very well. Try not to scratch the paint."

He remained on the bridge while Hall suited up. Even in the heavily insulated wetsuit, Hall would have to work quickly in the freezing water before hypothermia set in or his regulator iced up. He ordered the portable underwater lights lowered over the side to provide illumination in the murky water. He almost suggested Hall carry a shark stick with him, but decided it might be overkill. Hall would have his hands full just clearing the intake port. However, he did order the .50 calibers manned and ready. The 25mm chain guns, operated remotely from a console inside the cabin, covered the bow and stern.

Hall communicated with Will on the bridge through the headset inside his mask. "Going in now," he said.

Will leaned out the open cabin door and gave Hall a thumbs up. He hated leaving Hall exposed with no one else suited up to help if he got into trouble, but that was the problem of a small crew— everyone had a job to do. He watched Hall drop over the side from the starboard step-down cut out near the stern. One of the crewmen fed Hall his white nylon safety line from a spool attached to the hull, as Hall's head disappeared below the surface.

"It's a damn mess down here," Hall announced two minutes later. The wheezing of the regulator punctuated his short, clipped sentences. "Lots of gunk. Clogging the intakes of both thrusters. It's a wonder the other engine is running."

"What is it?"

"Looks like seaweed, but it's the color of ... moldy cottage cheese." After a long pause, he said, "I think I can clear it."

"Good. Be quick about it and get back up here ASAP. I don't like sitting here like a duck on a pond."

He listened to Hall's ragged breathing, punctuated by softly muttered curses, until Hall announced, "Got it. Start the starboard engine on low power to test it."

Will saw both needles on both tachometers move into the green and sighed with relief. "All good here, Rich. Come on up."

"Just a little more cleaning around the edges of the screens and I'm through," Hall replied. "Might as well do it right. I don't want to do this again later after dark. It's spooky enough down here as it is, Will, er, Skipper."

"I'm picking up something on the sonar, sir," Electronics Technician Zeke McGee announced.

Will went cold inside. "What is it?"

"Several objects moving relative to each other at a speed of twenty knots."

With a sinking feeling, he asked, "Where away?"

The tech looked up. "Off the port beam headed this way."

"Anything on radar?"

"Negative."

"What's the ETA?"

"Four minutes."

Barely time for Rich to get out of the water. "How big?"

"The largest is twenty meters."

"Sixty-five feet. Maybe it's a whale."

McGee shook his head. "They don't sound like whales, sir. Listen."

He switched his headphones to the cabin speaker. Instead of the low-frequency rumblings of whale song, Will heard a series of high-pitched clicks and groans. He swore they sounded like crickets on a summer's eve.

"Are they communicating?" he asked, incredulous at what he was hearing.

"I don't know. Maybe."

"Rich, get out of the water. Now! We've got company."

To his credit, Hall did not argue or ask questions. "Right. Almost finished. One more minute."

"You don't have a minute. Now!" Will turned to the watch officer, Petty Officer Cal Grayson. "Sound battle stations."

The klaxon sounded throughout the boat. All hands were already at battle stations, but he wanted them alert. Hall would hear the klaxon reverberating in the water from the hull and get a move on.

"They increased speed, sir," McGee informed him. "They're now moving at thirty-two knots."

They're attracted to sound, Will noted. He leaned out the bridge hatch and yelled to the crewman standing on the cut out. "Get the exec out of the water on the double. Drag his ass out with his safety line if you have to. Portside gunners, stand ready to fire at my command."

He had to wait for Hall, but as soon as his second's head cleared the surface, he would open up with all guns on the objects fast approaching his boat. Then, he would push the *Sunfish* for every knot he could coax from her engines. He had no doubt the sonar objects were sharks, megalodon. His boat displaced 72 metric tons, but multiple objects ramming her at thirty-two knots could do some serious damage to her aluminum hull. He hoped he could outrun them.

"New object coming straight up from the bottom!" McGee yelled. He looked up at Will with terror in his eyes.

"Ready the depth charge racks. Set distance at fifty meters, depth at twenty." Exploding depth charges that near the boat was risky, but he did not have time for a depth charge run. He would have to fire them from a standstill.

"Where's Lieutenant Hall?" he yelled.

"Just coming up, sir," he heard from the stern boat launch deck. A few seconds later, "He's on deck."

"Hang on, sir!" the sonar tech called out.

He barely had time to grab a ceiling support. The ship rang like a Chinese gong, and the bow lifted five feet from the water. The force of the impact broke his grip on the support and slammed him to the deck. The boat resettled hard, groaning as she rocked back and forth. The Christmas tree, the presents, coffee cups, and assorted charts and paperwork scattered across the deck. He picked himself up and grabbed the microphone. "Get the exec. We're getting underway."

"He's gone, sir," the crewman announced.

"What?" he asked stunned, as he stared at the microphone in his hand.

"He was lying on the rear deck removing his mask when the bow lifted. He rolled back into the water. I don't see him."

"Pull him out."

"I can't, sir. The rope broke."

Will swore. He spoke into his headset mic. "Rich, are you okay?" No answer. "What's your condition, Rich?" Still no reply. He could not roll depth charges with Hall still in the water. The aft MK-38 25mm opened up, firing 3,000 rounds per minute. Then two of the .50 calibers began chattering.

"They're circling us, sir."

The engineer, Chico Rodriguez, reported in from below decks. "Water's coming in from a sprung bow plate, Skipper. It should hold for now, but we can't take much more of that ... that whatever the hell it was."

"Rich," he called again, knowing he would get no answer. His second officer was gone, and he could not risk his ship any longer. One more collision like the last, and the *Sunfish* would split open like a rusty soup can, and they would be on the bottom.

A flash of pale gray flesh drew his attention as it sailed airborne by the port window. Seconds later, a bloodcurdling scream reached him from number four .50 caliber machinegun position. With the sound of shearing metal, the .50 caliber went silent.

"Mason's gone, sir!" one of the crew shouted over his mic. "He's just gone."

Mason was the young gunner from Georgia. Now, he had two men dead. He had to think of his boat.

"Full throttle ahead, helmsman." He felt sick at giving the order to abandon his friend, but he had seven other men and his mission to consider. "Drop a full spread of depth charges in our wake."

He knew if Hall was still alive, he had just ordered his death. He felt the *Sunfish's* bow lift as the boat picked up speed; then, felt her shudder, as two depth charges detonated just behind them, followed closely by twin geysers of water. Two more depth charges followed the first two. The chain guns and the remaining .50 caliber machineguns peppered the water, but he paid them no attention, as he watched the sonar screen. One of the smaller objects had disappeared from the screen, destroyed by a lucky depth charge hit. As he had hoped, the sharks were capable of rapid bursts of speed, but could not match the patrol boat's endurance. He watched them fall behind the boat's wake.

However, the larger shark was another matter. He had no doubt it could it could catch them, but it seemed more intent on eating the smaller ones, ignoring the *Sunfish* in its feeding frenzy.

He turned to Grayson, his communications officer. "Call in a report to Barrow. Advise them we encountered megalodon and suffered minor damage. Give them the GPS coordinates."

"What about Ensign Hall and Seaman Mason?"

He shook his head. "No, I'll report their deaths in person."

He had read the Navy reports and had even seen a grainy photograph purporting to be a megalodon over ninety-feet long, but he had dismissed them as incredulous. Now, he knew the truth, and it sickened him. They were in a war with giant prehistoric killing machines for the privilege of sailing the oceans of the world, and they might very well lose.

He glanced back at their wake in the fading light and whispered, "Merry Christmas, Rich. Hell of a present I gave you." A sob escaped his throat. He looked to see if any if the crew noticed his brief emotional outburst. "I'm sorry, buddy."

6

December 25, 2018, 5:30 a.m.   *Drillship Vanguard*, Beaufort Sea, Arctic Ocean –

Asa wasn't sure how he felt. He now had an ally, someone who believed him, but what could two men alone do? Like Simon, he was certain the giant sharks would follow the prevailing current and eventually reach the Beaufort Sea. That was why he had chosen the *Vanguard*. He just hadn't considered much beyond that. Perhaps he simply wanted to see a megalodon again to prove to himself that he wasn't crazy. *Completely crazy*, he added as a postscript.

He didn't know whether to thank or to curse fate, kismet, or whatever that the one man with whom he had allied himself was the brother of the woman he could not save. His troubled heart had almost climbed his gullet when he saw the name on Simon Thorin's chef diploma. Until that moment, he had not made the connection. Simon's chef jackets simply read Chef Simon.

After that, he had held his breath waiting for the one question he did not want to answer—how had Ilsa died? For some reason, Simon had refrained from asking it. *Perhaps he doesn't really want the gory details.* What could he tell Simon? That he had saved her from going over the side, only to lose her when the ship floundered. He didn't know if she drowned, if the ship landed on her and crushed her, or if she wound up in the belly of a king-sized shark. Simon might not hold him responsible for his sister's death, but he still did. He had taken on the responsibility of saving her, and he had failed.

He rubbed his right shoulder, soothing the imaginary ache from the long-healed dislocation. Like his mental wounds, it still haunted him. He glared at the face in the mirror as he dressed for work. His sunken, bloodshot eyes and the lines around his eyes made him look older than his thirty-four years. The months of heavy drinking after his rescue hadn't helped matters. The booze eased the nightmares, but it was just a slow form of suicide. If he were going to kill himself, a gun would be quicker.

He ran a comb through his unkempt brown hair. "Merry. Fucking. Christmas. Asa," he told his reflection, jabbing the mirror with his finger to punctuated each word.

He didn't mind working Christmas Day. The double-time pay was nice, and he had nowhere else to be, no family, and no friends that had survived his bout with the bottle. It was just another dreary day in what had become a long line of days extending into a tedious, uncertain future. In an emergency or during a tragedy, some people put their lives on hold to cope, to deal with the circumstances. He had put his in reverse, as if he were eager to crawl back into the womb before his miserable existence began.

He didn't see Simon in the cafeteria as he ate a breakfast of toast and jelly with six pieces of bacon slipped between slices of toasted bread, but he wasn't sure he wanted to renew their earlier conversation just yet. He finished his first cigarette of the morning and jabbed the butt in a glob of jelly on his plate. He filled his thermos with coffee for the job, hoping not to come back to the cafeteria and risk running into Simon.

Settlemires, his new apprentice, was waiting in the mechanic's shack, his toolkit in hand, a smile on his face, and carrying his own thermos of coffee. Asa suppressed a grin at his eagerness. The kid showed promise. If Brock had to saddle with an apprentice, he could have done worse.

"Good morning, Mr. Iverson," Settlemires said with far more enthusiasm than Asa had for the new day. "Merry Christmas."

"Mornin'," he returned gruffly, grabbed his toolbox, and left with Settlemires tagging along like a puppy.

On their first job of the day, he smoked a cigarette and watched on as Settlemires dismantled a hydraulic pump to replace a worn diaphragm, noting the young mechanic was careful to wipe it down before resealing it. He had deft hands with long, dexterous fingers he moved surely, reminding Asa how sloppy he had become lately. He vowed to do better. He did not want to teach his young apprentice any shortcuts until he had the fundamentals down. Settlemires carried a notebook in his pocket to jot down notes. Asa liked that. It showed a willingness to learn. Maybe he would not become as brash as Asa had before the *Global Kulik*.

"Nice job, son, but next time keep the screws in your pocket or wrapped in a rag. It wouldn't do to have one roll away if the rig shifts. It's a long walk back to the shack for a replacement."

Settlemires nodded. "Got it." He stared at Asa. "You look worried about something."

Asa exhaled a cloud of smoke and shook his head. "It's my normal look, kid. Don't let it bother you."

They worked amid relative silence. The drilling crew had taken the holiday off, leaving only two mechanics doing essential maintenance work and a crew of roustabouts whose hammers pounded rust from the deck, while others followed scraping, priming, and painting, one of the perpetual, mindless tasks aboard a ship at sea. That left only the constant hum of the generators and the rhythmic squeaking of metal against metal as the rig bobbed on the waves. The silence was a welcome relief, but it made conversation easier, and Asa wasn't sure he liked that. Settlemires seemed intent on talking a steady stream.

"Most of the guys warned me to stay away from you," he said with no obvious rancor, just stating an observation.

Asa smiled. He had expected the others to give Settlemires the scoop on him. "I take it you like living on the edge."

"Mr. Brock says you're good. I want to learn from the best. Too many others I've worked with take shortcuts or want to keep their little secrets."

"No secrets here, kid. If you can remember righty-tighty and lefty-loosey and don't fall for the 'fetch me a skyhook' line, you'll do fine."

"Why do you call me, kid?"

Asa took a last drag from his Pall Mall and tossed it over the side. "Because some days I feel like I'm a hundred years old, like today. No offense meant. I'm lousy with names. Give me a few weeks."

After the hydraulic pump, they replaced two waterline valves on a saltwater tank for the mud mixer, repaired a leak in a hydraulic line in the Number Four column, and tightened the loose bolts on a section of ladder. On each job, Settlemires took the lead, while Asa watched on, offering advice on technique or safety. His apprentice performed well, but the incessant chatter began to play on Asa's nerves. He didn't want to slap the kid down. He needed to ask questions, but he preferred they remain job-related. After his tenth or eleventh question about the *Kulik*, Asa chided him as gently as he could.

"Look, kid. Did it occur to you that I don't want to talk about the *Kulik*? A lot of men and women died. I didn't. End of story."

"But ..."

"Enough," Asa snapped. Lack of sleep had pushed him near the brink, and his emotions were raw. "Look, I don't know what the others told you. I can guess, but here's how it is. I was in the lab when the drill broke through into a cavern and released a large volume of air beneath the ship. I barely made it onto deck before the ship flipped onto its side and went under. I floated on a tool chest until a chopper picked me up. Anything else you've heard is either a lie or speculation. I don't remember much, and I was there. End of story."

Settlemires did not look convinced, but he kept future questions pertaining to work matters.

Asa skipped lunch. He didn't want to chance running into Simon. *Ilsa's brother*. That had been a shocker, like seeing a ghost. He had let Simon talk him into an alliance, and he didn't know if he could carry through on his promise. He had agreed because he felt he owed Simon, for Ilsa's sake, but he wasn't sure if their goals meshed. Simon said he wanted answers, but Asa suspected he wanted revenge. Asa wasn't sure what he wanted. Answers for certain, but beyond that he hadn't decided. That could wait until he saw for himself that the sharks were real. Simon was convinced. It sounded as if the Navy were convinced as well. They wouldn't send a task force so near Russian territory otherwise.

As he stood along the portside rail finishing his after-lunch cigarette, he spotted a dark smudge on the horizon, growing larger as it approached. He hoped it was the supply ship. The commissary was getting low on Pall Malls. The blur soon became distinct enough for him to recognize the silhouette of a small Navy patrol boat. A sense of dread swept over him. The Navy meant trouble. When the dull black sail of a nuclear submarine broke the surface less than two miles from the drillship, his stomach did flip-flops, his mind recalling the looming gray dorsal fin of the monster megalodon. Then he saw the bright yellow submersible with its red conning tower sitting on the rear deck of the submarine and knew the shit was about to hit the fan.

* * * *

Simon sat in his cubbyhole office composing a list of supplies to order. The cold weather encouraged the crew to eat more soup, and he was running low on stock. He usually made his own fresh stock from meat scraps, bones, and the trimmed bits of vegetables and herbs, but demand was outpacing supply. He had prepared a red pepper coulis soup for the Christmas meal that seemed to be a big hit, as well as roast turkey with all the trimmings, rum-glazed baked ham, candied yams, garlic-basil mash potatoes, green bean casserole with fried tobacco onion garnish, sweet baby carrots, cornbread dressing, and roast asparagus. His mind was not entirely on the job. His first meeting with Asa had gone better than he had hoped. Asa's admission that he had known Ilsa had been a shock, but he had carefully refrained from prying. He had a dozen questions about her, about her death, but knew Asa was a little gun shy. He didn't want to drive him away with too much information too soon. His plan required Asa's help.

His laptop chimed, notifying him of a message from a chef friend in Barrow. He saved his order for later—he still had plenty of time—and opened the message.

"Greetings, Simon. Navy DSV team left Barrow at 2000 hours 12/24 aboard patrol craft for rendezvous with *USS Utah*. Captain reported encounter with school of megs. Lost two men. Believe sub and DSV headed your direction. Good hunting. Antonio."

Simon smiled. It always amazed him how easily military personnel talked in a restaurant in front of the wait staff, especially in an innocuous pizza joint. He sent a reply.

"Thanks for the heads up, Tony. Simon."

He checked his watch. If they cruised at full speed, the sub should arrive within the hour. That meant the sharks were close as well. His pulse quickened and his mouth turned to cotton. He licked his lips. After months of searching, this was as close to the megalodon as he had gotten. Until now, it had been almost like a game—gather information, then wait for the sharks, repeating the procedure throughout the Arctic. Now, at last, he would have his chance at killing a megalodon. *If all goes right.*

He had no doubt that the Navy would be hunting them as well, and he did not begrudge them their opportunity to kill the creatures. By all accounts, there were enough to go around. He only wanted to see one of the megs close up, stare into its dead eyes, as he used his secret weapon to kill it. He didn't know if it would be an act of revenge or one of atonement. He and his sister had parted on bad terms the last time they had met. Since her death, he had regretted not reaching out to her. Words left unspoken were less than useless. Now, he would never have the opportunity to beg her forgiveness. Avenging her death was his only recourse.

A shadow fell across him. He looked up to see Asa standing in the doorway, his face ashen and crisscrossed with tension wrinkles.

"You've got to fucking see this," Asa said.

* * * *

2:50 p.m.–

Asa stood by the door in the cafeteria, the only space large enough to accommodate the entire crew of the *Vanguard*, even if they sat or stood elbow to elbow. Farris Wheeler, the Offshore Installation Manager, flanked by the rig captain and Chief Mechanic Brock, stood in front of the serving line, while cooks prepared coffee and sandwiches behind the line, glancing up occasionally with worried expressions. He didn't see Simon anywhere. He had disappeared right after Asa had informed him of the Navy's arrival.

Wheeler cleared his throat. "The Navy has just notified me that we must evacuate the rig." He glanced at a young Navy officer standing at the edge of the room. The lieutenant bore a grim look on his face that made him look older than his years, but he otherwise ignored the proceedings. Wheeler waved his hand in the air to quell the instantaneous outburst of questions and comments from the crowd. "I cannot go into any details at this time. We will institute the emergency shutdown procedure in fifteen minutes. Helicopters are in route to transport crew to a Navy carrier. You will carry only essential personal belongings."

The room erupted in questions despite Wheeler's efforts. Two stood out. One was from one of the roughnecks. "Why not simply move the rig?" Wheeler's answer was enlightening to Asa.

"The Navy has a use for the rig."

Asa recognized Simon's voice as he asked the next question. "Who's staying? I need to know how much food to cook."

"The Dynamic Positioning Officer, the Chief Mechanic, and two crane operators will remain until things are squared away. Then, they will be airlifted out as well."

He suspected Simon had asked the question for a reason other than to learn how many for dinner. Asa wondered just how the Navy wanted to use the drillship. He had seen the DSV on the sub and suspected it would not end well for the rig. He knew one thing—he had to remain on the *Vanguard*. He hadn't come all this way, waited all this time, just to leave when things were getting dicey. He glanced at the serving line and saw Simon's head appear from behind a steel column. His gaze fixed on Asa, and he nodded. The cook was thinking along the same lines.

"What about the riser?" one of the drillers asked. "If we simply disconnect, we'll lose 4,000 feet of pipe."

"It can't be helped," the OIM answered. "We'll shut down the subsea BOP and activate the emergency disconnect system."

"But we've found traces of oil."

Asa understood the driller's plight. Leaving oil in the ground was tantamount to sacrilege. They might be able to set up on the Blowout Preventer again, but only after they removed the twenty-five-hundred feet of drill pipe that would collapse over the BOP when it disengaged.

Wheeler's jaw clenched tight, as he said, "It can't be helped. I have no say in the matter. Just do it." From the look on his face, he was having a difficult time keeping his frustration in check.

Though they were not friends, Asa felt sorry for him. He, too, had dealt with the Navy and had come out on the short end of the stick.

Wheeler raised his hands in the air palms forward. "Okay, no more questions. We don't have time. Do your jobs. Work fast but safely. Gather one bag of personal effects and wait on the deck below the helipad. We'll assign you numbers to indicate which helicopter to take. The first chopper arrives within the hour."

Asa hung back, pretending to pour a cup of coffee from the urn, and waited for Simon. Simon brought out a fresh pot and poured some of it into the top of the urn, which was still almost full. Few had an appetite for coffee after the hard-hitting news of evacuation. Speaking almost too softly for Asa to hear him over the clamor of hundreds of work boots scuffing the tile floor as people filed out of the cafeteria, Simon whispered, "Meet me in my quarters." He then turned and left, leaving Asa confused.

By the time he left the cafeteria, Asa had determined not to allow anything to deter him from his goal, as tenuous as it presently was. He knew that if he left the rig now, he would probably never be back. He would continue to live his life a scarred and broken man. His only chance at reuniting the tattered remnants of his life lay on the *Vanguard*. Whatever happened, whatever was in store for the drillship, he would be a part of it. His face went hard and his jaw clenched so tightly it began to twitch. *This time, I won't abandon ship.*

"What do we do?"

He whirled to find his apprentice, Settlemires, standing behind him. He had forgotten about his new watchdog. He shifted his thoughts back to the present.

"We try to stay out of the way as much as possible. The Roughnecks can handle the shutdown."

"Shouldn't we—?"

"Look, kid," Asa snapped. "You worry about getting aboard one of the choppers out of here. I think things are going to get bad around here damn fast."

Settlemires stared at him without comprehension, but he nodded, accepting Asa at his word. "What about you?"

"I have a chess game to finish. Go on, report to the mechanic's shack, and pick up your tools. You'll make a good mechanic someday. Whoever you work with will be lucky."

Settlemires stared at him. "You sound like you're not coming back."

Asa shrugged. "Who knows what's going to happen. We may not come back to the *Vanguard*." He reached out and offered Settlemires his hand. "Good luck, kid."

Settlemires shook it, but looked unconvinced by Asa's story. "Yeah, same to you."

Settlemires left, but looked back over his shoulder before disappearing down the corridor. Asa hated to abandon him, but he didn't need anyone following him around. He knew he should have returned to the mechanic's shack with Settlemires to help shut down the rig, but his mind was elsewhere. There were enough mechanics to do the job. He waited in the corridor until he saw Simon leave the cafeteria and head to his quarters, and then followed him at a discrete distance. Simon left the door open a crack. Asa slipped inside and closed the door behind him, feeling somewhat like a frat boy sneaking into the girl's dorm.

"What now?" he asked, breathless from the intrigue.

"I was hoping for more time," Simon replied, "another day or two, but it looks as though time has run out."

"Do you have a plan?" Asa asked. He hoped they were not a tiny cabal of wannabe conspirators with no more purpose than to witness a naval battle between man and monster.

Simon smiled. "Being a chef allows me a little leeway bringing material onto the ship, like the Scotch. Over the past six months, I've been accumulating a stash of a poison that should be capable of killing anything that swims–*saxitoxin*, a neurotoxin made from a secretion of the dinoflagellate *Nitzchia occidentalis.* You may have heard of it as Red Tide."

Simon's resourcefulness stunned Asa and frightened him a little. The chef had put a lot more effort into learning about the megalodon than he had even considered. "You have neurotoxin here?" He glanced around Simon's room as if expecting it to be sitting on a shelf in plain view. "How much?"

"About two hundred milligrams in the cooler."

He whistled. "My God, how did you manage to accomplish that?"

"I have a friend in San Francisco, a marine researcher who manufactured it for me from cultures in his lab. He used to make it for the military until they banned biological weapons."

Asa wondered what kind of friend would be willing to break international treaty laws on bio-weapons manufacturing. Did he, too, have personal reasons for wanting the megalodon dead?

"Is that enough?"

Simon drummed his meaty fingers on the desk. "Half a milligram can kill a human."

"How do you propose we use it, some kind of spear gun?" The idea of actually swimming in close proximity to the megalodon frightened Asa almost to immobility. A horrid vision of the pale gray ghost from the *Global Kulik* slowly circling him with its blind eyes staring at him, as if it could see into his soul, sent shivers running up his spine. What had he gotten himself into? He wondered if it was too late to back out.

Simon smiled. "We use one of the ROVs. You're a mechanic. You should be able to build a simple injector mechanism to attach to one of the manipulator arms, something powered by compressed air from the ROV tanks. I have a rough diagram I drew up."

Asa considered Simon's proposal. Using one of the rig's remotely operated vehicles used to uncouple the undersea Blowout Preventer might just work. Anything that placed distance between him and the megalodon was worth considering. "How do you propose we do all that with the Navy on board?"

"As quietly as possible. I figure it will take an hour or so to adapt the ROV. Whatever use the Navy has for the rig, they're not going to notice a little activity for a while. Then, we lay low until the megalodon arrive." Simon's face broke into a macabre mask of hatred that threatened to split the flesh around his suddenly cold eyes. "Then, we kill them."

Asa knew a lot could go wrong with the plan, but it beat anything he could have conceived. If they were caught, the Navy would not be as lenient on him the second time. Still, it was better than doing nothing. Trying to live his life in the shadow of the megalodon hadn't worked out so well for him so far. Some fears must be faced; some futures must be risked.

"What if they don't show up for a while? We can't hide out indefinitely."

"I overheard that lieutenant talking to Farris. A storm front is due to hit us by early morning. The storm will herd the megalodon this direction. I'm betting that's why the Navy showed up when they did. The *Vanguard* is right in the middle of the front's path." He stared at Asa. "Well?"

Asa didn't want to answer. Saying yes would set him on a path that could send him to prison or to his death. However, doing nothing, joining the others in their exodus, would leave him where he was, and that was unthinkable. He swallowed hard and nodded. "I'm in."

Some of the tension faded from Simon's face, but the coldness remained behind his eyes. "We have to beat the Navy. I didn't plan all this just to watch someone else finish the job."

Asa knew how Simon felt. He, too, wanted to strike out at the creatures that had taken his future from him. "Okay, let's do it."

7

December 25, 2018, 4:14 p.m.   *USS Sunfish* –

Captain Will Cobb shifted his weight slightly to keep his balance, as the *Sunfish* banged against the floating dock attached to one of the rig's vertical columns. The waves were increasing in size as a rapidly building weather front fifty miles to the southwest moved relentlessly toward the drillship. The hope among the Navy Brass was that the storm would herd the megalodon their way. Observations from unmanned drones seemed to verify the fact that they were coming. Will hoped they were right. He was tired of waiting. He just wanted it to be over.

"Give her some slack," he said to one Able Seaman Zeke McGee and watched him loosen the line on the cleat to allow the boat to drift farther from the dock to ride the waves more easily. He didn't want any additional pressure on the damaged hull plates. The workers in Barrow had performed the refit quickly, but that had not included reinforcing the weakened bow. The crew had reinforced them as best they could with pieces of four-inch diameter steel pipe and two-by-fours. Under normal circumstances and in a calm sea, the makeshift repairs would be adequate, but against giant sharks in the midst of a storm, he wasn't as positive.

The bizarre contents of the starboard and port freshwater tanks caused the *Sunfish* to ride lower in the water than usual. Water for drinking, cooking, and the toilet now came from a supply of five-gallon plastic jugs. The shower was inoperable. If anyone wanted to clean up, they would have to avail themselves of the drillship's facilities.

He backed away from the railing, as a wave crashed against the side of the boat, creating a fan spray of frigid salt water. He glanced over at the *Utah* floating four clicks off his port beam, barely discernible as a black smear against a dark sky. Her seventy-nine-thousand metric ton displacement kept her steady in the rising swell, though her deck was awash. He had rendezvoused with the submarine and delivered the DSV crew as planned, but because of his ill-fated encounter with the megalodon, his superiors had amended his orders to deliver the civilian scientists directly to the drillship *Vanguard*. Keeping pace with the slower-moving submarine had tried his patience, likening it to walking a short-legged dog on a long leash.

The civilians, three men and one woman, all tight-lipped about their mission, had kept to themselves below decks, poring over their laptops with only the occasional word passing among them. He didn't like secrets aboard his boat, especially ones to which he was not privy. For his part, he had ignored the scientists, even the woman, who, in his opinion was much too good-looking for a scientist. He had always pictured female scientists as dowdy spinsters with their hair in a tight bun and wearing thick, heavy-framed glasses. This one looked as if she had stepped off the pages of *Elle* magazine. He realized some might misinterpret his views as misogynistic, but his only acquaintance with female scientists was through 50s sci-fi movies. If nothing else, the trip had raised his esteem of female scientists.

The three Navy divers had been almost as reticent about their mission. The chief diver, Haig, had hinted at secret weapons but refused to elaborate further. He seemed to take delight in withholding information from the *Sunfish's* curious captain.

Will's orders after delivering his passengers remained unclear. He did not like that either. He wanted to be in the upcoming fight. In fact, he needed to be in it. He had lost two men to the sharks, two friends. The pain of their loss still soured his mouth. Only the blood of a megalodon could wash the bitter taste from his tongue.

Blood. That's what this all comes down to. It's what all battles come down to—blood. Whose would spill first, his men's or that of the megalodon?

When he had delivered the orders from the admiral to the Offshore Installation Manager to evacuate the platform, the OIM had made his disdain of the Navy's heavy-handed usurpation of his power very clear. That a mere lieutenant had delivered the orders made the humiliation even more difficult to swallow. The OIM had Will's sympathy, but he was just the messenger boy.

The one thing that gave him hope that the *Sunfish* would take an active part in the coming battle was her refit in Barrow. The repair crew had broken speed records by replacing one of the .50 caliber machineguns, as well as the one ripped away by the megalodon, in just over two hours. In their places, they had mounted two MK-60 launcher systems, each capable of launching four BGM-176B *Griffin* missiles. After witnessing the destructive power of the megalodon firsthand, he approved of the added firepower. The *Sunfish* now also carried a *SeaFox* mini-ROV for underwater surveillance and four aerial mini-drones for surface detection of the megalodon.

He vaguely understood the Navy's reasoning in choosing the drillship *Vanguard* as its center of operations. The megalodons' path before the storm took them in a generally easterly direction, and the rig offered a stable platform from which to spring the trap they were preparing to stop the creatures' eastward advance. For his money, evacuating the area and launching a BGM-109 *Tomahawk* cruise missile tipped with a W80 nuclear warhead set for a 20-kiloton blast would be simpler and surer, but Russia might not look too kindly on a nuclear explosion so close to her northern border. No American president wanted to be the first president to use a nuclear weapon in almost three-quarters of a century. Besides, they could not be certain all of the sharks were in the same general location. A handful of smaller megalodon sharks and giant crabs had been spotted as far away as the Aleutian Islands, but most of the large ones had remained in frigid Arctic waters.

He looked up at the drillship towering above the *Sunfish* and watched the last MH-60 *Seahawk* helicopter leave the helipad carrying the last of the rig crew to the USS *Kirby,* an *America*-class escort aircraft carrier less than fifty miles away. Once there, they would transfer to MV-22 *Ospreys* for the flight to the mainland. When the soft *whumph* of the rotors died away, the only sounds remaining were the waves pounding against the hollow columns and the sizzle and bright actinic glare of arc welders, as engineers mounted missile launchers to the rig's deck.

Unlike his *Griffin* missiles, the launchers were part of a RUM-139 ASROC air-to-surface system capable of launching Mark 46 Mod 5A torpedoes, a five-hundred pound, eight-and-a half-foot long instrument of destruction. Unlike legendary whale-hunting, metal-tipped harpoons of yore, the Mark 46, tipped with a ninety-eight-pound warhead packed with PBXN-103 explosives, could sink a frigate. It was quite capable of delivering death in large doses to a megalodon.

The same *Seahawks* that had delivered the ASROCs and evacuated the drillship's crew had also delivered dozens of large crates, a modified anti-shark mine, which ordinance technicians had been assembling all day. In essence, they were transforming the drillship *Vanguard* into a stationary weapons platform.

He wondered what kind of chaos would be unleashed when the orders came to attack. Missiles and torpedoes he understood, something quantifiable. They delivered a measurable amount of destructive power. He knew nothing about the new weapon the scientists were preparing; therefore, he could place no faith in its effectiveness. He had watched too many *Godzilla* movies to know that secret weapons seldom performed as well as predicted. He placed his faith in high explosives and the men who knew how to use them.

He turned to Chico Rodriquez, former engineer newly promoted to executive officer. The twenty-three-year-old from San Bernardino was still uncomfortable with his new position as second-in-command, but Will trusted him.

"Launch the aerial drones, Chico. Let's see if we have any company."

He watched Rodriquez and another crewman pull the four drones from their crates and assemble them. Twenty minutes later, all three were buzzing along on their four rotors and six-foot wingspans six-hundred feet above the surface, relaying high-resolution images to the split-screen monitor on the bridge. The rapidly changing view of the surface was dizzying. He didn't know how technician Cal Grayson could keep up with everything. It was multi-tasking in the extreme. Like most young people, the nineteen year old had probably grown up attached to a video game controller. Except for the whitecaps dotting the surface like a sprinkling of meringue, the ocean was empty. Recharging their batteries from solar cells built into the body, the drones could have remained aloft all day and for long hours into the night, but he had seen enough.

On their return flight, Will ordered Grayson to buzz the *Utah*, allowing him a close-up view of the three-man DSV sitting on her aft deck. He was curious about the submersible and what part it would play in the operation. In his mind, the DSV looked too small and fragile to operate in the midst of hungry giant megalodon. After landing safely on the *Sunfish's* bow, the crew disassembled the drones and returned them to their crates in preparation for the next day's use.

As evening fell, a golden glow spread across the horizon, creating deep shadows beneath the rig. It was a moment of quiet time for him. Leaning against the rail on the leeward side of the boat out of the spray, he watched the buzz of activity aboard the drillship. Light towers burst into life, washing the deck with bright lights, allowing the workers to complete their tasks. The crews worked quickly but methodically, installing the launchers and making the necessary modifications to turn the rig into a base of operations. By morning, the installation would be complete. Later in the day, the leading edge of the storm would be upon them, and, hopefully, the megalodon. They would learn if all their preparations had been enough.

Will sighed. *Hurry up and wait.* That was the Navy way. He was ready for some payback.

"It looks like we're going to have some company, Skipper," Grayson announced. "I just received a message from the *Amberjack*. They'll arrive in two hours."

Will nodded. The USS *Amberjack* was a Mark VI patrol craft, the *Sunfish's* sister ship, one of four in the Arctic. He had met the boat's captain, Mark Eisner, at the operations briefing in San Diego. Eisner, at 46, was old for a small boat captain, but he was experienced and had contributed some good points at the briefing. The *Amberjack's* assignment had been Wrangel Island farther west of the *Vanguard*, but he was glad for the added firepower.

"Good, we could use the help."

The *Amberjack* had not undergone a refitting in Barrow, as had the *Sunfish*. She retained her .50 caliber and 25mm chain guns and the depth charge racks installed in San Diego, but did not carry *Griffin* missile launchers. Even so, a second highly maneuverable boat could make a difference in the success of the operation.

He reached for the headset to speak with Eisner. "Welcome to nowhere, Mark."

"There's a lot of nowhere in the Arctic. We just left another little bit of it yesterday. We came through the storm front. It left us pretty beat up. The Mark VI wasn't built for heavy seas. We need to tidy up and shift some cargo. Maybe I'll get a chance to drop by later for coffee."

"Pot's on anytime. Did you see any megalodon?"

Eisner's voice took on a harder edge. "No, but we passed through the wreckage of a Russian trawler earlier today. No survivors. It looked like it had been run through a car shredder."

"We'll stop them."

"We had better. Well, I've got to get my crew cracking. I'll talk with you later. Good hunting."

"Same to you, Mark."

Eisner's report left a hard knot in Will's stomach. The megalodon were on their way.

8

December 25, 2018   Shell Oil Drillship *Vanguard,* Beaufort Sea–

The unexpected arrival of the Navy cast a cloud over Simon's plan to kill the megalodon. He and Asa maintained a low profile, avoiding the staff rounding up workers and assigning numbers for transport, by remaining in Simon's quarters until dark. Throughout the day, a steady stream of helicopters arrived and departed ferrying rig crew off the ship. Others delivered Navy engineers and crates of equipment. Even amid the hustle and bustle, Asa was afraid someone would confront them and send them packing. Simon could not hide his eagerness to implement his plan, but the anxiety of waiting allowed doubt to creep into Asa's resolve. Fear gripped him so tightly he could feel it on his skin, like cold clammy hands.

"Are you sure this is a good idea?" he asked Simon. His mouth was dry. He badly wanted another sip of Simon's *Bunnahabhain* Scotch, but the chef had not offered any. He wasn't sure even good Scotch could ease his nerves.

Simon's head snapped up from the pile of papers on his desk to glare at him. "Having second thoughts?"

"When the repercussion of getting caught was being fired, I thought it was worth the risk. Now ..."

"I'm going through with this with or without your help." Simon paused. "I could use it though."

"Look, the Navy warned me to keep my mouth shut. If we're caught, it won't take them long to discover who I am. Now, with the neurotoxin in our possession, they might decide we're terrorists and drop us out of a chopper on the way back to the mainland. No questions asked."

Simon's features softened. "I have to avenge my sister's death. I see her ghost every time I try to sleep. Her shade won't let me rest." He studied Asa for a long moment, and then said, "I can't begin to understand what you must have gone through—the doubt, the guilt, deserved or not, the threat of prison for trying to clear your name. You're the shell of the man you once were. I can tell. Don't you want your life back? Don't you want redemption?"

Simon's words sounded sincere, but Asa wondered if anything could ever heal the scars of the *Kulik's* sinking. "Redemption?" He shook his head. "Killing these bastards isn't redemption. It's revenge. Maybe the Navy can do a better job of it than we can."

Simon hissed, "I don't trust them. They've had a year to do it."

Neither did Asa, but he was hesitant to admit it to Simon. He needed a way out of his promise, not to ensnare himself deeper in Simon's plan.

"How can we do it with the Navy all over the rig?"

"We do it tonight after things quiet down. I checked the weather station. The storm front will be here early tomorrow and with it, the megalodon. We have to be ready." He stared at Asa, waiting. "Are you in or out?"

Asa sighed. What more did he have to lose that he had not been taken from him already? "I'm in."

Simon relaxed his stance and nodded. "Good. We can do this."

"I hope the hell you're right."

Simon glanced at the photo of his sister. "I *have* to be right."

* * * *

By six p.m., things had quieted down on the drillship. Whatever the technicians had been assembling behind a wall of canvas screening was ready. Most of the work installing the ASROC torpedo launchers was completed as well. The large, box-shaped metal launchers on each swivel mount each held eight missiles with a range of twelve miles. The drillship looked like the deck of a missile frigate. Only a handful of Navy men and the four scientists remained aboard the *Vanguard*. The Dynamic Positioning Officer, the Chief Mechanic, and the two crane operators had left on the last helicopter. Simon checked the corridor outside the room and found it clear.

"It's now or never," he said.

Asa sighed and joined him. His legs felt leaden, but he knew it was only his fear holding him back. They reached the mechanics shack undetected. Working from Simon's crude drawings, after adding a few modifications of his own, Asa gathered the necessary items and began assembling them using the TIG welder. For a delivery system, he modified a small oxygen tank to contain the deadly *saxitoxin*. He attached a pressure regulator to control dosage. A thin tube extended from the regulator into the cylinder to pressurize it, and a length of flexible, metal-fiber coated tubing served as an oxygen line. He cut one end of a three-foot-long, ½-inch diameter hollow tube at a sharp angle to create a bevel and welded it to the regulator's outlet.

His final modification was a bracket to attach the injector to the ROV's manipulator arm and use the claw of the arm to activate the injector. The task took two hours to complete. By eight o'clock, they were ready to attach it to the ROV. His eyes burned from the welder flash even through the darkened glass of the shield. It had also given him a headache that threatened to split his skull.

Simon admired Asa's work and grinned. "It looks better here than on paper."

"It should do the job."

Working in the mechanic's shack had been easy. No one could see them. Preparing the ROV was another matter altogether. It sat on the drill platform where the roustabouts had left it after decoupling the Blowout Protection Valve. They would be in plain sight to anyone bothering to look in that direction.

Trusting to luck, they worked quickly to make the necessary modifications, and then acquainted themselves with its operation. The ROV's construction was basic—a buoyancy tank, a frame containing five thrusters for movement and positioning, a motor, work lights, and a high-resolution NTSC camera. Various plug-in attachment packages included manipulator arms, cable cutters, and a welder. For their purpose, they would use the modified manipulator arm.

Attaching their giant shark-sized hypodermic syringe to the manipulator arms allowed them some degree of control in hitting a vital spot on the shark. The mechanism would release a predetermined amount of pressurized *saxitoxin* upon impact. A second blast of air would clear the nozzle of any flesh or cartilage to prepare for a second injection. Holding the regulator open would empty the cylinder in one burst. Asa began to feel more confident that Simon's plan would work. *Work once, anyway*, he corrected himself. He doubted they would get a second chance. Once would be enough. Their goal was not to eliminate all the megalodon, simply to strike a blow, a token gesture. *If the creature doesn't swallow the ROV whole.*

"It's as ready as I can get it." He stared at Simon. "I wish we could test it."

Simon's face was grim. "Either it works or it doesn't. You did a great job putting it together. It'll work. I'm sure of it."

While he appreciated the chef's vote of confidence, Asa was still worried. Too many things could go wrong. There were too many variables. They had no idea on the proper dosage necessary to kill a megalodon, so they erred on the concept that more was better. With the makeshift tank filled to maximum, the pressure regulator would allow them three injections of sixty-six milligrams each, if luck gave them the opportunity. Much of the success depended on the thickness of megalodon skin. Their calculation was all conjecture and supposition based on the nearest relative, the Great White shark.

A thought occurred to Asa, one he had neglected to consider in his haste to aid Simon. "These megalodon are blind. I've seen it. How do they find their prey?" he asked, feeling foolish for not thinking of the creatures' blindness earlier.

"Sharks have an excellent sense of hearing and sense of smell. Loss of visual acuity probably enhanced their other senses to a remarkable degree."

"So how do we attract them? Does one of us offer a pint of blood for the water?" He envisioned slicing his arm and letting his blood drip into the water. "Do we chum the rig with Porterhouse steaks?"

"I considered using blood as bait, but decided we might have better luck with an auditory signal."

"What kind of …?" Asa began; then smiled. "The sonar on the ROV. You intend to use the sonar as a beacon."

Simon smiled as well. "The scent from any other type of bait would disperse quickly, too quickly to sustain for long periods. We can set the sonar to broadcast as wide a frequency as possible for as long as necessary. Sharks have an organ called the ampullae of Lorenzini, electroreceptor in their snouts. They can detect very faint electromagnetic fields."

Simon's thoroughness heartened Asa but did not alter the fact that he now proposed competing with the United States Navy in a battle to kill megalodon. Asa could think of a hundred ways for the plan to fall apart, several of which ended with the two of them dead or in a federal prison. He knew broaching the subject with Simon would be useless. Simon had already made up his mind, and nothing would sway him from his course of action, his vendetta. For better or for worse, Asa had enlisted in Simon's army. He would not let him down. Neither death nor imprisonment could be worse than the agony he had suffered for the past year. In a way, he had nothing to lose.

"Shall we get started?" Simon asked.

Asa took a deep breath, released it slowly, and said, "It's why we're here, right? Let's do it."

As they carefully filled the converted oxygen cylinder with the *saxitoxin*, Asa thought, *too late to back out now. I'm committed.*

* * * *

11:00 p.m.–

Will leaned against the rail on the leeward side of his boat out of the salt spray. The bitterly cold wind did not howl, but it did growl as the storm front drew closer. The *Sunfish* bobbed like a cork on a line downwind from the dock. He had watched the flurry of activity all day aboard the *Vanguard*, the constant stream of helicopters, the welders installing the torpedo launchers. Now, the drillship was quiet. The furtive movements of two civilians outlined in the rig's lights drew his attention. What were they doing? For a moment, he considered calling in a report, but then decided to investigate himself. He needed the exercise.

He pulled the *Sunfish* closer to the dock by hand with the bowline and leaped the gap between the deck and the dock. The long climb up the stairs inside the hollow column winded him, but at least he was out of the cold. The lack of any sentries surprised him, but supposed they assumed there was no need. After all, the enemy they faced was not man but a beast. Everyone was inside the building enjoying the evening or asleep with the exception of the two mystery men. He located them near the drill platform inside the glass-fronted control room out of the cold wind. He watched them work for a few minutes to determine if their actions were innocent or nefarious. He had his sidearm in case of the latter.

The pair, a taller man and a shorter, heavy-set one, huddled around a stack of instruments set up on a table. Two of the cases held video monitors. A third looked like a sonar screen. The taller man held a toggle control in his hands. Will crept closer until he stood just outside the door, where he could better eavesdrop on their conversation.

"Camera clarity is good," the taller one said. "Range is one-twenty-five to one-fifty yards."

"Switch to Infrared," the overweight one suggested.

"Still clear," the first answered few moments later.

"Try sonar."

"Operating within specs. Range is six-hundred yards."

"Good! Now, disconnect the umbilical and see if we maintain control."

The taller one glanced up from the screen and replied in a nervous voice, "If we disconnect now, Simon, we can never recover the ROV, not without help."

"Look, Asa, if we survive this, the company can sue me. If not …"

Will saw the speaker's shoulders lift in a defiant shrug.

"Ok. We still have control." There was relief in Asa's voice.

"We'll practice operating the ROV for a while. At dawn, we'll bring it to just below the surface and moor it to a pontoon. When the megalodon show up, we'll move it to the dock and load the syringe."

"What if the Navy catches us," Asa asked.

Taking the words as his cue, Will stepped into the control room, his right hand resting lightly on the butt of his .45. "That's an interesting question. The short answer would depend on just what you two are up to."

The pair froze, staring at him. Finally, Asa said, "You're the lieutenant from the meeting in the cafeteria. Cobb, right?"

"What are your intentions?" the heavy-set man, Simon, demanded in a gruff voice, as he noted the pistol at Will's side. Asa placed his hand on Simon's shoulder to restrain him from attempting anything foolish.

"The real question is what your intentions are," Will replied. He sensed defiance in the pair, but no danger. He moved his hand away from his sidearm to ease the tension.

"We're hunting giant sharks," Simon said. "We're going to kill as many as we can."

Will suppressed a grin at their audacity. "That's the Navy's job."

"You've been taking your own sweet time doing it. We deserve first crack at them," Simon snapped. "They killed my sister." He nodded at Asa. "He barely survived an attack."

Will stared at Asa more closely, recognition finally dawning. The three-day growth of beard had disguised his features. "I thought I recognized you. You're the survivor from the *Global Kulik* disaster."

Asa sighed and shook his head slowly.

Will turned to Simon. "What do you do?"

Simon rubbed his ample belly and smiled. "I'm the chef. Never trust a skinny cook."

"You both have my sympathy; I lost two crewmen yesterday, but you could endanger the operation and risk Navy personnel, not to mention your own lives. I cannot allow that."

"It's not right," Simon burst out.

"Just what did your plan entail? I assume that's the rig's ROV down there."

The two men stared at one another for a moment; then, Simon spoke. "We rigged the ROV to deliver a large dose of *saxitoxin*, enough to kill a megalodon."

Will whistled. The two men were resourceful, as well as foolish. "I won't even ask how you came by an illegal chemical agent. Even if your plan worked, it wouldn't matter. There are dozens of megalodon—fifty by last count. We've killed a few, but they're fast and deadly. Killing one won't do much. I'll call a chopper for tomorrow morning. Fly out of here and leave the killing to the Navy."

"If we refuse?" Simon asked.

"Look, I don't want to lock you up, but I will if necessary. If I report you, it will be out of my hands. Why not make it easy on both of us and return to your rooms? I assure you conditions are much better there than in the brig of a *Virginia*-Class submarine."

Simon continued to stare at Will in defiance. Asa returned to the ROV controls. "I'll set the ROV down on top of the pontoon."

Will nodded. "That will suffice for now. We can recover it later."

"You had better not screw this up," Simon warned, jabbing his finger at Will, "or you'll never stop me."

"We have a plan of operation in place."

Simon sneered. "You think those missiles will do the job?"

"They're not missiles. They're ASROC torpedo launchers and quite formidable. We have a special weapon ready for the sharks, a new type of mine. If it works as predicted, we'll finish them here."

"If?" Simon growled. "And if it doesn't?"

Will smiled. "Then you can use your ROV. It won't matter by then anyway. Please, gentlemen, return to your rooms."

"Come on, Simon," Asa said, tugging at Simon's shoulder. "We can't do anything more."

Will watched the pair until they entered the main building; then shook his head. "Damn, they've got some balls. Neurotoxin."

He was certain he hadn't heard the last of them.

* * * *

12:05 a.m.–

Simon stomped the room as if tromping down an enemy, his anger written plainly on his scowling face. Asa sat on the bed with his legs out of the way of Simon's pacing. Unlike the chef, his feelings were less clear. Once he had decided to help Simon, he wanted to get the job done, but a small part of him felt the same relief of an undersized schoolboy whose fight with a large schoolyard bully a teacher has just stopped. Now, the fear that had been gnawing at his gut could subside. It was out of his hands.

"Damn! What do we do now?" Simon asked.

"Do? We do nothing," Asa replied. His head still pounded from his blinding migraine. The confrontation with the lieutenant had not helped matters. All he wanted was a couple of aspirin and a glass of water. *And sleep, but good luck with that.* "The lieutenant could have arrested us. He won't be as lenient next time."

"I didn't come this far just to ..." He stopped speaking and cursed, "just to sit here twiddling my thumbs."

Asa tried reasoning with Simon. "Look, Simon, if the Navy has a plan, let them carry it out. As long as the megalodon die ..."

"No," Simon growled. "That's not good enough." He made fists of his hands. "I need to do something personally. I need to make things right."

"You can't make things right, Simon. Your sister is dead. My friends are dead. It's all been about revenge. Revenge is for the living, not the dead. Hold on to the memory of your sister and get on with your life. Life is too precious to waste on grieving, or on self-doubt," he added. "I'm beginning to learn that."

Simon shook his head. "So close. We were so damn close."

"At least we have front row seats for the battle," Asa reminded him.

"If the lieutenant doesn't ship us home in the morning on a helicopter."

"If you're right about that storm, he won't have time."

"I'm right," Simon replied, nodding. "Can't you feel the change in the air?"

Now that Simon had mentioned it, Asa, too, felt something different about the air, not just the slight ionic change in the atmosphere before a storm. The air bore a strange odor previously masked by the normal smells aboard a drillship, and then by the tang of a dozen welders burning metal, the same stench fouling the water and the air after the *Global Kulik* had broken through the cavern ceiling and sunk. The megalodon were coming and bringing the foul air of their primeval world with them.

"Well, there's nothing we can do now." He paused before continuing, "Maybe the lieutenant is right. Maybe we should leave in the morning. I have a bad feeling about this whole Navy versus megalodon thing. Maybe dying for a front row seat isn't such a good idea."

Simon stared at Asa for a moment before replying. His voice was softer than Asa expected. "Go ahead. I won't hold it against you. You kept your part of the bargain." He grimaced and shook his head slowly. "I can't go. I have to see this thing through, one way or another."

"But—"

Simon stopped him. "Somehow, I'll get the chance to strike my blow. That's all I want, one good lick; then, after that, it doesn't matter."

"Surely, your sister wouldn't want you to die to avenge her death. We weren't close, but I knew her a little. She enjoyed life. I don't think she would want anyone to die for her, especially for revenge."

"It's not for her; it's for me."

The knock at the door startled Asa. He glanced at Simon, who shrugged and opened the door. A young Navy ensign with a solemn look on his face and an armed sailor stood outside the door. Asa's heart sank. It did not look good. Lieutenant Cobb had turned them in anyway.

"Gentlemen, I'm not sure why you chose to remain on board the *Vanguard*, but your presence here is unauthorized." He looked at Simon. "You, sir, will remain in your room. Mr. Iverson, you will return to your room. Tomorrow, you will both be airlifted off the drillship. Tonight, you will remain confined to your quarters."

"What if we refuse?" Simon challenged.

The ensign grinned. "I wouldn't advise it. The corporal is armed for a reason …" He looked at Asa. "Mr. Iverson."

Asa pretended to stretch and yawn. "I think I'll go to my quarters and get some shut eye. No matter what happens tomorrow, I want to be bright-eyed and bushy-tailed for it." He smiled at the ensign.

"Yeah," Simon said. "Go ahead. Looks like nothing is going to happen tonight anyway."

He left Simon in his room staring at the large Arctic Ocean map on the wall with all its telltale pins and cryptic notes. Simon had dedicated a large part of the past year to his quest for revenge. Asa feared he would not lightly abandon this dark desire in spite of their incarceration.

He stopped in the corridor. "Did the captain of the *Sunfish* turn us in?" he asked the sailor.

"I don't have that information, sir," the sailor said. When Asa stood there, he frowned. "Please move along, sir."

Asa stared at the young sailor for a moment, ready to refuse, but then decided his fight wasn't with the sailor, but with Lieutenant Cobb.

9

December 26, 2018, 2:40 a.m.   *USS Sunfish* –

Will wasn't certain if he had even fallen asleep before his new second, Chico Rodriguez, was shaking his shoulder vigorously. At first, he saw Rich's face leaning over him. He mentally banished the foggy veil that lingers between sleep and wakefulness and snapped awake instantly. "What is it?"

"We just got a call from the *Utah*. The storm is moving faster than anticipated. The timeline has advanced by six hours. They want us on station in twenty minutes."

He nodded. He could tell by the roll of the boat that the storm was almost upon them. The waves pounded the hull like fists hammering a punching bag. "Start the engines and alert the crew."

"Already done, sir."

Will nodded at Rodriguez's thoroughness, rose from his bunk, and splashed water on his face from the basin on the wall to wash the sleep from his eyes. He wanted to brush his teeth to remove the taste of last night's microwave dinner of Penne Alfredo from his mouth, but didn't have the time. Instead, he grabbed a stick of peppermint gum from the pack on his table and tossed it in his mouth. He had slept fully dressed. He straightened his shirt and donned his cap; then stepped from his cabin onto the bridge to find the crew standing by. He noted the time on the clock above the com – 0240 hours.

"What about the *Utah*? Where is she?"

"She's still two clicks off the drillship's windward side, but they deployed the DSV three hours ago. It's placing the last of the mines in position."

Mines. He wondered if one could truly call the Navy's new secret weapon mines. Each three-hundred-pound modified mine, nicknamed *Porcupines*, contained a twenty-five-pound high explosive core, but unlike conventional mines, the core was surrounded with twenty, four-foot-long metal spikes, or harpoons, designed to impale the megalodon when detonated. The velocity of the five-pound harpoons ensured maximum damage to flesh and internal organs. At twenty yards, a fifty-foot-long shark would receive five or six of the lethal spikes. At forty yards, two or three.

From previously observed megalodon behavior, the blood in the water should incite a feeding frenzy, where shark ate shark, further reducing their numbers. It also bunched them closer together. Exploded among the tightly packed sharks, the mines could kill or severely injure several creatures at a time. Altogether, the DSV was deploying twenty of the *Porcupines* around the drillship.

Now the trap needed baiting. That was where the *Sunfish* came in.

"Take up the lines and move us away from the drillship," he ordered.

Moving up the timeline concerned him. With a dozen last minute things that needed doing, he would have to trust his crew to get them done without his supervision. He did not doubt their ability. They were a good bunch, well trained and eager to get the job done.

"Have you heard from the *Amberjack*?" he asked McGee.

"They report nothing on sonar. They're making a wide sweep north to south; then, they'll head in closer to the *Vanguard* and stand by."

"Good. Our overlapping sonar sweeps will give us better coverage."

The chop had increased throughout the night as the wind picked up in velocity. Powerful six-foot waves battered the boat as it headed into the wind, slicing through the sea of whitecaps. The *Sunfish* shuddered as she nosedived into the deep trough between waves. Will winced at every creak and groan, but the boat held together. Once they reached their station twenty clicks from the drillship, Will surveyed the area through his binoculars, continuously wiping the lenses as waves splashed water over them and drenched him. The wan moonlight and choppy water made seeing anything impossible. A roiling mass of black, lightning-streaked clouds darkened the horizon to the southwest, ominously closer than just a few hours earlier, indicating the forefront of the storm bearing down on them.

The original plan had called for using the *Sunfish's* aerial drones, in conjunction with unmanned drones and helicopters from the *USS Kirby*, during daylight to scan the surface for movement, giving the crews some lead-time for their preparations and to move resources to intercept the sharks, drive them toward the minefield. That scenario was now a bust. The storm had picked up speed. The megalodon would arrive early. At night, his small drones, not equipped with Infrared cameras, were useless. He hoped the UAVs from the carrier arrived soon. Their night vision cameras could come in handy. He didn't want to be caught with his ass hanging out.

"Anything on sonar?" he called out.

"Nothing yet, but I'm getting false echoes from heavy thermal layering."

"Hmm. Keep sweeping the area."

Lack of sonar made them effectively blind and deaf, but he still had a job to do.

"Helm, take us in a slow arc relative to the drillship. Keep speed below ten knots." He nodded to Rodriguez. "Chico, start dumping the fresh water tanks."

Will winced as the wind bore the smell to him, the sickening stench of five-hundred gallons of congealing blood. Fish blood from the docks in Barrow, bovine blood from slaughterhouses, the blood of two hundred butchered caribou, and expired human blood from hospital blood banks filled the tanks. The megalodon with their supersensitive sense of smell would be able to detect the faintest traces of blood from miles away, placing his small boat in the center of ground zero. He did not like being a target, especially one barely able to outrun the megalodon.

He hoped the Deep Sea Vehicle managed to position the *Porcupines* before the sharks arrived. Waiting until the last minute was risky, but they could not anchor the mines, and time and current would disperse them quickly. The buoyancy tanks on the mines allowed the crew to place them at various depths, but that took time. He felt a moment of pity for the DSV crew, but then remembered that the Hy-100 steel hull of the submersible, designed to withstand the crushing pressure at sixty-five hundred feet, was three times as thick as the hull of the *Sunfish*. Maybe they felt sorry for him.

Will worried about the very real possibility of friendly fire. The ASROC launchers on the *Vanguard* provided Offensive Ring One. The rocket-launched Mark 46 torpedoes were faster than the sub's Mark 48 ADCAP torpedoes and had a greater range. When the megalodon entered the twelve-mile mark, the ASROCs would begin launching and continue until the sharks entered the minefield. The *Porcupines* were Offensive Ring Three, deployed in a wide arc at a distance of between five-hundred yards to twenty-five-hundred yards from the drillship and between fifty feet and four-hundred feet in depth, but they were stationary and avoidable. The *Utah* was Ring Two, patrolling the area between the two rings. Armed with twenty-two Mark 48 ADCAP torpedoes, it was well equipped for the task of preventing any megalodon from retreating.

The *Sunfish* and the *Amberjack* would perform the roles of mop up, staying out of the main fray. Both were equipped with .50 caliber machineguns, 25mm chain guns, and depth charges to kill any strays. The *Sunfish* had the added capability of her *Griffin* missile launchers. If all went as planned, the megalodon threat would end today.

Nothing ever goes as planned—an old Navy maxim.

"We'll never get those water tanks scrubbed clean," Rodriguez complained.

"Maybe the Navy will spring for new freshwater tanks," Will said. He continued to keep an eye on the horizon, though the frigid water tossed up by the waves had drenched his clothes and was chilling his body.

His orders called for two swaths of blood spaced two hundred yards apart. As the *Sunfish* completed her first arc, he called out, "Bring her around for a second run. Mind your distance."

Now, they headed directly into the wind. He held onto the rail as the boat's bow rose and fell, looking at times as if it would continue to plunge beneath the dark surface. As the tanks of blood drained into the ocean, the boat became lighter, becoming a piece of flotsam tossed about by the waves without mercy. She lingered dangerously long atop the crest of each wave before plunging down the back slope. Will prayed the boat held together long enough to complete her run.

"The tanks are dry," Rodriguez called out a few minutes later with obvious relief in his voice.

"Good. Take us back to the drillship. We'll drop a sea anchor on the leeward side of one of the pontoons and wait."

"Are you scared, Skipper?" Rodriguez asked.

"Mr. Rodriguez, a boat skipper is never scared. He is merely concerned." He smiled at his second. "Besides, this wet uniform won't let anyone see me piss my pants."

In spite of his remarks to Rodriguez, he was not afraid. He felt a strange eagerness to do something, to strike a blow for his fallen comrades. He remembered the two men he had caught with the ROV on the drillship and figured they felt the same way. If things took a nosedive, they might yet get their chance.

Now, every light on the drillship was on, casting undulating pools of luminescence on the surface of the water. However, the light did not penetrate the murky water. Below the surface, in the inky depths was where the coming battle would take place. The giant ancient sharks would be in their element, equipped by millions of years of evolution to be lords of the depths, while man, a land creature, and a newcomer by comparison would rely on his technology—animal cunning versus human engineering. Will was betting on technology.

"The *Utah* is picking up something on her sonar. The images are fuzzy, but it looks like thirty or forty megalodon. They're less than twenty-five clicks out."

Will nodded. *Let the battle begin.*

10

December 26, 2018, 4:30 a.m.   DSV *Christophe*, near Drillship *Vanguard*–

Lieutenant Stuart Haig peered out the central of the three forward facing, six-inch-diameter, acrylic observation ports, using the twin manipulator arms of the DSV to place one of the *Porcupine* mines in position at a depth of one-hundred-twenty feet. Operating the joystick with the delicate skill of a surgeon, he bled air from the mine's buoyancy tank and released it. To his relief, the mine remained in place.

"Two to go," he told Specialist Ron Foreman sitting beside him in the submersible's cramped seven-foot-diameter pressure cabin piloting the craft.

"Good!" Foreman replied. "My ass is frozen. Let's get it done."

Able Seaman Brian Leeds made up the last of the three-man crew of the re-fitted *Pisces IV* submersible. He lay in a prone position below the pair observing through one of the portholes. "After five hours on my belly," he called up, "I could use a stretch."

"Another hour and we're done. One more dive."

The *Christophe*, a *Pisces*-class submersible built in 1985 and operated by the National Oceanographic and Atmospheric Association, was currently on loan to the U.S. Navy. After a complete overhaul and refit, including more modern electronics and updated hydraulic systems, the DSV had made the journey from Hawaii to Nome, Alaska, aboard a C-130 transport, and then loaded aboard the *Utah*. Haig and his crew had flown into Barrow, Alaska, and traveled to the *Utah* aboard the *Sunfish* with the group of civilian scientists in charge of the project. Of all the dives he had made in his twelve-year career, this was shaping up to be the most bizarre.

The *Christophe* could carry only two of the special mines on each dive, making it a tedious and laborious process. The cabin's temperature registered 38 degrees. He could either heat the cabin or conserve battery power for the dives. The DSV had a 7-10 hour operational window, and he did not want to wait for the batteries to recharge before completing his job. Haig considered the safe delivery of the mines more important than crew comfort.

They surfaced twenty feet from the Vanguard in a pool of light cast by two spotlights, bobbing on the rough sea like a cork in a tempest, as the crane lowered a basket containing two of the *Porcupine* mines. The heavy waves made transferring the mines on the rolling surface impossible. He blew ballast and followed the basket beneath the surface to smoother water. Using the twin manipulator arms, he settled the mines onto the DSV's platform, folded the arms around them like an overprotective mother, and descended to a depth of sixty feet. Moving away from the drillship to a distance of two hundred yards, he positioned one of the pair using the GPS coordinates supplied by the scientists that would allow maximum coverage, creating a Death Zone of harpoons for the megalodon. He tried not to dwell on the results of a premature explosion while he was priming the mines.

The second mine, the last of the series, proved a problem. *Just my freakin' luck.* One of the harpoons had become wedged between the platform and the pressure hull. Using one of the manipulator arms, he gently rocked the mine back and forth to pop it free. In spite of the chill in the cabin, beads of cold sweat dotted his forehead by the time he finished.

"Son of a bitch," he muttered, as the mine stubbornly refused to budge.

"Easy, lieutenant," Leeds called up. "I don't want to become a shish kabob."

Haig swore softly at Leeds and the recalcitrant *Porcupine*. After almost seven hours, his half-frozen fingers were numb and swollen, difficult to control.

"Swing the *Christophe* around a little," he said to Foreman. "Jiggle her like a Hula dancer. See if you can shake it loose."

Foreman wiggled the joystick, shaking the DSV like a dog shedding water. Finally, the *Porcupine* loosened from its bind.

"All right. Hold it steady while I set the depth."

Foreman grimaced. "Like a rock," he replied with a white-knuckle grip on the joystick.

"Oh, shit!" Leeds groaned.

"What is it, Leeds?" Haig asked, resisting the impulse to glance down at him.

"I just received an update from the *Utah*. The megalodon are less than fifteen clicks out. The ASROCs on the drillship are about to begin launching."

"We're screwed," Foreman said, almost shouting the last word.

"Can it, Foreman," Haig snapped. "Keep the vehicle steady and let me finish the job. We have time. Then we can get the hell out of here."

Minutes later, the first faint concussions of the Mark 46 torpedoes reached them. Haig tried to keep his hands from trembling, as Foreman concentrated on steadying the DSV. The manufacturers had not intended the claw on the end of the manipulator arm for delicate work, but it was the only tool available. His only other option was to go outside and do the job by hand, a task he did not relish, especially with megalodon coming. He slowly bled pressure from the buoyancy tank and followed the *Porcupine* as it sank a few feet into position.

"Done," he said. "Take us up and out of here, Ron."

The shock waves from the Mark 46s were growing stronger as the ASROCs fired into the midst of the school of megalodon closing on the drillship. Haig estimated the last explosion had been less than two-thousand-yards distant. The sharks had almost reached the outer line of *Porcupines*.

Like his crew, he was eager to reach the surface before the megalodon arrived. Soon, the dark water would become a death trap, as the *Porcupines* released their load of lethal metal harpoons.

"We're not going to make it," Leeds announced.

"We've got time," Haig replied, trying to keep his concern from his voice, as he quickly calculated the distance back to the *Utah*. "We'll never reach the sub in time. Take us to the drillship. The sharks are blind. We can hide against one of the pontoons. The metal will mask our profile."

"I hope the hell you're right," Foreman replied, as he turned the nose of the DSV toward the *Vanguard* and pushed the thrusters to their two-knot maximum speed.

"They'll reach the first mines in thirty seconds," Leeds warned. "You'd better brace yourselves."

The *Christophe* was now less than thirty yards from the drillship's pontoon, but Haig knew it would be a photo finish. His pulse quickened when the DSV's lights outlined the dim profile of the pontoon. The sound of the first mine detonating reached them before the shockwave. The DSV rolled to port, but Foreman quickly steadied the small vehicle. The solitary detonations turned into a cacophony of exploding mines, as the school of megalodon entered the Death Zone. The DSV bucked wildly, standing on its nose and spinning like a top, as the barrage of underwater pressure waves ripped the controls from Foreman's hands. The three men clung to whatever they could reach and held on.

Instrument lights winked off as systems began to fail. Smoke curled from the sonar panel, quickly curtailed as Foreman fought the crushing G-forces and reached out to toggle an automatic extinguisher. The DSV rang like a church bell tolling the call to Sunday morning mass. A louder thud shook the vehicle as it careened from one of the drillship's columns. To Haig's relief, the pressure hull did not rupture and no observation port cracked.

"Almost there," he urged, but he was certain no one heard him over the rapid-fire cacophony of explosions growing louder as the sharks swam deeper into the kill zone.

"We lost the starboard thruster," Foreman called out, his voice barely shy of panic. He placed the DSV in a steep dive and shoved the joystick to starboard to compensate and to keep the craft straight.

Slowly, almost imperceptibly, the small craft rose above the pontoon and eased behind the column. *Safe!*

The shriek of metal shearing sounded like the ripping of a bed sheet. A jet of frigid salt water sprayed Haig in the face. He wiped it from his eyes and saw the water was red. Confused, he turned to Foreman. Foreman's head lay slumped over his chest and his hands hung limply at his sides. The razor-sharp point of a harpoon protruded from his chest. The jet of water sluiced away the blood from the blood-splattered control panel. The projectile had completely penetrated both sides of the drillship's column and pierced the bottom of the DSV, slicing through the thick HY-100 steel like cardboard and skewering both Leeds and Foreman.

Haig had no time to dwell on their deaths. The submersible was out of control. He reached over Foreman's corpse and cut power. The *Christophe* settled gently onto the top of the pontoon. He was safe from sinking, but the cabin was rapidly filling with water. He could still drown. The pontoon was only thirty feet below the surface. He had no air tank, but he could hold his breath long enough to reach the surface. He popped the upper hatch and bled the air from the cabin. When the pressure equalized, he opened the hatch and swam out. The water was near freezing, sapping his strength after his exhausting five-hour dive. He did not struggle to swim to the surface, but allowed his buoyancy to ascend him to the heaven of warmth and air.

He felt a presence nearby, pressure in the water, and turned to see a pale gray shadow three times the length of the twenty-foot-long submersible slide by him silent and deadly, illuminated by the submersible's lights. Three harpoons protruded from its massive body. A trail of blood stained the water behind it. As he watched, two more of the creatures struck at the injured megalodon, their sixty-inch jaws ripping side-of-beef sized chunks of flesh from its body. He floated for a moment watching the surreal scene unfold, and then kicked his legs to reach the surface, careful not to attract unwanted attention to his presence. Waves slammed him against the column as he tried to suck air into his oxygen-starved lungs. His numb fingers struggled to find purchase, finally gripping a small flange between metal joints of the column. He clung to it desperately to prevent the waves from washing him away. He did not have the strength to reach the dock. If he let go, the waves would sweep him out to sea, and he would die of hypothermia. *If the megalodon don't get me first.*

A spotlight blinded him. He looked up to see the patrol boat that had delivered his crew to the *Utah* riding the waves a twenty yards away and approaching slowly. Someone tossed him a line. With trembling hands, he released his grip on the column and wrapped the line around his chest and under his arms several times. He grasped the line with his remaining strength, as the thrower pulled him toward the boat. He expected one of the megalodon to snatch him from the water at any second, but instead, hands reached down to pull him aboard the boat.

"Welcome back."

He recognized the boat's captain, Will Cobb. "Get me out of the water," he said.

* * * *

4:15 a.m.–

Will watched the plumes of water rise into the air in the distance as the ASROC torpedoes detonated. The explosions, muffed by wind and water, were dull reports, like the sound of crashing surf. Beneath the surface, he knew the torpedoes were producing results that were more dramatic. The arc of fire from the rocket-launched torpedoes lit up the sky above the drillship, their arcs growing tighter as the distance between the megalodon and the drillship grew shorter.

"Man the guns," he called to his crew. "Chico, you take the port *Griffin* missile launchers."

He wanted to get into the fight, but his orders were clear. He was to maintain a safe distance unless needed, but he would not let the megalodon catch him unaware. Louder explosions lifted plumes of water as the first of the *Porcupines* exploded. Between the *Porcupine* mines and the torpedoes, the sea around the drillship had become a kill zone.

"There's someone in the water!" Able Seaman Patrick Levitt yelled, pointing toward one of the drillship's columns.

He swung a spotlight around and saw a figure in the water hugging the column as the waves sought to break his tenuous grip.

"Move us closer."

When they were close enough, he tossed a line to the figure and watched him wrap it around his body. He and Able Seaman McGee pulled the figure aboard. When the half-drowned man rolled over onto his back, sputtering out water he had swallowed, he recognized the DSV dive team leader, something-or-other Haig.

"Welcome back, lieutenant. We'll get you into something warm and dry." He glanced out to sea expectantly. "Where is the rest of your crew?"

Haig coughed up a mouthful of water. "Dead. One of the mine's harpoons struck the *Christophe*. I'm the only survivor."

"Sorry to hear that."

He nodded to two crewmen standing nearby. They lifted the exhausted lieutenant to his feet and carried him inside the cabin and down the stairs to the wardroom. As Will's gaze returned to the sea, a gray dorsal fin taller than the *Sunfish* rose from the water alongside the boat. One of the 25mms cut loose, peppering the water around the fin, but it slid back beneath the surface in a leisurely manner. Mindful of his orders but against his instincts to join in the fight, he ordered the *Sunfish* away from the drillship and back to her original position. The fate of the DSV aptly conveyed the all too real danger of lingering too near the *Porcupines* when they exploded.

From a safe distance, he watched the battle unfold. It was a surreal battle between unseen opponents. The only indications of the event were the dull thuds of underwater explosions and plumes of water sent skyrocketing into the air as a result. He saw the occasional dead shark float to the surface, but they quickly became the centers of cannibalistic feeding frenzies that took them back to the depths. One harpoon from an exploded mine, having missed its target, soared thirty feet into the air before falling back into the sea. The ASROC launchers were now firing almost directly into the water less than a thousand yards from the drillship. Occasionally, one of the Mark 46s struck a *Porcupine*, causing a double explosion of gigantic proportions.

The radio chatter from the *Utah* painted a more accurate picture of the battle, and it was not the news for which he had hoped. She remained at a safe distance from the drillship and the minefield picking off stray sharks. Unfortunately, her torpedoes had proven next to useless. Of sixteen fired, only six struck their intended targets. A large concentration of megalodon had centered their attention on the *Utah*, battering her hull and opening several leaks in her seams. The forward torpedo room was flooding, and her ruptured starboard ballast tank made maneuvering difficult. The sharks attacked the sub unmercifully and without let up. Even metal would soon give way to flesh if the flesh was relentless enough.

The *Porcupines* proved more effective than the torpedoes, but even with their overlapping fields of fire, there were far more sharks than mines. A series of explosions ripped the depths, churning the water. In the spotlights, the water was red with megalodon blood.

Slowly, the concentrated firepower began to whittle down the number of megalodon sharks, but not quickly enough. The blood in the water had driven them insane. Drawn by the vibrations of the drillship as it launched the torpedoes, the megalodon began attacking the pontoons as it had the submarine. The hollow structures rang like bells from a drowned church. Unlike the hull of the *Utah*, designed to handle the extreme pressure of the deep, the pontoons were relatively fragile. A continuous assault would sink the drillship. It was time for the *Sunfish* to join the fray.

"Take us in to the drillship. Prepare for a depth charge run." He quickly estimated the safest distance from the pontoons he could drop his depth charges without damaging the drillship. "Keep us twenty yards away as we circle the drillship. Gunners, fire at any target that presents itself."

The twin thrusters of the *Sunfish* roared to life, and she shot like a dart toward the *Vanguard*. He wasn't sure how much damage he could do to the megalodon, but he could draw attention away from the *Utah* and the drillship, giving them a fighting chance at survival. The *Sunfish* was a fast boat, designed for speed, maneuverability, and lightning-fast attacks. She might not outrun the sharks in a flat out race, but she could run rings around them.

In spite of the mines and torpedoes, the sonar screen was alive with active pings. At least twenty of the megalodon had survived the conflict. Some of the *Porcupines* had not yet exploded, and both the *Utah* and the drillship were still firing torpedoes. He would not risk straying too far from the drillship.

"Fire!" he yelled and watched two depth charges soar through the air before lancing into the water. Seconds later, they exploded at a depth of fifty feet. The .50 caliber machineguns and the 25mm miniguns fired streaks of tracer bullets into the water amid a sea of shark fins. Will's heart thundered in his chest. This was his first real combat experience. The quick fight in which he had lost two men had been spontaneous, a reaction to events. This was deliberate, calculated. He could not afford to err.

"Again!" he yelled.

Apone spun the boat in a tight turn, reversed direction, and made another pass. This time, two of the megalodon rose to the surface and converged on the ship as if challenging it. The gun crews concentrated on the nearer creature, pouring streams of bullets into its head and sides. Its blind eyes betrayed no emotion, no sense of fear or realization of what was happening to it. One moment it was attacking, and the next it died less than twenty yards from its goal.

Chico fired one of the *Griffin* missiles at the second shark. It struck the creature in the back near the dorsal fin and exploded, shredding tons of flesh from its body amid a fountain of blood. Even mortally injured, it did not give up pursuit of its prey. A second missile struck near the gill slits, decapitating it. Almost immediately, both dead megalodon became targets for their brethren.

"Let's take out a few more," Will called out.

The *Sunfish* released two more depth charges set to detonate just below the surface. The explosion lifted the surface of the sea behind the boat, scattering bloody parts of shattered megalodon across the surface, providing more food for the feeding frenzy. The blood-filled water around the drillship was alive with giant man-eating sharks. The *Sunfish* picked a torturous winding path between them to avoid a collision, as the gunners sprayed the water with .50 caliber and 25mm fire. Chico fired another missile at an unseen target in the distance.

"Save the missiles," Will warned. "We might need them later." The boat shuddered when it slammed into a dead shark, and then catapulted into the air. He grabbed a railing to prevent hurdling over the side. The boat landed with a splash but kept moving forward. Sensing that he was pushing their luck operating the boat among the feeding sharks, he ordered, "Take us out of here."

The gunners, reluctant to halt their carnage, continued firing as the boat sped away. Understanding their need to strike a blow for their fallen comrades, he did not stop them.

Farther to the south, explosions and machinegun fire from the *Amberjack* rocked the night, as she fought a deadly battle of her own. He wanted to go to her assistance, but his orders were to remain near the *Vanguard*. Abandoning his post could place the entire operation in jeopardy. Eisner and the crew of the *Amberjack* were on their own.

* * * *

5:25 a.m.–

The sun rose on a dismal day, casting a soft golden glow across the eastern sky, but the sky above and to the west roiled with dark, ominous clouds. Lightning danced between clouds and lanced into the water. The leading edge of the storm was now fully upon them, and it looked to be a big one. It would be rough riding it out on the small *Sunfish*, but he could not run to a safe port. His boat still had a job to do. If the *Amberjack* could do it, so could the *Sunfish*. His faith in his boat and his crew were absolute, and he knew both would give him all they had.

The Navy had determined the drillship to be the best spot to stop the megalodon and prevent them from continuing east into the North Atlantic. They had just one chance to end the megalodon problem before it became endemic, a primeval disease infecting all the world's oceans.

He spotted half a dozen fins breaking the surface but knew more were still alive beneath the waves. They had whittled down their numbers considerably, but had not eradicated them. Sporadic explosions from *Porcupine* mines still roiled the waters, but both the *Utah* and the drillship seemed to have depleted their supply of torpedoes. The *Amberjack* and the *Sunfish* were the only offensive weapons available until air support from the helicopter carrier arrived.

He looked at his men, weary, wet, and half-frozen, but they each wore a grim look of satisfaction on their faces. They had struck a blow against the enemy. He feared they would have to summon strength from the exhausted bodies and do so again.

11

December 26, 2018, 3:30 a.m.   *USS Utah–*

Like most *Virginia*-Class fast attack submarines, the *USS Utah*, designation SSN 801, was a floating weapons platform capable of both surface and undersea operations. Her one-hundred-thirty-two man crew were highly trained and the best in their fields. The seventy-nine-thousand-metric-ton behemoth carried a complement of twenty-one MK-48 torpedoes and *Tomahawk* ASM/LAM missiles. Her S9G nuclear reactor produced thirty-thousand kilowatts and could propel her at over thirty knots submerged.

Her captain, Lieutenant Commander Charles Raeburn Prescott, at thirty-three, was one of the youngest attack submarine commanders in the fleet, and one of only a handful of black skippers. He did not blame undue prejudice for the low number; few blacks aimed at the job of sub commander. He certainly felt no prejudice from his crew. He had proved his capabilities, and they accepted him. He watched the DSV *Christophe* position the *Porcupine* mines through a feed from the DSV's camera. The work went immeasurably slow compared to deploying regular mines, but the new weapons were untested and particularly sensitive. It would not do to have an accident at this stage in the preparations.

"How far away now?" he asked the sonar technician.

"Eight clicks, sir, holding steady."

He checked his watch. It was going to be close. The megalodon were moving at a rapid clip. He could gain the DSV crew a little time by delaying the sharks. "Driver, take us away from the drillship. Give the minefield a wide berth."

If anyone had suggested, even in jest, that he would be attacking a school of megalodon sharks, creatures that supposedly died out twenty-million-years ago, he would have punched them in the nose, and yet, here he was and here they came. No one from his old neighborhood in Strawberry Mansion would believe him.

"Hold her steady at twenty knots," he advised.

The ASROC system installed on the drillship would be engaging shortly, and he did not want to wander into their field of fire. Their rocket-launched Mk-46 torpedoes were sonar guided and might not distinguish between an eighty-foot ancient shark and a three-hundred-seventy-foot submarine. The ASROC torpedoes had a range of fifteen kilometers. The battle plan called for using the torpedoes as artillery, employing a reverse walking barrage as the megalodon advanced; then, a Zone and Sweep to inflict maximum damage and reduce their numbers by attrition.

When the sharks entered the *Porcupine* minefield, the mine's proximity fuses would target groups of sharks first; then, as their numbers reduced, individual mines would be detonated by remote control using data provided by sonar buoys the Utah had anchored to the bottom of the sea. It was here they hoped to break the enemy's back.

The *Utah's* assigned task was that of mop up, hunting and attacking stray megalodon and preventing a retreat. Prescott was not happy about his mission. The *Utah* was a fast attack submarine, the newest in the fleet. He should be the one firing the first salvo. Instead, command had relegated his boat to ferrying the DSV to location and rounding up stray doggies like a cowboy. Command had ignored his requests for a change in his orders, and he was too much a naval officer to question orders.

"The *Vanguard* is signaling they are commencing fire," his executive officer, Lieutenant Tack Hardin, reported.

Prescott nodded to Hardin. He noticed his first officer licking his dry lips nervously. It was Hardin's first fight, and his apprehension was natural. "Inform them we are in position and will provide area assessment reports. Maintain a running commentary of megalodon positions."

Prescott leaned against the chart table with his hands pressed against the latest weather map printout. He worried that they were already operating under a disadvantage. The storm front driving the megalodon had moved much faster than anticipated. The plan had called for the use of MQ-4C *Triton* drones from the *USS Kirby* to provide blanket surveillance of the area and warn of the megalodons' approach. Armed X-478 UCAVs would then pick off any creatures on the surface and keep the school herded together. Unfortunately, neither vehicle could operate effectively at night in such inclement weather. The same drawbacks applied to the V-22 *Osprey* VTOLs and *Viper* helicopters. Throughout history, the weather had contributed to the success or failure of military campaigns. In spite of their advanced electronics capabilities, the sharks had the advantage of weather.

"First torpedoes are in the water," Hardin announced.

Prescott walked over to the sonar station and stood behind the technician.

"Multiple explosions," the technician announced. "On target."

Prescott smiled. Perhaps his worries were unfounded.

"Picking up multiple contacts closing."

"Lieutenant, load tubes one and three. Calculate a firing solution. Set for twenty-five-hundred yards. Fire on my command."

He could feel the tension in the command and control center thicken as Hardin relayed his orders. This was what they had been waiting for. Any fear or doubts he might have harbored faded, as if flushed from his system by a flood of adrenalin.

"Targets within range, sir."

"Fire tubes one and three," he ordered.

He felt the sub wobble slightly as the torpedoes left their tubes, propelled by a blast of compressed air. He imagined their piston engines powering their pump jet drives, sending the thirty-seven-hundred-pound, nineteen-foot-long projectiles toward their targets at sixty-five miles per hour. The Mark 48 Mod 7 ADCAP (Advanced Capability) torpedo could determine its target by acoustic homing using both its passive and active sonar guidance systems. Its revamped electronic guidance hardware allowed it to ignore false signals and pursue its target.

"Ninety seconds to target." A minute and a half later, the sonar tech said, "One explosion on target. Second torpedo missed. The torpedo can't maneuver as quickly as the megalodon." He glanced up at Prescott with concern in his eyes. "One target still approaching fast."

He nodded to Hardin, who said, "Sound the collision warning."

The collision klaxon began blaring. He held onto the desk waiting for the impact. The megalodon struck a few seconds later. The entire submarine shuddered and rang as if someone had pounded it with a hammer. He had not expected such an impact from a flesh and blood object. A second impact indicated the shark was still unharmed and determined to sink his boat.

Red lights began flickering on the damage control panel. One was in the torpedo room. He grabbed the intercom and hit the torpedo room button. "Report."

He waited until the weapons officer picked up. The sound of shouts and hammering filled the background. "Two seams ruptured. We have about a foot of water in the torpedo room. Tube number three is out. We're working on sealing the leaks. I'm pressurizing the compartment."

"Keep me advised." After a moment's thought, he said, "Switch the other torpedoes to guide wire control. Damn things can sense the sonar and outrun them."

In spite of the flooding, the *Utah* fired eight more torpedoes. The guide wires allowed the torpedoes to get closer to the megalodon before detection, but the sharks still outmaneuvered them. Of the eight, only three struck targets. The megalodon, drawn by the sub's sonar, began attacking in larger numbers. Prescott worried about the pounding his boat was taking. Numerous small leaks opened up throughout the boat, overwhelming the damage control crew's ability to keep up.

The sub suddenly rolled to port and nosed downward.

"We're taking on water in the aft port dive ballast tank, sir," the steering officer reported.

"Damn!" Prescott groaned. He had not expected the megalodon to be so aggressive. They had geared most of the action plans toward preventing the sharks from escaping, not on defense. "Move us away from the sharks. Skirt the edge of the minefield."

It would be risky. They could avoid the mines. The mines were marked on his charts, but if one exploded too near the submarine, it would cause more damage than the megalodon. As dangerous as it seemed, remaining close to the edge of the minefield might be their only hope. Everyone in the control room understood the risk, but no one questioned his order.

"Aye, sir."

The external acoustic microphones picked up the sound of exploding mines. He hoped they were killing sharks.

As they neared the edge of the minefield, the number of attacks lessened, as if the sharks could sense the presence of the mines. He left a distance of a hundred yards between his boat and the mines. He hoped it was enough.

"We're still taking on water," the driver called out. "I can't keep the rudder steady."

"Steer to starboard to compensate," he replied. "Keep the nose steady."

A few seconds later, the boat groaned and shuddered. "No good, sir. The controls are sluggish."

"Lieutenant, go aft and see if you can vent that ballast tank."

Hardin sprinted down the passageway, grabbed the top of the first hatch, and swung through feet first. Sailors fell to the deck to allow him quick passage.

Their present course took them too close to the mines. Their only hope lay in passing beneath the minefield.

"Dive! Dive! Dive!" he ordered.

For a full minute, he thought they might succeed. Then, a megalodon struck one of the *Porcupine* mines. The lights flickered; then, failed, as the boat rolled to starboard. The deck canted forward twenty-five degrees, as the sub's nose pointed at the ocean floor. He grabbed onto the edge of the table to remain on his feet. A few crewmen, caught off guard, slid along the deck and slammed into bulkheads or equipment. The dim emergency lights came on. He didn't need to glance at the damage control board to know they were in trouble. The thundering sound of water entering the compartment under high pressure echoed in the compartment and down the passageway.

"Two holes in the torpedo room from harpoons," the damage control officer reported. "Another in the engine room. Eight dead, six injured, two seriously. Exterior and interior hatches sprung in the aft lockout trunk. The exec is seeing to repairs. No report from the reactor watchman. Intercom is out past crew's quarters."

Now, I've done it.

"Dispatch men to check on the reactor room and weapons compartment. I need visual confirmation of the damage. And fix that damn intercom. I need to know what's happening with my boat." *That was a lie*, he thought. He knew what was happening. He had made a bad decision, and his boat and his crew were paying the cost. His boat was no longer effective as a weapon. The drillship was on its own. He slammed his fist into the console. "Damn it! Get us away from here."

A few minutes later the runner returned to the control center, soaking wet. Prescott glanced up at him. "We're still tail heavy. Inform the exec to pump more air into the engine room before it floods."

It was several seconds before he realized the runner was still standing there. He noticed the look of shock and disbelief on his face. "Well, go inform the exec."

"The exec's gone, sir."

"What the hell do you mean gone? I need him to ..." He stopped. An icy cold gripped his chest, foreshadowing the answer to his next question. "Where's the exec?"

"Lieutenant Hardin is dead, sir. The blast sprung both hatches in the aft lockout trunk. The inner hatch wheel sheared on the exterior side of the chamber. We couldn't seal it from the outside. Mr. Hardin climbed inside the trunk and sealed it behind him. We pressurized the chamber, but it continued to flood."

"Did he have a breather?"

The runner shook his head; then, realizing the captain was staring at the deck, said aloud, "No, sir. He said he didn't have time."

Prescott was silent while he absorbed the news of his friend's fate. Hardin had died a hero saving his crewmates, but that didn't lessen the pain.

"Very well, tell the engineer to pressurize the engine room to force the water out."

Hardin's death was his fault, as were the other eight men. He had made a grave mistake in underestimating the megalodon and their unexpected ability to cooperate. He hoped he hadn't doomed the entire operation to failure because of his error in judgment. If the megalodon reached the open North Atlantic with its rich feeding grounds, there would be no stopping them. The oceans would belong to the megalodon. He could not allow that to happen.

12

December 26, 2018, 3:45 a.m.   *Drillship Vanguard*, Arctic Ocean–

Asa awoke confused and in a sweat. In his nightmare, the *Global Kulik* had shuddered beneath his feet and stood on its bow for a long, agonizing minute before crashing into the sea. The water had been so cold that his body had gone instantly numb. He could not move a muscle, as the waves slowly lapped over him. All around him, like Comanches on the warpath, pale gray fins dotted the surface, circling slowly, moving inexorably closer.

He had awoken from his nightmare before they had reached him. For that, he was thankful. What had awoken him? He sat on the edge of his bed and glanced at the clock—3:45 a.m. He had been asleep less than an hour. The drillship was eerily silent. No crew worked the nightshift. He and Simon were the only crew members left aboard. The deck bounced beneath his feet; then, again a few seconds later. Alarmed, he quickly threw on his pants and shirt. He did not bother lacing his boots. He grabbed his parka from the rack by the door and went out into the corridor. The rig shuddered again, harder this time.

His guard was not there.

"What the hell?" he muttered and raced for the stairs.

He opened the door and stepped into chaos. The ASROC launchers were lancing their deadly load of torpedoes into the water a few miles from the drillship. That was what had awoken him. Sailors ran back and forth cross the deck tending to the launchers. From the darkness, he heard muffled reports of explosions. The wind whipped the sea into a fury and blew saltwater spray into his face sixty feet above the surface. The storm had arrived earlier than expected, and with it the megalodon.

He peered into the darkness beyond the pools of light cast by the drillship's spotlights, but could see nothing. Whatever was happening seemed so far remained confined to the depths. The *Utah* was no longer in its original position. He guessed it had submerged to attack the sharks.

A wedge of light bathed him as the door opened behind him. He turned to see Simon outlined by the light with a grim look on his face.

"They're here," he said.

Asa nodded. "I guess the Navy has bigger problems to deal with than us."

Simon ignored the activity around him. His focused his gaze with a laser-sharp intensity on the water, as if able to pierce the blackness and peer beneath the surface. His clenched fists hung limply by his sides, but his tensed body gave the appearance that he would gladly use them to fight the sharks if necessary. His entire body trembled with barely suppressed rage. Oddly, Asa felt nothing—no fear, no thirst for revenge, no desire to strike a blow. He was not sure, if his mind had not yet fully grasped what was happening, or if his fear had grown so strong that it had shut down his emotions. Perhaps seeing the reality of the nightmarish creatures was enough to convince his troubled conscience that he was sane. He waited for some of Simon's rage to spill over into him, fill him like an empty cup, but it did not happen.

Larger explosions breached the surface—the secret weapon Lieutenant Cobb had mentioned. The dark depths became fulgurous with streaks of light. Several gray dorsal fins rose from the depths and broke the surface, followed by a gigantic fin, much larger than any of the other creatures were, twice as long as the one he had witnessed at the sinking of the *Kulik*. The enormous megalodon's broad back and tail joined it, cutting the water like the wake of a ship. Using the edge of the drillship as a handy ruler, he estimated the megalodon to be well over a hundred-eighty-feet long, twice as large as some of the other creatures fleeing before it. He recognized it as the granddaddy megalodon that had spared him. The sight broke through the emotionless shell that had enveloped him. His legs trembled and his palms began to sweat. An intense fear gripped him like two frozen hands. He looked into the white eyes of the pale gray monster and saw death. The creature had come to finish the job it had started.

He took several steps backwards away from the edge of the platform, gasping for breath.

"Is that it?" Simon asked. "Is that the one you saw?" The chef's voice was a mixture of excitement and fury.

Asa shook his head. "I don't know," he lied. "No. This one is bigger. It's a monster." He didn't know why he refused to acknowledge it as the same shark. It was unlikely there would be two that large. He thought if he ignored it, it might go away, like a bad dream. But those had not gone away either.

Around them, the ASROC launchers began firing their modified Mark 46 torpedoes almost at the base of the drillship. The long graceful arcs had become straight lines as they struck the water two hundred yards from the drillship. Minutes later, a series of explosions illuminated the depths. The water churned and roiled above the explosions. He urged the torpedoes onward, as if by his will alone he could guide them to their marks. Dead sharks floated to the surface, becoming a free meal for their cannibalistic kin. He almost let out a whoop of joy at seeing the creatures suffer the same fate as so many of his friends on the *Kulik*.

They watched the carnage for two hours, paying little heed to the wind and the rain, entranced by the epic conflict. Most of the battle was invisible beneath the waves, requiring imagination to see the torpedoes lancing toward the sharks and the mines exploding, blowing sharks to bits. Occasionally, a megalodon surfaced, giving them a ringside seat to the ancient creatures. He winced inside at the memory of the *Kulik*, but could not tear his gaze away from the creatures. Especially, he liked the way the creatures ripped into their own dead and injured in a feeding frenzy. He considered it justice.

The Navy had erected a tent on the deck near one of the ASROC launchers. Curious, Asa wandered over to it and peeked inside. He recognized a bank of sonar screens with two technicians monitoring them. He assumed the screens displayed data from sonar buoys moored somewhere beyond the minefield. All of the screens showed activity—the megalodon. His heart sank at the number of blips. As he watched, one of the screens went blank.

"We lost the Number Five buoy," one of the technicians reported.

Less than a minute later, a second screen died. Asa had a bad feeling about the coincidence.

"Number Two is gone." The technician looked at his superior. "You don't think they know, do you?"

His superior looked incredulous. "They're dumb fish, for God's sake. It's the torpedoes. They must be taking them out."

"They're homing in on the sonar signal," Asa said.

Both men glanced up at him. "Who the hell are you?"

Asa shook his head. "It doesn't matter. They can detect the sonar signals."

Two more screens went blank. "No," the technician said, but doubt filled his voice. He looked at his superior. "Two more buoys and the ASROCs will be firing blind."

Asa didn't wait to see what they did. He raced back outside and saw Simon still staring out to sea.

"The shit's going to hit the fan." He quickly explained what he had overheard.

Simon shook his head. "Damned Navy. I knew they would screw this up."

Asa stumbled when the drillship rocked from a solid hit. He turned to Simon. "One of the torpedoes?"

Simon shook his head. "That was no explosion. The megs are ramming the pontoons."

He had not considered that. "Can they sink us?"

"Probably," Simon replied, "given enough time."

Not again! "Crap! What do we do?"

Simon grinned. "We can use the ROV as we planned."

Simon's suggestion floored Asa. "Are you freakin' kidding me? It's a war zone out there."

"Do you propose we just stand here watching the battle? We might be in the water soon if the *Vanguard* sinks no matter what happens. I'd rather die striking a blow now while we have the chance than drowning meekly doing nothing."

The sound of motors below drew their attention. Asa looked down and saw the patrol boat speeding past the drillship with her captain, Lieutenant Cobb standing on the foredeck shouting orders. The machineguns mounted fore and aft began firing into the water at the sharks. Two large explosions split the water behind the boat, lifting twin plumes of water into the air. The drillship vibrated from the concussions.

"They're dropping depth charges," he yelled to Simon.

Although he was still angry with her captain for reporting them, the timely appearance of the patrol boat energized him. If it could keep the megalodon away from the drillship, it lessened the need for them to retrieve the ROV and join in the fight. He had much rather watch the battle from the safety of the deck than to participate.

The ASROC launchers fell silent as the last sonar buoys failed. A few minutes later, the first of the mines began exploding. It seemed to Asa that too much time passed between explosions. He wondered if the mines were a bust, too. The patrol boat continued making passes around the drillship, running a zigzagging course through the sharks, dropping depth charges, and peppering any shark that surfaced with machinegun fire. Three missiles flew from her deck and lanced into the water, adding their firepower to the depth charges and smaller weapons fire, but Asa saw that it was not enough.

To his dismay, more fins broke the surface, fewer than before, but more than enough to cause serious damage to the drillship. When he saw the monster megalodon again almost two-thirds the length of a football field cut a swatch through the water at the pontoon directly below them, Asa braced for the inevitable crash. Moments later, the entire ship shuddered and tilted to port. Chains and drums rolled off the decks.

"That had to do some damage," he said. "Come on. I want to check the underwater structural integrity." Forgotten was his fear of the megalodon. His fear of sinking outweighed that grim fate.

For a few moments, Simon did not reply, his gaze still steadfastly fixed on the megalodon. Then, he nodded. "All right. The water's too cold for a swim."

"Help me carry the portable welding rig down. I think we'll need it."

The *Vanguard* continued to take hits from megalodon, as the pair picked up a portable TIG welder from the mechanic's shack and descended the stairs inside the column. Though portable, the TIG welder still weighed almost fifty pounds. Manhandling it down the stairs was no simple task. Simon stopped several times to catch his breath. The overweight chef, at home in his kitchen, was out of shape for rapid stair climbing. The drillship now had an obvious list to the deck as it rapidly took on water. He only hoped he could repair the leak before they sank.

When he opened the bulkhead hatch into the pontoon, the sound of rushing water echoed in the dark depths of the steel tank. He played the flashlight around, and the sight that greeted him was disheartening. Swirling water stood two feet deep in the bilge and rose higher as he watched, indicating a dangerously large rupture. He despaired that it might be too big to seal. His only hope lay in doing the best job he could to reduce the amount of water coming in. If he could slow the leak, it would give them more time, perhaps enough time for a more permanent repair.

He plugged the welder into a power outlet inside the base of the column and waded through the icy water, clenching his teeth at the sudden numbing shock to his feet and legs. Simon followed carrying the power cord, cursing under his breath. Still winded by the stairs, his ragged breath reverberated in the hollow space. Asa hoped the overweight chef didn't have a heart attack. He would never get him back up the stairs.

When he saw the leak, Asa's hope diminished. Two jets of water sprayed across the pontoon and cascaded down the opposite wall. He examined the source and cursed.

"Damn! It's ruptured between two braces. I can't get to it."

"Can we pack it with something?"

"Too much pressure. Besides, we still have the same problem. We can't get to the crack." He stood back to think about the problem. There had to be a way to stem the leak.

"So what do we do?"

Asa's mind raced for an answer, but the only solution he came up with brought them back to the ROV, a subject he did not wish to broach with Simon. Finally, faced with the likelihood of drowning, he said, "We could change out the ROV's tool arm I jury-rigged for a welder. Maybe I can seal the crack from the outside," he paused, rubbing his chin in thought, "but that would mean winching it back aboard, replacing the arm, and lowering it back into the water. I estimate it would take us an hour." He glanced at the leak and the speed at which the water entered the space. "We don't have that much time."

"What about the crane?" Simon suggested.

"Yes!" Asa burst out. "Quick thinking. We can move the ROV to the dock; then, you lower the welder kit, the control cases, and me by basket. I'll attach the welder kit down here. It won't take ten minutes."

"I've never operated a crane," Simon protested.

"It's your suggestion. You just need to worry about one control that raises and lowers the basket. The crane is already in position at the edge of the platform." He smiled at Simon's sour look. "No problem."

Simon wasn't convinced. "Yeah, so you say."

"We don't have much time, Simon."

"Okay, okay, I'll do it, but I'd advise you not to stand under it."

"Fair enough."

He followed Simon back into the column. Simon had more difficulty climbing the steps than he had going down them. Asa wanted to hurry him, shove him up the steps, but felt compelled to keep Simon's slower pace. By the time they reached the deck, the drillship had canted another six degrees. As Simon leaned on the railing catching his breath, Asa surveyed the bedlam on the deck. It appeared all bets were off. Sailors and technicians paid them no attention as they scrambled to the emergency lifeboat stations. Like Asa, their biggest concern was the sinking drillship. Asa demurred from that route. He had rather take his chances in the open sea than in the lifeboats. They made good targets for megalodon.

While Simon familiarized himself with the crane controls, Asa operated the ROV's remote control and quickly moved it to the dock. In the rough sea, keeping it in position was difficult. He finally hit upon the idea of clamping the manipulator arm to the dock to moor it. He grabbed the welder arm kit, carried it to the crane, and placed it in the basket. Then, he returned for the two cases containing the ROV controls and the camera monitor. They were all he would need for the job.

He stepped into the basket, nodded to Simon, and held on. He almost lost his grip when Simon jerked the basket ten feet off the deck. With the slope to the deck affecting the crane, the basket swung wildly for a moment, banging against the railing. He saw Simon mouth an apology as he fought the controls. More gently the second time, he swung the basket over the side and lowered it. As the churning sea grew closer to the bottom of the basket, Asa wondered if he was about to get wet, but at the last moment, the basket jerked to a halt and bounced for a moment before Simon set it onto the dock with barely a bump.

Relieved he had survived the harrowing descent, Asa quickly laid the control cases and the welder arm on the dock. Reaching the bobbing ROV was more difficult. It remained in place because of the manipulator arm, which he had to remove. He tossed a loop of line around the top of the ROV and tied it off on a cleat. Then, timing it carefully to avoid the dock crushing him, he leaped onto the ROV's small platform with the welder arm kit held under one arm. The cumbersome package threw him off balance, and he almost fell off. He grabbed on with his free hand, avoiding the lethal tip of the homemade injector arm and its deadly load of saxitoxin. Bleeding the hydraulic line loosened the arm's grip. He quickly disconnected the injector mechanism and tossed it across the gap onto the dock. He mounted the welder arm in position, holding his breath as he tightened the connections while the waves crashed over him. His task completed, he waited until the ROV rose above the dock on a high wave and stepped down onto it.

Just inside the open door of the column, out of the wind and spray, he set up the control cases on the deck. Sitting cross-legged on the deck before the controls, he turned on the spotlights and camera. The image on the monitor of the dock bobbing up and down and rolling side to side tightened the knot in his stomach. Submerging the ROV beneath the waves stabilized the dizzying camera image. He used the thrusters to propel the ROV well away from the drillship to prevent the waves from slamming it into the hull. Moving it along the pontoon, scanning for the rupture with the camera, he located the leak in a large indentation. To his dismay, several other dents and large parallel gashes marked spots where the megalodon had attacked the pontoon, anyone of which could cause a leak. The power of the creatures amazed him. Their primitive instinct for survival was matched only by their natural impulse to strike out at anything unknown.

From the outside, the leak was more accessible, a six-inch long gap between two plates. He fired up the welder. Only after the bright actinic flash half-blinded him did he remember to use the filter on the monitor screen. He had no time to weld a plate over the gash. He started at one end, and using flexible welding rod fed from a spool, slowly built up a lip along the edge of the gash, adding more metal until the edges almost touched; then, drew them together with a final bead. Operating the welder by remote control was more difficult than doing it by hand. He had a hard time getting the feel of the welder. Satisfied with his progress so far, he began on the other end. The wider middle gap was more complicated. He had to build a bridge almost two inches wide between the two sections of hull plating. Several times, the lip he was adding broke away, forcing him to begin afresh.

His weld job was temporary at best. The uneven bead would have drawn a hard glare of contempt from George Gibson, his welding instructor in trade school, but it was doing the job. The leak was almost sealed.

A silvery gray body moved by the ROV just at the edge of the camera range. He risked panning the camera and saw several indistinct shapes milling around the pontoon. The glare of the lights and the welder had drawn the megalodons' attention. He cursed and worked faster. Suddenly, the ROV seemed to leap skyward, as one of the sharks slammed it from beneath. He fought the controls to stabilize it, but the sharks were knocking it about like a soccer ball, each one seeking it as a prize. The lights extinguished, leaving him in darkness. He switched to IR but saw only indistinct hazy shapes. Then, the camera too failed. He had lost the ROV.

Not satisfied with destroying the ROV, the megalodon began crashing into the pontoon near the weld with renewed vigor, drawn, he supposed, by the warmth of the fresh weld. Their frantic attacks became more violent. The column vibrated like a plucked violin string. The deck tilted, sliding him across the floor. He glanced into the pontoon and saw water gushing in from fresh leaks. He had done all he could, but in spite of his valiant attempt, the drillship was doomed.

He glanced up to see Simon clambering down the steps.

"Did it work?" he yelled.

"No," Asa replied. "I just drew more sharks. We're sinking."

"One of the men on the deck said a helicopter was on the way to pick them up. We need to get back up there and go with them."

Asa sighed. It looked as if all their plans had amounted to nothing. They were still evacuating the drillship on a helicopter. "Okay."

He climbed the stairs and joined Simon. The megalodon continued battering the drillship as if determined to send it to the bottom. Several times, they were forced to stop climbing and hold on as the drillship rolled. Just as they reached the deck, in the pale early light of dawn, they saw the Navy M1-60 *Seahawk* taking off from the helicopter pad.

"No!" Simon yelled, waving his arms as he stumbled across the deck.

Asa knew it was too late. The pilot did not look back as he flew the chopper around the derrick and quickly disappeared into the storm.

"Come back," Simon whined.

"It's no use," Asa told him. "They forgot us. We're stuck here." He glanced at the row of bright red lifeboats. It looked as if his worst fear was soon to be realized—floating around like a snack on a tray among the hungry megalodon.

An amplified voice boomed out from below. "Ahoy up there!"

Asa looked down over the side of the drillship and saw the patrol boat alongside.

"Need a lift?" Cobb called to them.

"Hell yeah," he yelled down. He turned to Simon and grinned. "Looks like we ain't quite dead yet."

13

December 26, 2018, 5:20 a.m.   *USS Sunfish*, Arctic Sea–

"Glad to see you," Asa called out to Will, as he hopped aboard the *Sunfish*.

Simon waited until the boat rose and dropped again before making the crossing. "Yeah, your buddies took off and left us here," Simon growled. "That's for squealing on us."

Will glared at the chef. "I'm not sure what you mean."

"Yeah, sure," Simon grunted, and then pushed past Will.

"Damn, forgot something," Asa said. He ignored the boat captain's, "Stay here," and leaped back across to the dock. He went into the column and retrieved the injector arm he had designed for the ROV. "Can't leave this behind," he said, smiling. He stepped onto the deck just as the drillship groaned and listed several more degrees.

"Take us out of here, Chico, before debris rolls off the deck on top of us," Will said.

"I saw that big mother-loving shark earlier," Asa told him. "It's not over."

"No," Will agreed, "but we cut them down a bit."

"What now?"

"We get out of the way," Will replied.

The boat picked up speed and moved away from the drillship. Seconds later, a pair of sleek, stealth Northrup Grumman X-478 UCAVs arrived. The drones' sixty-two feet wingspan gave them the appearance of raptors. The unmanned drones swept low over the sea seeking targets for their load off AGM-84 *Harpoon* missiles. The twelve-foot-long anti-ship missiles, with their four-hundred-eighty-pound explosive warheads, could sink a frigate. Asa hoped they would be a match for the megalodon.

"We remain here a while and hope more targets present themselves," Will answered.

Almost in the wake of the two UCAVs, two white MQ-4C *Triton* surveillance drones appeared in the sky, scouring the area for targets for the UCAVs to attack.

"More help is on the way. A squadron of AH-1Z *Viper* attack helicopters left the *USS Kirby* just after the drones launched. They will arrive on station soon."

The *Vanguard* groaned loudly, followed by the sound of gear rolling and sliding across the deck. The drilling derrick swung back and forth like a conductor's baton. It would not take much more for the entire drillship to topple over. Watching the *Vanguard* sinking left a hollow spot in Asa's chest. It had been home for the last two months, and he would miss it.

"I tried to weld the crack in the pontoon, but a megalodon ate the ROV. Then they played hell with the pontoons." He tried to keep his emotions from his voice, but Will stared at him as if reading his thoughts. The *Vanguard* was the second drillship the megalodon had sunk out from under him. Was he was tempting fate?

"We anticipated losing it," Will replied. He looked pointedly at Simon. "That's why we evacuated the crew."

Simon glared at the *Sunfish's* captain. "If you hadn't stopped us, we could have made a difference."

"The ROV would have suffered the same fate as it did during the welding attempt. These things are more intelligent than their modern shark cousins are. If they were just big sharks, we could have wiped them out months ago. These creatures are smarter. It's more likely you would have died for nothing."

"It's my life," Simon countered.

"And it's my job to pull your ass from the fire. My crews' lives are important to me. I've already lost two close friends in the last few days. I don't want to lose anymore, especially saving someone who doesn't want to be saved."

Simon stared at Asa as if asking him to choose sides. Asa said nothing. Simon was angry and bitter, but the captain was right.

Asa knew now would not be the time to speak out. Chastised, Simon stomped down the stairs. Asa followed him to the cabin to try to talk some sense into him. After all, despite turning them in, the captain of the *Sunfish* had saved their lives, and he was grateful. Simon ignored the stares from a sailor wearing a diver insignia on his bloodstained uniform and poured a cup of coffee from the urn in the small galley. He sat down opposite the sailor, took the bottle of *Bunnahabhain* from his jacket, and poured a splash into his coffee.

"Don't feel too bad. He pulled my ass out of the fire, too. I was on the DSV that deployed the mines. The megalodon hit us hard. I'm the only one who escaped."

Simon grumbled something unintelligible and sipped his coffee. He held out the bottle. The diver offered his cup and Simon poured a liberal amount into it. "Cheers."

Asa decided to leave Simon alone in the small galley to brood. After months of planning and single-minded forethought, his carefully conceived plan to kill a megalodon had failed. Asa had never invested that much effort in anything, but he felt some of the chef's disappointment. For a short while, sharing Simon's vision, he had felt alive again. Now, he was back in simple survival modem swept along by events instead of controlling them. He had gotten used to that over the past year.

He went back up on deck to smoke a cigarette. He hadn't had a chance to quench his nicotine habit in hours, and he badly needed to calm his nerves. He found a spot just outside the bridge door, fumbled through the damp pack, and found a dry cigarette. As he took a drag off his cigarette, the *Amberjack* appeared on the horizon. As it drew nearer, Asa noted that it had sustained some serious damage—a large indentation marred the starboard aft hull, and a chunk of the bow was missing, shorn off by massive megalodon jaws. The boat limped along on only one engine. He heard Will contact them by radio. He eavesdropped.

"Looks like you've been in a fight," Will said.

"You should see the other guy," the *Amberjack's* captain replied.

"Do you need assistance?"

Asa wondered how they could not. The boat looked ready to roll over and sink.

"One thruster is gone, and we're leaking like a sieve, but we're still afloat. I lost three men, including my engineer and exec. I would appreciate the use of your engineer for a while to help control the leaks and see if we can get our sonar working."

Will glanced at his exec, who nodded his approval. "Come pick him up. Then, I suggest we both move away from the area and let the Flyboy's take over."

"I'm out of depth charges and 25mm ammunition anyway. I still have two .50 cals and my .45," he added defiantly.

A few minutes later, the battered *Amberjack* pulled alongside the *Sunfish*. Close up, Asa got a fuller extent of the damage. Long gashes along the deck and hull marked where the megalodon had gnawed the boat like a dog's rawhide chew toy. Empty .50 caliber and .25mm shell casings rolled around on the deck. The *Amberjack* had settled into the water until waves washed over the step down cut out deck. The crew, however, looked ready to go at it again. Their young, eager faces showed no fear, only dogged determination and the weariness of a hard-fought battle against a nightmarish enemy.

The *Sunfish* divided its remaining 25mm ammunition with its sister ship.

"Appreciate it, Will," Captain Eisner said. "I'll try to return the favor."

"We can tie off together while you make repairs," Will suggested. "We can have that cup of coffee I promised you."

Eisner shook his head. "I think it best we make repairs underway. Even with one engine, I feel safer moving than sitting."

"Take good care of Chico. He's my exec officer now."

Eisner scowled. "I lost my exec, Grace Browning, as well as my engineer, David Helmuth, and Able Seaman Troy Adams."

"Life sucks," Will said.

"Then you die. Yeah, tell me about it. I have to write letters to their next of kin." He shrugged. "That's war, I guess, even against mindless beasts. I'll return your exec in as good condition as I found him."

"I would appreciate it. Good luck."

Asa watched the *Amberjack* pull away, beaten but not defeated, and felt a swelling of pride in his throat. "It's hard to believe little boats like this can take so much punishment."

Will looked up at him. "Little? Don't you know size doesn't matter? The Navy built the fleet of Mark VI boats for river and shallow inland water operations, aiding the Coast Guard. No one believed them capable of operating in open sea; and yet, the *Amberjack* and the *Sunfish* have proven they can. I hope it means a broader role in the future for the fast attack patrol craft."

Asa tossed his cigarette butt over the side of the boat. "What now?"

"Now, we get out of the way." Will pointed to four AH-1Z *Vipers* approaching the sinking drillship. "The drones will find them something big and gray to shoot at."

The helicopters circled the area only a hundred feet above the surface, their pilots peering into the depths with electronic eyes aiding the drones' efforts.

"How about some coffee?" he asked Asa.

Even with the drones and *Vipers* in the air, nothing was happening. Asa nodded. "I could do with a cup."

As they entered the cabin, Electronics Technician's Mate Levitt called out, "I'm picking up something big on sonar, Skipper. It's rising fast from the bottom."

Will stopped walking. "Whereabouts?"

Levitt looked up, his face ashen. "Directly beneath the *Amberjack*."

"*Amberjack* has no radar." He grabbed the radio mic and yelled, "Eisner! Get the hell out of there! You have sharks coming up from your keel. Take us in," he yelled to the coxswain. Asa realized the *Sunfish's* captain knew it was too late to save any of them, but he had to try regardless.

Six megalodon breached the surface. Three immediately scattered and swam away from the boat, but the other three focused their attention on the *Amberjack*. Her guns cut loose on them, but with only one engine, she was practically sitting still. One of the helicopters made a pass firing its 20mm M197 Gatling gun to ward off the megalodon closest to the boat. Stung by the fusillade, the megalodon submerged again. The other three helicopters joined the fray, standing off and firing AIM-114 *Hellfire* missiles from their wingtip pods. One missile struck a megalodon in the back, leaving a smoking crater three feet across. The sixty-foot-long shark stopped swimming and rolled over onto its flank, thrashing the water with its massive tail. A pool of bloodstained water spread outward from its leeward side. The remaining shark attacked the still-struggling creature, tearing wheelbarrow-sized chunks of meat from its body. A second pass with the Gatling gun dug gouges in both sharks' bodies with 20mm bullets.

Drawn by the scent of fresh blood, the three megalodon that had swum away returned to participate in the feast. Two of the *Vipers* emptied their remaining *Hellfire* missiles into the gam; then, concentrated their Gatling guns on them, killing two.

The *Vipers* had barely cleared the area when the *Amberjack* shot into the air amid a spray of water as if plucked upward by invisible hands. The cause of the geyser of water, the one-hundred-eighty-foot mammoth megalodon, rose from the water beneath the boat like a behemoth from the abyss until it stood on its tail, with the *Amberjack* clutched in its massive jaws. The damaged boat snapped in half just behind the cabin, and both sections of hull fell separately back into the water. The smaller aft section sank immediately. Men spilled into the water from the cabin and bridge. The megalodon landed atop the bow section, smashing it to pieces. One of the smaller, sixty-foot megalodon seized one of the men in its mouth, snapping the man in half. Two more men floundered in the water around the shattered boat, but quickly disappeared, dragged under and swallowed whole by the remaining rampaging sharks.

Too far away to aid the stricken boat, the stunned crew of the *Sunfish* threw off their initial shock and opened up with the forward 25mm minigun and two of the .50 cals. It was like pelting a rhino with Nerf darts. The giant megalodon ignored the machinegun fire as it circled the stricken vessel. One of the *Vipers* flew low over the *Sunfish* to warn her off. Her captain's blood was boiling, but he ordered a sharp turn to port to give the *Vipers* their chance. A hail of 70mm *Hydra* rockets lanced from one of the *Vipers* and sprayed the water around the sinking *Amberjack*, killing two of the creatures, but the behemoth megalodon ignored the rockets' sting as if mere mosquito bites.

Another *Viper* pursued a fleeing megalodon, its landing struts almost brushing the water as it fired its 20mm gun directly into the creature's broad back. The daring pilot veered with the shark each time it tried to move away. Suddenly, the shark turned and leaped into the air, slamming broadsided into the side of the helicopter. The *Viper* tiled until its rotors dug into the water, pulling it farther over. The pilot fought the controls, but gravity won. The rotors shattered and spun away. One piece of rotor broke away and impaled the shark, killing it instantly.

The *Viper* struck the water at a hundred-sixty miles per hour, bouncing end-over-end and scattering pieces of the craft for a hundred yards. It came to rest upside down and sinking rapidly. Only one of the crew survived the crash. He popped to the surface and clung to the wreckage, as sharks circled it. One of the X-478 drones closed in to drive the sharks away with *Harpoon* missiles until a second *Viper* could join it in protecting the hapless crewman.

One of the sharks broke away in pursuit of the *Sunfish*. Asa watched the creature drawing nearer, his heart pounding in his chest from terror. The aft 25mm minigun stitched a row of holes across its snout and head, leaving one blind eye a ragged mess, but the enraged megalodon did not stop. The shark launched itself at the stern. Asa braced himself for the impact. The seventy-foot shark struck the boat like a battering ram, lifting the stern and shoving the boat forward, throwing Asa to his knees. The sickening screech of tearing metal lanced through Asa's ears. The microwave antenna on the cabin roof, toppled and collapsed, crashing to the rear deck less than a foot from Asa. Bosun's Mate Second Class Brad Pierce operating one of the .50 calibers was not so lucky. The antenna crushed him beneath it. His dead eyes stared at Asa.

The boat remained afloat, but the pitch of the engines changed and a column of fuliginous smoke rose from the exhausts. From his knees, Asa watched the shark charge again, seeking to finish the job. Then, as if an attacking watchdog snapped short by its leash, the megalodon stopped abruptly. The enormous mouth of the giant megalodon, which had grabbed onto its tail, closed around the creature and drew it deeper into it cavernous maw. The two-feet-long, razor-sharp teeth sliced into its flesh like a thrashing machine, grinding away chunks of flesh. The injured shark emitted a high-pitched squeal before disappearing down the behemoth's gullet like a large-mouth bass swallowing a minnow. Asa stumbled backwards to the cabin wall in relief.

"It's leaving," Will said.

The giant megalodon abruptly reversed course and glided off to the west, leaving the area. For whatever had called or driven it away, Asa was grateful. For a heart-stopping moment, he feared the *Sunfish's* captain would order his crippled boat in pursuit, but it appeared he had had his fill of carnage for now.

"Let it go. We'll search for survivors." He went to the downed crewman and checked Pierce's pulse, and then knelt beside the dead man and closed his eyes with his hand.

A loud metallic groan drew his attention back to the *Vanguard*. It had dropped another ten feet into the water and now listed twenty degrees to starboard. The portside crane broke away, tumbled across the canted deck, sweeping tents, ASROC launchers, and outbuildings with it as it slid into the water. Made top heavy by the drill derrick, the drillship slowly collapsed onto its starboard side and sank. He watched the last bit of one of the pontoons disappear beneath the waves and felt a sense of impending doom. His willingness to join with Simon in an attempt to kill a megalodon had almost gotten him killed. No. He couldn't blame Simon. Simon was only the catalyst. The megalodon had drawn him back to the Arctic like a magnet, and they had homed in on him as if equally attracted to him.

He could not be positive, but he believed only the granddaddy megalodon remained alive. The Navy had killed most of the creatures. The few survivors had become food for their fellow megalodon and the giant. Whatever the outcome, he knew the fight was not over. They had won a battle but not the war. The battle between the giant megalodon and humans would come soon, but to Asa's relief, not today.

14

December 26, 2018, 3:00 p.m.   *USS Sunfish–*

The battle was over, but there was no clear winner. They had eradicated almost all the megalodon, but the largest one had escaped. The human losses were devastating, both human and material. The drillship *Vanguard* had taken the long journey to the bottom of the ocean, a seven-hundred-million-dollar pile of scrap metal resting atop the well it had been drilling. The *Amberjack* and her crew were gone, the *Sunfish's* own new executive officer and a bosun's mate among the casualties. They had rescued only one of the *Viper* pilots. His injuries were not life-threatening, but he required more medical expertise than the *Sunfish* could provide.

He had contacted the *Utah* to arrange a transfer of the injured pilot, Anderson, and Haig, the DSV diver, but the captain of the submarine was in pursuit of the last megalodon and could not linger for fear of losing it. The *Utah* had suffered damage to her hull and had lost nine crewmembers, including her executive officer. Will noted it had been a bad two days for executive officers. With the drillship gone, the helicopters had no place to land to pick them up, and the two-man *Vipers* could carry no one. Transferring his passengers to the sub would have to wait until the *Sunfish's* repairs were complete.

The tally of the dead was disheartening. Will took no pride in a battle well fought. Their enemy had been mindless, prehistoric megalodon whose only instinct was to feed. He had not outwitted or outmaneuvered his foe. He had simply beaten them into submission with high explosives and survived. It was nothing for which he could claim bragging rights.

Presently, he was elbow deep in grease helping Asa repair the starboard engine. He scratched an itch on his shaved pate and left a smudge of grease, realized what he had done and wiped it with his sleeve. He could barely focus his attention on the repairs from lack of sleep and exhaustion. With no heat, the engine room was cold, but beads of perspiration dotted his forehead. He and the *Vanguard* mechanic had been working for three hours and were just now learning the true extent of the damage. With Chico Rodriguez, his second-in-command and former chief engineer gone, he was glad for any help he could get, even a civilian's.

The visible damage was daunting. The engine's supports had sheared away during the impact with the megalodon, and the entire engine had shifted forward and crashed into the generator, rendering both inoperative. Asa crawled out from under the engine housing and sighed.

"The main bearings are frozen," he reported. He plopped down in the engineer's chair in front of the screen that should have displayed the engines' status. Like all the boat's electronics, it was blank. He wiped his greasy hands on a rag and shoved it in his back pocket. Will noted the grease stains he left on the chair but said nothing. "I can replace them easily enough. However, the heat exchanger is cracked. Unless you have a spare lying around, you'll have to run it on low power or shut it down every few hours to cool."

"What about the generator? I need power." He didn't like sitting helpless in the middle of the ocean. If any of the megalodon were still around, the *Sunfish* would make a tempting target.

Asa shook his head. "That's not gonna happen. Most of the control panel is shot, the shaft is warped, and the solenoid is fried from a power surge."

It was unwelcome news. Without power, the remaining 25mm minigun was useless, as was most of the hi-tech equipment on the bridge.

Asa continued, "I might be able to coax enough power from the solar panels on the drones you're carrying to run your most critical systems, but it's a big maybe. No computer for the engines. Someone will have to run them manually."

Will frowned. He had four crewmen left, and Asa was telling him he would need one of them to operate the engines. "We need sonar and radar. Make that your top priority after the engine. I'll see what the *Utah* can spare from her stores when we catch up with her. Will both engines run?"

"Yeah, but I wouldn't push them too hard. They both took a beating."

"Just as long as they get us where we're going."

Asa glanced away. He tapped his crescent wrench against the console as he asked, "Just where is that?"

Will hesitated. "First, we rendezvous with the *Utah*. The giant megalodon is still moving in a westerly direction, and the *Utah* is following at a distance. They think it's returning to familiar waters."

"The underwater cavern?"

"So it seems."

"What about after we rendezvous with the sub? What then?"

"We accompany her in the pursuit."

Asa's face clouded. It was clear he was not happy with the answer. "Why? The Navy has other ships in the area. Why are you so eager to expose your crippled boat to the megalodon again? Isn't twice enough?"

Will stared at Asa. It was difficult to put in words. The megalodon had bloodied him, making it personal. If anyone knew how he was feeling, the mechanic would. They both shared a hatred for the creature. "I want to see it dead," he replied.

Asa's sardonic grin as he slowly shook his head conveyed his low opinion of Will's logic. "You sound like Simon. He was willing to die for his revenge, probably still is. Are you? More to the point, are you willing to kill the rest of your crew?"

"My crew is my business," Will snapped, stung by Asa's question. It had struck a little too close to home. In his book, the loss of four men under his command was difficult to justify, but he had a job to do. He could not shirk his duty. "You just get my boat operational."

Asa's eyes flashed with anger. He threw Will a mock salute. "Aye, aye, sir!" he growled, and returned to the engine. He buried his face in the bowels of the engine, grumbling.

Will decided he needed some fresh air before he choked his only mechanic. His first act when he caught up with the *Utah* would be to transfer the two civilians with his other two charges to get them out of his hair, but he needed the mechanic for a while longer, and Asa refused to work unless Simon stayed as well. The pair had his nuts in a bind and delighted in squeezing them. He needed the *Sunfish* operational as quickly as possible.

The list of damages to the *Sunfish* was long and varied. The megalodon impact had warped the stern drop ramp and rendered it unusable. They had lost the Zodiac, the aft 25mm chain gun, and one of the .50 cals. The blow had opened a dozen leaks in the aft section. They crew had sealed or patched the worst of them, but all of them needed a permanent repair. The bracing to the previously damaged bow had shifted, opening even more leaks. Even Haig was lending a hand with the repairs. Both bilge pumps were working full time and barely making headway against the incoming water.

As if that wasn't enough, half of their plastic water bottles had ruptured, leaving them low on drinking water.

On the deck, he stopped Apone as he raced by with a hammer in his hand. "Set up a portable pump and flush the water tanks with salt water. Maybe the *Utah* can spare some fresh water."

Apone nodded, his exhausted, dirty face showing no trace of emotion. As damage control officer, his duty was to oversee the repair crews, but the multitude of tasks kept him running from one calamity to another. The crew continued to function, but they had endured more than their fair share of loss. Like their captain, they were running on caffeine, adrenaline, and stubborn bullheadedness, but their store of energy was not limitless. Soon, they would be crashing, the full weight of their experiences bearing down on them. As their captain, he would have to be there to keep them going. *If I can keep it together*.

"Soup?"

The question brought him out of his reverie. Simon stood there holding a tray of bowls of soup and sandwiches. The aroma wafting from the steaming bowl of soup made his mouth water. He shook his head. "Not now." He started to leave, but the chef moved to block his path.

"You've been at it for nine hours, Captain. You're beat. Your crew is beat. I made a hearty beef and lentil soup and a pile of corned beef and Swiss cheese sandwiches with horseradish mayo and dill pickles. Eat something." More quietly, he added, "If your crew sees you eating, they'll eat something. Right now, they're afraid to stop working long enough to eat. You need a break. None of you can go on like this much longer."

As much as he resented Simon, he made sense.

"Fifteen minutes. We'll break fifteen minutes; then, we'll get back at it."

Simon smiled. "Good decision. I have a little Scotch I salvaged from the *Vanguard*. A drop or two all around might perk everyone up."

Will cocked his head and looked at Simon. "You salvaged a bottle of Scotch from a sinking drillship?"

Simon drew himself to his full height. "It's very good Scotch."

"Very well, food and a shot. Happy?"

"Delighted. How's Asa?"

"Pissed at me. He's elbow deep in the starboard engine."

"From what I hear, he's a good mechanic. If it can be fixed, he'll fix it."

"I hope so." He noticed the grin on the chef's face. "Why are you so happy? I thought you resented the Navy."

"Oh, I still do, but as long as I'm on this boat, I still have a chance to kill a megalodon. That is where we're going, isn't it?"

A thought occurred to Will. "You put Asa up to demanding you stay aboard if he did."

"We spoke of it. It looks like we both need him, cCaptain."

"I don't appreciate being manipulated."

"You're shorthanded, Captain. I can cook, and if you show me how, I'll man one of the machineguns. I'm fat, but I'm ornery. Asa will keep us afloat. Besides, you owe us."

"How do I owe you?"

"You said you wouldn't report us. Thirty minutes after you left, a lieutenant showed up with an armed escort to confine us our rooms."

Will nodded. "And you think I reported you."

"Who else?"

"Did it occur to you that the Navy had the drillship under observation?" When Simon looked confused, he said, "The ship's monitor cameras were still operational. Someone spotted you on camera and reported you. I didn't."

"I see," Simon said. He squared his shoulders and faced Will. "I have one quality you're going to need when we catch up with that monster."

"What's that?" Will asked curtly. His conflict with the chef was growing tiresome.

"Your crew is scared. I'm not. I *want* to find it. I'm eager to kill it."

Will shook his head. The chef might be insane, but if so, so was he. "You're a crazy son of a bitch, I'll grant that. Okay, take the food back to the wardroom. I'll round up the crew and join them there."

As Simon walked away, Will said, "Thanks."

Without turning around, Simon replied, "De nada."

By the time he had gathered his crew from their various chores and reached the galley, he found Asa waiting for him. He sat at a table with a cup of coffee in one hand and a sandwich in the other. He eyed Will as he entered, but said nothing. Will picked up a cup of coffee and sandwich and delivered it to the injured *Viper* pilot, Anderson, lying on a bench. The pilot's leg was broken, along with several cracked ribs. Grayson had given him a shot of morphine and set the broken bones, but he needed more care than they could offer him on the *Sunfish*.

Anderson took a sip and grinned. "Your cook makes good coffee."

"He's not Navy. He's a civilian chef off the *Vanguard*."

"Nevertheless."

"How's the leg?"

Anderson studied his splinted and bandaged leg for a moment. "No much pain, but that could be the morphine kicking in. My ribs hurt like a son of a bitch when I move. All in all, I'll live."

Will smiled. "Good. No patients die on my watch."

In spite of his injuries, Anderson seemed in good spirits. He wasn't sure about his crew. They were exhausted; he saw it in their blank faces. Conversation was minimal. No one wanted to talk about what had happened or showed any interest in where they were going. Were they scared, as Simon had suggested? He knew they would fight if the need arose, but how much did they have left to give. They looked drained, walking automatons. *Like me.* How much could he demand from them?

When they got the engines back on line, and if he could count on a steady thirty knots, they faced a challenging twenty-hour journey to the site of the *Global Kulik* sinking. That allowed him time to rotate his crew for some much-needed sack time. If the *Utah* had sent a message, or if he managed to send one with their quirky battery-powered radio, they would rendezvous with the rest of the Arctic Fleet. With that much firepower available, they could end the battle for dominance of the oceans. Then, a systematic extermination of any of the primitive sea life that had escaped its eons-long tomb could begin.

It sounded easy, but he doubted it would be that simple.

* * * *

December 26, 2018, 7:00 p.m.–

Asa felt like a shanghaied sailor, except instead of from seedy port side bar, the captain of the *Sunfish* had been plucked from a sinking ship, the *Vanguard*. It wasn't that he minded pitching in and helping. After all, until the engines were operational, he was stuck in the middle of the ocean. However, Will had made it abundantly clear that he want neither him nor Simon on his boat and that only the direst circumstances prevented him from dropping them both overboard for a helicopter to pick up. Having endured one such experience, he was not eager for a second attempt. Simon had explained that the *Sunfish's* captain had not reported them, but he wasn't ready to kiss and make up. He resented the captain's commandeering him.

The boat had taken a beating. Only a shipyard could repair the cracked plates, the warped keel, and the savaged stern, but he had made headway on the damaged engine. It would run, after a fashion, but it would require some finesse and a steady hand to keep both engines in sync without burning them out. They had power of sorts. Stripping the four UAVs of their solar panels, added to the 60-Watt portable roll up panel used for SEAL team operations, gave them just enough power to operate sonar, radar, and the boat's electrical system, including the refrigerator and coffee urn, in his opinion, the boat's two most essential systems.

The heating system operated from waste heat from the engines, so they would not freeze, although without the heat exchanger for the number two engine, it would get cold. However, they had no ship's computer, hence no 25mm chain gun, no long-range communications, or GPS navigation. The captain would have to pilot the boat by dead reckoning using the stars and the sun for position.

They had set out after the *Utah* just before sunset and still faced a long, arduous journey. They had left the storm behind them like a dark testament to the sunken drillship and the *Amberjack*. The sea was calm with long, gentle swells. In her present condition, Asa doubted the *Sunfish* could have held together in a rough sea.

He was in a quandary about his present circumstances. After surviving two ships sinking out from under him, he was leery of his presence on a third vessel of dubious hull integrity. The crew had stopped most of the leaks, at least temporarily, but if the bilge pumps failed, they would sink. *Third time's a charm!*

On the other hand, Simon was delighted. He was still in on the hunt for the giant megalodon. In spite of Asa's assurances, Simon had convinced himself that the behemoth was somehow responsible for his sister's death. He had focused his entire being, his reason for living on pursuing and killing the creature. For his part, Asa had had enough. The slaughter around the *Vanguard,* both human and megalodon, had sated his appetite for blood. His personal quest had ended. The megalodon were real. He wasn't crazy. He felt vindicated, relieved. Killing them no longer appealed to him. He was willing to let the Navy, or even the Boy Scouts, finish the job. His part in the Great Arctic Megalodon Extermination Sales Event was finished. He was ready to resume his life, what bits he could salvage.

He had coaxed thirty-five knots from the engines, though the higher speed made it more difficult to keep the revolutions even. He was eager to get where they were going, not to kill megalodon, but to transfer to another ship, one from which he could hitch a ride back home on a helicopter. He nudged the throttle down a bit on the damaged engine with the heel of his hand until the tone sounded right in his ear, more in sync with the number one engine.

"Keep it up, baby," he urged them. "Daddy wants to go home."

He looked up and saw Simon standing in the engine compartment door.

"Do you always talk to engines?" he asked. His voice rose to project over the noise of the engines.

Asa grinned. "Sure. They never sass me. They just listen."

"An admiral character trait, I suppose. It's a bit one-sided though."

Asa stood between the two engines, his hands resting on each one, feeling the vibrations hoping to detect any problems before they arose. He felt more in touch with inanimate objects than he did humans. Machines he could understand. They operated by a fixed set of physical laws. The vagaries of human psychological did not influence or corrupt them. Machines might try to kill you, but they didn't try to fuck you over.

Simon sat down at the useless engineering console. Asa decided the overweight chef looked more exhausted than the *Sunfish's* battle-weary crew. Both of them had experienced an eventful twenty-four hours, but he doubted Simon had slept.

"The captain gave you an offhand compliment about your mechanical skills."

Asa grimaced. He was still sore at Will. "Any other time, I'd be delighted in his vote of confidence."

"You should give him some slack. He's doing what he has to. He's in a tight situation."

Asa arched an eyebrow at the change in Simon. "I thought you were anti-Navy. So you're okay with it now because he's taking you where you want to go."

Simon looked puzzled. "And you don't? I thought you were still in the fight. Isn't that why you went back for the *saxitoxin*?"

Asa shrugged. "I brought it on a whim. Multiple brushes with death have forced me to rethink my position. I've decided I'm not ready to die."

Simon's face clouded, and he got that far away look in his eyes Asa had seen in them more and more often. "Neither was Ilsa."

Simon had not asked how she had died. Asa wasn't sure if he did not want to know, or if he wanted to spare him the burden of reliving the events of the *Global Kulik's* sinking. It was time he knew. Maybe then, he would abandon his unhealthy quest for revenge.

"Look. The shark didn't kill her; at least I don't think it did. Certainly not the big mother we're chasing. I killed her." He waited for Simon's reaction. To his surprise, Simon's mien barely changed. "Not directly," he added as he continued. "I was with her in the lab when the ship drilled into the cavern and it collapsed beneath us. The ship was going down. We raced for the lifeboats with the rig crashing down around us. The *Kulik* was like a bucking bronco. When it stood on end, we slid across the deck. I almost went over the side. Ilsa did." Simon's eyes widened. "I held her with one hand, while clinging to a cable with the other. That's how I dislocated my shoulder." He rubbed his injured shoulder. "I managed to pull her up, and we scrambled back on board." He paused, as the emotions of the event flooded over him, threatening to overwhelm them. He had suppressed them for so long, it was reliving the event. He could even taste the salt water; smell the methane-and-sulfur-laced air.

"The ship rolled and we both went over the side. When I came up, she was some distance away. The ship came down between us. I … I didn't see her again." He closed his eyes and shook his head, shivering from the cold of that fateful day. "I don't know if the ship landed on her or if she drowned. I almost did. I pulled myself on top of a toolbox and floated until a chopper picked me up. That's when I saw the giant megalodon, or imagined I had. Now I know it was real. If I had … If we hadn't been separated, I might have saved her."

Simon said nothing for a few moments; then, said, "No, it's not your fault. Maybe a megalodon didn't kill her. Maybe it did. It doesn't matter. There's still one left, and I want to kill it."

Asa shook his head in disappointment. He had hoped his explanation would make Simon see some sense, draw him back from the brink of abyss over which he teetered. He liked the outspoken chef and didn't want to see him die. He didn't want to see anyone else die.

"This obsession is going to kill you."

"Maybe. It doesn't matter. Ilsa was the only family I had. She died hating me, and I can't live with that."

"She didn't hate you. She … she was better than that."

"Our last words were spoken in anger. She accused me of being emotional detached. I've had many girlfriends but none of them took. I'm lousy with relationships. I told her it's because being a chef took all my time and emotion. She said I was afraid of commitment. We argued and left on bad terms. I, I never got the chance to apologize and tell her she was right."

Simons sat slump-shouldered, his head bowed. Asa could see how much his admission had taken out of him. Two women would have hugged to show mutual support. Asa just grunted, the manly equivalent. After, in Asa's mind, and uncomfortably long minute, Simon raised his head. He looked at Asa as if seeing him for the first time.

"I shouldn't have involved you in this. I used you. I took advantage of your guilt and doubt and persuaded you to help me. I was wrong. I can't see a way out of this for me, but you're different. You've walked through the fire and emerged a new man. If you get the chance, promise me you'll walk away. You don't owe me anything."

It was exactly what Asa was hoping to hear, but somehow, it didn't comfort him.

The intercom, one of the few things operational, crackled to life. "Asa, cut the engines," Will said. "I think you two will want to see this."

What now? Asa thought

15

December 26, 2018, 7:20 p.m.   *USS Sunfish*, Beaufort Sea, Antarctica–

Will felt the engines shut down as Asa relinquished control of them. It was just as well. They were going nowhere anytime soon. With the exception of the small bay-like area in which the *Sunfish* floated, a dun-colored carpet blocked their passage, extending out of sight both left and right, and looking as if it extended all the way to the horizon. The gently undulating mass was a floating island. All it needed was a sandy beach, a thatch-roofed cabana, and hula girls. However, this was no tropical paradise. It was a lichen-covered biomass with spindly, fuzz-covered plants waving in the breeze.

The breeze bore the acrid odor of sulfur-rotting vegetation, much stronger than the sea around the *Vanguard* during the storm. The floating algal mat was so alien he knew it had originated from the subsea cavern. He could see no way around the mass, and the *Sunfish's* water jets could not operate in it. Unable to continue, he had to make a decision whether to go back or to make a long detour around it.

He did not like retreating.

Will climbed atop the cabin for a better view. From there, the solid-appearing mass became a series of various-sized islets separated by narrow leads of open water. Several such streams converged to traverse the entire width of the mass, but a hundred-yard-wide portion of the mat separated the *Sunfish* from the open water. Though benign in appearance, something about the mat troubled him. It reminded him of a kelp bed on the Pacific coast. Kelp beds usually swarmed with a myriad of sea life, both predator and prey. He decided to take no chances. He turned to Apone, standing behind and below him, waiting expectantly.

"Go to battle stations. No klaxon." He didn't want to draw any creatures that might be lurking on or beneath the mat, especially the giant megalodon. "Anything on sonar?" he asked.

"Nothing, sir," McGee reported.

Still, he felt uneasy but wasn't certain why. He stared at the mat for several minutes but saw only clouds of flying insects. Small crustaceans he did not recognize scuttled among the mounds of lichen, and a few Arctic terns swooped down to pluck the crabs into the air to feed on.

Up close, the tightly interwoven strands of kelp and mucilage nodes of bacteria resembled a sisal welcome mat, but Will doubted they would find a smiling face greeting them if they knocked on the door. He wrinkled his nose at the stink. He was no biologist, but he understood algae. Unlike autotrophic algae, the alien alga— if alien was the correct word for something of this earth, merely from a different time—lacked chloroplasts, hence the pale color. Unable to fix carbon from sunlight in the sunless cavern, the chemoautotrophic bacteria derived their energy by the process of osmotrophy, absorbing sulfur dioxide, hydrogen sulfide, and carbon dioxide dissolved in the water through cell membranes, and releasing oxygen as a byproduct. By all rights, the algae should not have thrived in a sun-rich environment.

He noticed streaks of color, darker brown, green, and red threading through the otherwise uniformly taupe expanse. The new alga mass had adapted and began to incorporate existent autotrophic cyanobacteria, including blue-green algae, into its evolving body, cannibalizing them for their chloroplasts, a melding of prehistoric and modern worlds.

He glanced down and saw Apone staring up at him, waiting for orders. The *Sunfish* had drifted until her hull brushed against the fringes of the mass.

Curious, Apone poked the mat with a boathook to test its density. He pushed with all his strength, but the hook sank only four inches into the mass. His actions disturbed a swarm of tiny black flies that dove for his face. He sputtered as he swatted at them and spat them from his mouth.

"It's like a friggin' putt-putt golf course," he said. "You know; the artificial turf kind."

Simon and Asa walked out onto the deck. Asa stared at the mat with dark wonder in his eyes, but Simon's reaction was instant and antagonistic.

"It's trying to take over the world," he growled.

Will wasn't sure if he meant the algae or the megalodon. "It looks harmless enough," he replied, but his palms itched, to him a sure sign of danger. He was glad he had ordered battle stations. He climbed down from the roof.

Simon immediately turned on him, his face twitching with rage. "It's not just the sharks. It's the whole primeval ecosystem. It could supplant ours; make the earth more suitable for Miocene creatures than their present-day descendants. It's like a virus, rewriting the DNA of the planet."

Asa stared at the delicate fronds waving in the breeze with muted terror. "We should go around it."

"Nonsense," Simon replied. "It would take hours, maybe a full day."

"To you, this is just another megalodon, something to kill. I think it's much worse."

Will watched the intense interchange with interest. This was the first sign of disagreement he had noticed between them. "It's an algal mat, Asa," Simon said, "like kelp or seaweed. It's not an animal."

Simon's assurances did not placate Asa. "For millions of years, it derived energy from sulfur-eating bacteria in symbiosis with the algae instead of sunlight and released oxygen in the cavern's closed system; yet, here it is, alive and thriving in an oxygen environment in full sunlight. That's strange, don't you think? It's like an iceberg. It's what's beneath the surface that we have to worry about."

Will thought it ironic that Asa's thoughts mirrored his own.

"Oh for God's sake, Asa!" Simon snapped. "I use seaweed and kelp in my recipes. Let's burn this shit and get going."

Asa looked at Will and shrugged. "Do what you want. I'm just a passenger."

Will and Simon exchanged questioning glances. Whatever doubts Asa might have planted in Will's mind, he still had to follow the *Utah*, which could pass safely beneath the mat. The *Sunfish* could not.

Apone interrupted them. "I see something out there, about five points off the starboard beam, two hundred yards out."

Will raised his glasses and spotted a dark mass that appeared to be the wreckage of a small boat. "Good eyes, Apone," he said.

"Could there be survivors?" Asa asked, shading his eyes with his hand to see.

"Unlikely," Will responded.

"But you don't know for sure," Asa insisted.

Will lowered his binoculars and cast an annoyed look at Asa. "No, how could I? However, it seems unlikely." He paused. "What would you propose we do?"

"Go look."

At first, Will thought the mechanic was joking, but his expression remained deadpan. "We can't get to it. The *Sunfish* can't hike its skirt and walk over this stuff."

"No, but we can. The mat looks firm enough. Send someone out to check."

"Are you volunteering?" Will asked Asa.

Asa glanced at the object in the distance and swallowed hard. Will knew he had hurt his pride, but he was curious to see how the mechanic responded. After a few moments consideration, Asa nodded. "Yeah, I'll go, but not alone."

Simon shook his head and patted his ample belly. "Not me. No way. I'll fall through."

"I'll go, sir," Apone volunteered.

"No, I'll go with Mr. Iverson. You take command of the boat while I'm gone." He looked at Asa. "Ready?"

"Sure. Let's go."

Will admired Asa's courage, but he would never give him the satisfaction of telling him so. He realized Asa had volunteered just to put him on the spot. *We're both fools.*

"I thought you were afraid of this stuff," Simon said to Asa.

Asa's expression turned grim. "I've been shipwrecked twice now. If there's someone out there, I know how they feel."

The tension between the two drained away. "Good luck."

Asa nodded.

Armed only with his Model 1911 .45 caliber pistol, Will climbed over the side and onto the mat. He sank three inches into the growth, but it held his weight. He took a tentative step and found it akin to walking on a trampoline. The substance yielded to the pressure but pushed back as he lifted his foot. He motioned to Asa.

"I think it's safe. Come on."

Asa hesitated for a moment, but then climbed down onto the algal mat. He waved his arms for balance, as he walked out to stand beside Will. Their passage stirred clouds of small black flies that swarmed their faces. Will fanned his hands in front of his face toward them off. Black beetles scurried among the undergrowth, avoiding their feet. Small grayish-blue crabs crawled around the mat, their pink claws snapping off fronds and shoving them in their mouths. The bundles of filaments of colonial blue-green alga insinuated itself in the mass like colored thread running through the taupe lace.

As they neared the wreckage, Will saw that the chance of survivors was small. The wooden-hulled craft looked like an Inuit whaleboat that had passed through the gut of a boa constrictor. The boat was a crushed bundle of splintered wooden planking wrapped in a net of algal threads. The only sign of life was the mob of tiny blind crabs scurrying around the area.

"No one survived that," Will said.

"Or if they did, the crabs got them," Asa added, making a face of disgust at the tiny creatures. He glanced around the mass of algae. "My original objection still stands. We can't get through this."

Asa's willingness to give up irked Will. The enemy was still out there, and his gut told him he needed to be where it was. "We'll see," he answered and started back toward the boat.

A series of concentric ripples swept along the mat, almost knocking Asa off his feet. Will's sea legs allowed him to shift his weight and ride them out. They seemed centered around the boat. The algal mass bulged upward.

"What the hell is that?" he asked Will.

Before Will could make a guess, cracks appeared in the mat; then, the mat split open, revealing the horrors lay beneath it. The first giant crab crawled up onto the surface and stood staring at them, its six-foot-wide taupe carapace ringed with thorny protuberances like a knight's mace. Then Will noticed that the eyes on the end of the meter-long eyestalks were blind. Born in the dark, it did not need eyes. It knew where they were by their movement on the algae mat. The creature raised its three-feet-long chelae in the air and clacked them together, producing a sound like a rock hammering on a hollow log. Within seconds, several more of the creatures had joined the first, as if summoned by its call.

"They must live on the underside of the mat, feeding on it."

Asa began backing away from the advancing crabs. "Well, now they see something else on the menu—us."

"Let's go back to the boat. Move slowly."

As the crabs gave chase, they picked up the pace. Will quickly discovered that the spongy mat allowed him to take long, bounding steps, like walking on the moon. Asa joined him. One of the .50 caliber machineguns began firing, but the bullets only ricocheted from the hard exoskeletons. The sudden noise more than the stream of bullets, slowed the crabs. They milled around as if uncertain of where their prey had disappeared. By the time they decided to attack the source of the sound, Will and Asa had reached the boat. Simon and Apone helped them aboard.

"What the fuck are those things?" Simon shouted. He paced the deck agitated, wiping his hand through his hair. "I read about giant crabs, but I never ..." He turned to Will. "I noticed quite an arsenal in your SEAL ready room. If you don't mind, I'll borrow one of the machineguns."

"We have a few FN SCAR Mk-46 5.56mms, and a couple of Mk-48 LWMG 7.62mms. Take your pick."

Simon cast another glance at the approaching crabs. "I'll go with the biggest damn gun you've got."

Haig stood in the doorway describing the scene to the bedridden Anderson. He moved aside to let Simon enter. "I can man a .50 cal."

Will pointed to the starboard gun on the opposite side on the mat. "Careful firing over the boat," he warned.

Tracers from Apone's .50 caliber ignited the dry upper fronds of the algae. Fanned by the breeze, the flames spread outward from several spots, creating billowing clouds of dense, acrid, ocher smoke. Ignoring the smoke, the giant crabs pressed forward toward the ship like an advancing army.

Seeing the flames gave Will an idea. He yelled, "Fire in front of them. Start more fires."

The creatures feared the flames, but their long legs allowed them to step over the smaller blazes. When the leading edge of the creatures were less than fifty yards away, Will ordered the other three .50 calibers, manned by Haig, Levitt, and Grayson, to open fire. The heavy-caliber slugs chipped away at the crabs' carapaces, but did little real damage.

"Concentrate on the head," he yelled over the chattering of the machineguns.

The softer tissue surrounding the mouth proved more vulnerable. Several crabs succumbed to the withering crossfire. Will wished the remaining 25mm chain gun was operational. Its rapid rate of fire would have come in handy. Simon reappeared on deck with an FN Mk-48 machinegun, adding its 7.62mm stream of bullets to those of the four .50 caliber machineguns. His first volley went wide, but he quickly learned to control the recoil and began to hit his target. Within minutes, seven of the crabs were dead or too injured to continue. The smaller crustaceans immediately began feeding on the dead and injured, intent on a free meal even amid the burning algae. In spite of the .50 calibers, the giant crabs continued to advance. They need more firepower.

Will was now glad he had refrained Chico from using all the *Griffin* missiles on the megalodon. He had five missiles left, one in the portside launcher and a full complement of four in the starboard launcher. He knew he had to make them count. Without power, the MK-60 launcher's GPS guidance was useless. However, the hand-held laser for targeting operated on battery power. He painted the nearest cluster of crabs with the laser and fired a missile. The solid fuel engine propelled the forty-two-inch rocket across the intervening space in a flash of light and smoke. The explosion of the fragmenting warhead scattered half a dozen crabs, killing four of them. Bits of shell and crab blood and organs splattered the surrounding algae.

"That's more like it," he said.

He raced to the starboard launcher. Noticing the ten-foot-wide water-filled crater left by the *Griffin*, he got an idea. It was dangerous but could be their only chance. Rather than fire at the crabs, he aimed the missiles in a line along the narrowest point between the *Sunfish* and the open water. Apone saw what he was doing and looked confused. As he had hoped, the explosions blew away large chunks of algae, not enough to clear the path, but enough to weaken it. He knew the sea would do the rest. Within minutes, propelled by the current, the smaller raft floated away from the larger mass, widening the gap.

"Asa!" he yelled. "The engines!"

Asa ran for the engine room. Seconds later, both engines revved up. Will took the helm, guiding the boat into the narrow channel he had created. He kept the speed under ten knots to avoid sucking any of the kelp fronds dangling below the mat into the water jet intakes. The crabs, seeing their prey escaping, redoubled their efforts, racing along beside the boat. The gunners continued to kill them, but the creatures numbered in the hundreds. At the narrowest point in the channel, three of the creatures leaped the gap and landed on the deck.

One immediately attacked Apone, who backed away from his .50 caliber and fought it off with a boathook. The crab raised its body into the air as is scrambled over the gun mount. Simon noticed Apone's peril, sprayed the crab's softer thorax with his Mk-48, and then kicked its corpse over the side. Levitt dispatched a second creature with the .50 caliber. It fell dead across the mangled rear deck.

The third crab ignored the men on deck, concentrating instead on the men inside the cabin. It thrust its claws through the window, shattering it. The claws clamped closed inches from Will's head. He drew his .45 from his holster and emptied into the creature's face, but the small arms fire did not faze it. Unable to reach Will, the crab tried to push its bulk through the hatch, but the opening was too small.

Seeing the danger, Anderson, rose from his bench, and standing on his broken leg, leaned against the wall, firing his SCAR into the creature's head, his face wracked in agony in spite of the morphine. Sensing this new threat, the crab shifted its body, and in a blur stabbed the sharp tip of its claw into Anderson's abdomen. He screamed and fell backwards onto the deck writhing in pain. Blood streamed from between his hands clasped over his belly.

The crab made one last attempt at gaining entrance to the cabin. It ripped away a metal brace between two windows and enlarged the gap by pulling at the metal around the window's edge. It thrust its chelae through the larger rent. Technician Zeke McGee sat at his station, his attention focused on the radar screen in front of him, shouting directions through the maze of channels to Will. He noticed the crab's claw at the last second but did not move quickly enough. The large claw struck him in the head, knocking him senseless. The crab then clamped the claw around McGee's chest, crushing it instantly, and yanked him out through the opening. Will heard a SCAR Mk-46 erupt outside the window. The crab retreated, bearing its grisly trophy. Haig walked by holding the SCAR, his face twisted in a mask of fury. He poured a steady stream of 5.56mm rounds into the creature, chipping away at the carapace until he punched a hole; then, fired directly into the opening from a distance of five feet. The crab, injured, fell over the side, pulling McGee's lifeless body with it.

The *Sunfish* reached the wider lead. Will shoved the throttles forward, urging the boat through the winding waterway. Crabs continued to watch their passage from the shore, but did not attack. Behind them, the algal mat was a blazing inferno. He hoped it would kill the algae, but knew most of it was underwater. The same channels of water that aided their escape would prevent it from spreading. Nevertheless, the cloud of smoke billowing to the sky heartened him.

Apone, Levitt, and Grayson, all that remained of his crew, and Haig, their hitchhiking diver, gathered on the bridge. Simon sat by himself in the galley. Asa remained with the engines. They looked as if they wanted to hear a few words of encouragement from him. He didn't know what to say, as he waited on inspiration that did not come. He stared into their faces, feeling their anger, their pain.

Simon provided the words he could not find. He stood at the door. Crab blood covered his face and arms and stained his shirt.

"You did good. You're all heroes in my book. I know you lost comrades and colleagues. It hurts, but we're dealing with an enemy that will show no mercy. We have to stand strong. You saw the megalodon; know what they're capable of. Now, you've seen the giant crabs. Who knows what other creatures escaped their deep-sea cavern. They are part of Earth's past. They have no place in our present. We must eradicate all traces of them, or we face extinction.

"I'm sorry for your losses. I didn't know them, but I trust they were good people, good shipmates. These things have killed many people. They will kill a lot more if we don't stop them. I ..." He shook his head. "That's all I've got to say."

He walked back to the galley and began making a pot of coffee. Simon's speech moved Will. He saw that it had touched his crew as well. He nodded.

"What he says is true. The battle's not over yet. We're crippled, out of depth charges and missiles, the 25mms don't work, and we're low on .50 cal ammunition, but we can replenish our supplies when we rendezvous with the fleet or the *Utah*. We're not out of the fight yet. Now, get some rest. I'll man the con."

One by one, they left, leaving him alone with his thoughts. They were dark ones. He felt like a failed leader. Half his crew was dead. His boat suffered from severe damage and was barely afloat. He had lost someone they had rescued. He depended on two cantankerous civilians and a Navy DSV diver to keep his boat running. He knew the worst was yet to come.

They never said command would feel this heavy in command school.

16

December 28, 2018, 3:00 p.m.   *USS Utah*, Chukchi Sea, Arctic–

Twenty hours after the battle, the *Utah* was still tending to its wounds and grieving for its dead. Among them was First Officer Tack Hardin, killed when the aft payload lockout hatch flooded. To save the ship, he sealed himself inside the lockout to secure the outer hatch and drowned. Altogether, the *Utah* had lost nine crewmates, and the bilge pumps were working overtime to keep her from going to the bottom. In spite of everything, they were in pursuit of the giant megalodon, perhaps the sole remaining creature from the undersea cavern.

Captain Prescott had not slept since the day before the battle. He stood as rigid as a ship's mast in the command and control center, ready to handle any crisis that came up. They were numerous, chief among them his inability to contact anyone at a distance farther than a few miles. One of the photonic masts and all of the communication masts on the sail were gone, swept away during the battle. By all rights, he should make for a port and repair his boat, but unable to report the megalodon's location or the direction in which it was moving, the *Utah* remained the best chance of killing the last remaining megalodon. At the very least, he could track it and apprise the fleet.

On the way, they had passed beneath a miles-wide floating mat of algae from the cavern. He had risked a peek through his one good photonic mast, poking it through the algae, amazed at the mat's burgeoning ecosystem. It was just one more sign of the havoc the flora and fauna of the cavern were causing with the delicate ecosystem. He could do nothing about the algal mat, but he could stop the last shark, somehow. The *Utah* still had teeth. Four Mk-48 Mod 7 torpedoes and six *Tomahawk* ASM/LAM missiles remained in her arsenal, one tipped with a W80-1 nuclear warhead, although employing a tactical nuke required a higher authority, and he had no communications.

"Any luck on getting out a signal?" he asked for the fourth time in the past hour.

The communications technician was as weary as he was, but refrained from the obvious retort. "Short-range only, sir. The damage to the SATCOM mast is total. We lost the AN/BLQ-10 warfare mast, one of the AN/BVS-1 photonic masts, and the AN/BPS-16 radar mast suffered severe damaged." He sighed. "I'm sorry, sir. Unless someone is flying directly over us, we can't talk to them."

Prescott grimaced. Half blind, deaf, and mute was no way to fight a war. "Very good, sailor. Why don't you take ten and grab some coffee?"

The technician shook his head. "No thank you, sir. I'd rather remain at my station. Someone might come within range."

Prescott nodded. Such devotion to duty was typical of his crew. He was proud of them, especially Hardin. He had given his life for his ship and crew.

"Any sign of the megalodon?" he queried of his sonar technician.

"Not in the last hour. It's about ten clicks ahead of us, swimming at a leisurely pace."

"Yeah, it knows we can't catch it."

He was surprised the behemoth megalodon, half as big as the *Utah*, had so far ignored them. During the fight at the *Vanguard*, it had attacked and eaten everything in its path. Instead of finishing them off, it chose to return to familiar waters. He could only wonder why.

They rode the surface in hopes that some passing airplane, drone, or ship might spot them, anything that could signal the Fleet. He wondered why the *Kirby* had not sent surveillance drones in their direction following the megalodon. They had been in the air during the battle. Someone had screwed up and left him holding the bag. It had been his duty to follow the megalodon, even in a crippled boat. The trap at the *Vanguard* had for the most part been a success. Only one creature remained, and if he could catch up with it, he would end the threat for good.

"We're at the coordinates of the cavern, sir," Kyle Mason announced.

Some of the tension left his body. They had made it. He nodded to the bosun's mate, now acting as his first officer. He faced a hard choice. He could either remain on the surface, hoping that another ship made contact, or he could take his damaged boat down into the unknown depths of the cavern in pursuit of the megalodon. The safe course would be to bide his time, but how long could he afford to wait? If the megalodon slipped away or disappeared into the bowels of the cavern, they would have lost it, and with it, the war. He took one last look at the surface through the photonic mast camera, wondering how he had come to be surrounded by so much water. Back in his Strawberry Mansion neighborhood in North Philly as a boy, broken fire hydrants spraying the street on hot summer days were as close to a lake or ocean as he ever thought he would get.

Few neighborhoods in North Philadelphia were as tough or as impoverished as ill-named Strawberry Mansion. Bounded by 33rd Street to the west, 29th Street to the east, Lehigh to the north, and Oxford Street to the south, Strawberry Mansion was one of the most crime-ridden neighborhoods in the city. Abutting Fairmount Park, a place where discarded heroin needles outnumbered squirrels, and dealing and prostitution fueled the underground economy, the neighborhood, once home to John Coltrane, offered little incentive for success. Prescott had fought hard to get an education in a system on which most city planners had given up hope. Some people called it perseverance. He just called it his stubborn streak.

"Take us down, Mr. Mason."

With the damaged ballast tank, he took the sub into a steep dive to pass through the two-hundred-yard-wide mouth of the cavern. The sub shuddered and bucked as rising thermal currents buffeted it like a taxi ride down a pot-holed Philly street.

"I'm picking up metallic debris scattered along the bottom directly beneath the opening. It must be the *Global Kulik*. Should we investigate?"

"No. We can't help them. Keep her steady on course."

The entrance became a long sloping tunnel barely a hundred yards wide. He had doubts about entering the confined space, but he had come to investigate, and backing up solved nothing. To his relief, it soon opened into a wider chamber. Watching the monitor feed from the remaining photonic mast, the crew enjoyed a panoramic view of the cavern's interior. Exterior lights illuminated clouds of plankton so dense they absorbed the light like a solid wall. Billions of tiny dinoflagellates, diatoms, and bacteria, unable to synthesize nutrients from sunlight, thrived on sulfur and other compounds dissolved in the water. Zooplankton, composed of krill and the larva of crustaceans, consumed the dinoflagellates. Schools of fish darted through the cloud eating everything. Larger predator fish patrolled the edges of the cloud, devouring smaller fish. The vista presented a prehistoric circle of life that mirrored the one in the ocean above it.

The sonar reflections revealed an irregular-shaped cavern a dozen miles long and ten miles wide. The bottom, a series of underwater smooth ridges and jutting mesas, registered an average of eight-thousand feet in depth. A large opening in the center cavern's floor dropped into an abyss so deep the sonar could not find a bottom. Numerous clefts and ledges overgrown with pale gray kelp forests rimmed the interior walls of the cavern, providing food and shelter for a host of crustaceans ranging from miniscule to the size of small automobiles. Ominous dark openings of various sizes dotted the cavern walls

"It looks like a lava chamber," Prescott noted of the cavern's shape. "That might explain the heat." He glanced at the exterior temperature gauge. It read fifty-five degrees Fahrenheit. "Mr. Decosta, any sign of the shark?"

"I'm picking up large objects," the sonar technician reported, "but none as large as the megalodon we're chasing. Most are fifteen to twenty feet in length. Listen to this." The technician played the audio through the main speakers. A deep rumbling sound filled the room, haunting in its beauty.

"It's whale song, Mr. Decosta," Prescott said, smiling. "I wonder how the words have changed in twenty-million years."

"Well, whales are mammals," Mason noted. "They're breathing something."

"Yes, it would indicate air pockets in some of the side chambers. This cavern probably contained an atmosphere as well before the collapse."

If their quarry was not in the cavern, it must be in one of the side chambers. He chose an opening at random and pointed to it. "Take us in there. Make our speed ten knots."

"It will be a tight fit, captain. The opening is barely thirty yards wide."

"We'll just put our nose in. Don't scratch the paint."

He tried not to dwell on the many instances in which he had poked his nose in places it didn't belong. He had won a few fights and lost a few, but he had not let the experience quell his sense of curiosity.

The atmosphere in the control room grew tense, as the almost four-hundred-feet long, thirty-four-feet-wide *Utah* edged her nose into the opening. She had no maneuvering room. If they encountered an obstacle or if the tunnel became too twisting to continue, they would have to back out. The exterior lights exposed lines of small crablike crustaceans scuttling along the walls toward the main cavern. Unlike the larger denizens, many of the smaller crustaceans varied in color from pale blue to red to multicolored, a throwback to the ages before the sightless species branched off from their marine counterparts.

Pockets of plants resembling sponges and fragile spires of coral waved in the current.

"The tunnel widens out in six hundred yards. A larger cavern lies beyond that."

Prescott nodded. "Prepare tubes one and three for firing. If we meet our giant gray friend, I want to be ready."

The bow of the *Utah* nosed out of the tunnel into the cavern. The sonar image disappeared, indicating a cavern larger than the one they had left. Prescott began to imagine just how extensive the underwater cavern system might be.

"Increase speed to fifteen knots."

Before the engine room could reply, the bow of the sub shot upward, sending everyone not seated flying across the control room. The shriek of shearing metal sounded like screaming people. Prescott slammed hard into a console with his back. His head napped backwards and struck the hard metal. The lights began flickering, and he didn't know if it was the lights or his vision fading in and out. Moments later, the sub struck the roof of the tunnel. This time, the sound of grinding rocks mixed with that of the overstressed metal hull.

"All engines stop!" he yelled; then, pulled himself to his feet. "What hit us, Mr. Decosta?"

Decosta's face was grim. Blood oozed from one nostril. "It's the megalodon. Eighty yards away and coming for us again."

"Engine room, reverse engines. Take us back inside the tunnel." It would not stop the shark from attacking, but he would have a direct shot at it with the torpedoes. The concussion in such close quarters might damage the boat, but it offered their only chance. "Torpedo room. Fire both tubes on my mark."

"Tubes one and four inoperable," the torpedo room replied.

"Damn. Fire three. Mark."

Ten seconds later, the sub rocked violently with the blast wave of the explosion. The lights failed. Emergency lighting flickered on.

"Miss, sir. We struck the tunnel wall."

Prescott swore. They were sitting ducks inside the tunnel. "Back us out. Twenty knots."

The helmsman looked at him nervously, but pushed the throttle forward. They risked banging the walls and rupturing the hull, but if they didn't get away, the megalodon would do that for them.

As soon as they exited the tunnel, he took the sub in a steep dive along the cavern wall, hoping to mask the sub from the shark. It didn't work. The megalodon rammed them just forward of the engine room, between the engine room and the reactor. The chief engineer reported a massive leak, but then the intercom failed.

"Engine room completely flooded, sir," the damage control officer reported.

"Did anyone escape?"

"I don't think so, sir."

"We also have leaks in the missile launch compartment and the bow dome. A coolant line ruptured in the reactor. The engineer is shutting down the reactor and evacuating the reactor compartment. Switching to battery power."

They would soon lose power. They would never reach the surface. "Blow all ballast tanks and steer for the exit tunnel."

A few minutes later, he knew they would never escape. The megalodon rammed them twice more, rolling the sub like a log at a lumberjack logrolling contest.

"I'm losing helm control," the driver said.

"Try to set us down on that ledge."

The ledge was just inside the exit tunnel and barely wide enough to accommodate the *Utah*, but it offered the only hope to keep them from descending to the bottom below the sub's crush depth. The sub scraped the wall as it settled onto the ledge.

"Mr. Mason. Inspect the aft section. Secure all watertight doors and repair any leaks you can. Send the crew forward. I'll take the torpedo room and forward sections."

Mason took several deep breaths and nodded. "Yes, sir."

As Prescott took the ladder to the lower sections, he cursed himself for his folly. His decision had doomed his boat and maybe his crew. Unless help arrived soon, they would remain where they were until air ran out or the carbon dioxide built up to a lethal level.

And that damn shark is still out there.

Suddenly, Strawberry Mansion didn't look so bad.

17

December 28, 2018, 2:00 p.m.   *USS Sunfish*, Chukchi Sea, Arctic Ocean–

Asa perched atop the *Sunfish's* 25mm chain gun on the bow deck wearing a sour expression. Beside him stood Simon and Will. With the engines off, the depth of the silence around the boat was disconcerting. No wind disturbed the surface of the water. No squawking birds wheeled in the sky overhead. The odor of rotting vegetation and the stench of sulfur tainted the air, rising in a roil of bubbles from the depths as if escaping from hell.

"We'll, we're here," Asa announced, his frustration evident in his tone. "Where is everybody?"

Will glared at the mechanic and continued scanning the area with his binoculars, hoping he had missed something. As the radar had indicated, there were no ships in sight. The fleet had not arrived, and he saw no sign of the *Utah*. They were alone in the spot where it all had started.

"If the *Utah* sent a message, they'll be here," he said. "We beat them here." He could not allow his own reservations taint the crew, what was left of his crew. They had come to do a job, though he was not sure how to accomplish it alone.

"If," Asa snapped, clearly agitated. He had grown more belligerent as the journey had progressed. At first, Will had attributed the mechanic's hostility to lack of sleep and exhaustion, like almost all his crew, but Asa's ire seemed directed at him personally. "If we had remained where we were, we could have fixed this pile of scrap. Hell, we could have held up a fucking cardboard sign asking a helicopter pilot to drop us a few spare parts. Now, we're stuck in the middle of nowhere on a sinking boat, and no one else has a goddamned clue where we are."

"She'll stay afloat. Insult me, but don't insult my boat."

Asa slid down from the minigun and stood in front of Will. "For how long? One of the bilge pumps is out of commission, and we're out of fuel for the portable pump. It won't run on diesel, you know. Even I can't change that. In a few hours, we'll be getting our feet wet and for what? So you can play war games?"

"This is no game, Mr. Iverson, and yes, I'm well aware of the situation. I have five dead friends to attest to that. Now, why don't you make yourself useful and see if you can perform some mechanical miracle with what we do have and save our asses?" He allowed his voice to rise at the end of his tirade to the mechanic, hoping Asa would accept the challenge.

Asa spread his hands. "Well, as long as you've asked so nicely."

He swung and stalked away, quickly disappearing below deck.

"He's scared," Simon said. "He's been here before, you know." He sniffed the air. "I wonder if it smelled this bad when the *Global Kulik* sank."

Will stared at the bubbles rising around them, dark brown and unpalatable, like bubbles blown through a straw into a glass of chocolate milk. It surprised him that gas still leaked from the subsea cavern after almost a year. That meant some pockets of primeval atmosphere remained in the cavern. Instead of a single vast cavern that had lost its roof, the subsea opening could lead to a series of vast chambers filled with who knew what horrors. He shook his head to quell that line of thinking.

"I realize that. He just rubs me the wrong way," Will admitted.

Simon laughed. "I've been told I rub people the wrong way, but I'm a darling when you get to know me." His expression grew more serious. "Maybe he objects to being shanghaied."

Will winced. He had no defense against the charge Simon levied against him. That was exactly what he had done, shanghaied them. It might wind up ending his career, if he lived long enough to face court martial. "You were castaways, and I took you aboard. When the *Utah* set off in pursuit of the monster megalodon, I had no time to transfer you to another ship."

"You mean you wouldn't take the time. The *Kirby* was only a few hours away, but you chose to follow the *Utah*. Oh, I don't blame you. It's what I would have done, but Asa thinks differently." He paused. "Maybe your superiors will, too."

"Damn you!" Will growled. "I don't need civilians trying to run my boat or question my decision. If you've nothing better to do, go below and make some sandwiches, cook."

Simon narrowed his eyes. "That's chef to you, and you'd better watch it, Admiral. I'm as close to a friend as you have on this boat. I don't think you'd win any popularity contests with your crew."

"This is a Navy vessel. My crew will follow orders."

"Your crew is mostly dead, remember."

Will turned on Simon, his fists clenched, angry that the chef had reminded him of his failures. He fought the urge to lash out, to strike something in lieu of the megalodon they were after.

"You have a disgruntled Navy diver, a civilian mechanic, and a civilian cook aboard," Simon continued, ignoring Will's threatening posture. "In case of a mutiny, you might find yourself swimming home."

He left, leaving Will alone on deck. He glanced inside the cabin at Apone, who looked away. Had he overheard the conversation? Was Simon right? Was his crew near mutiny? Had he led them on a six-hundred-mile goose chase? So far, he had lost his First Officer Rich Hall, Chief Gunner's Mate John Mason, Chief Engineer Chico Rodriguez, Bosun's Mate Second-Class Brad Pierce, and electronics technician Zeke McGee—over half his crew. Add to that tally Anderson, the downed *Viper* pilot. Would he kill the rest?

Grayson cleared his throat. "Uh, Skipper, I might have a plan on establishing communications with someone."

"Speak up, Grayson."

"Well, Asa and I were talking. It would mean stripping away most of our power, but it could work." He paused, and then said, as if convincing himself, "Yeah, it could work."

"Spit it out, Grayson."

"If we replace the solar cells we stripped from the drones, adjust their telemetry, and stagger them just within range of each other and the *Sunfish*, it might be possible to piggyback a radio signal from drone to drone. We could extend our radio range out to a couple of hundred miles."

"It'll work?" he asked. It was almost too much to hope for.

"Maybe. Problem is; it'll leave us only with the emergency solar cell and what juice remains in the batteries. We'll need it all for the radio. That means no pumps."

Will rubbed the top of his head, noting the stubble of hair growing back. When was the last time he had shaved his head? When was the last time he had showered? Three days since Rich died. Two days since reaching the *Vanguard*. Only one day since the battle? It didn't seem right. The days jumbled together into one another with some events seeming out of place in his mind.

With no pumps, they would sink within half a day, but with no communication, they would eventually sink anyway. Not only their lives, but also the lives of the crew of the *Utah* depended on his decision, and so far, his record was less than perfect. He tossed a mental coin.

"Do it," he said.

He hoped he had made the right choice.

* * * *

It took Asa, Grayson, and Levitt two hours to replace the solar cells on the drones' wings and install the necessary electronics to piggyback their broadcast signal. During that time, another two inches of water flowed into the bilge. At that pace, they would soon be bailing with buckets.

"Ready," Grayson announced. In spite of the chill in the air, perspiration covered his forehead.

"Release the drones," Will said, hating his choice of words. It sounded too much like 'Release the Kraken' or some other movie lingo.

"I'll guide each one out as far as I can until the signal weakens; then, bring it back in a little and place it in a circular path around the boat. I'll piggyback subsequent drones to the first, ranging father out with each one. The farthest drone will make a long sweep, so it may take a while to pick up any signal."

Will nodded. "Do the best you can."

He watched the drones soar away one at a time and felt a moment of hope. If not a ship of the fleet, they might pick up a signal from a commercial fishing boat or aircraft, anyone with a radio. The megalodon had returned to its home, and he felt helpless sitting around doing nothing. If the creature decided to leave, they would lose it, perhaps for good.

He glanced at Asa watching the drones wing away. In spite of Asa's hard feelings toward him, the mechanic had performed well. If swallowing his pride would heal the rift between them, he would try. He didn't have the time or energy for a war on two fronts.

"Thanks for helping," he said.

Asa shrugged. "It's my ass in the sling, too."

"Look, I regret hijacking you and Simon. I condoned my actions at the time based on expediency. I should have waited and allowed you both, as well as Haig and Johnson, to leave. In my haste to do my duty, I placed your lives in danger. I was wrong."

Asa shuffled his feet. "It's a little late for apologies. I'm stuck out here." He waved his hand out toward the emptiness around them. A grimace rode the lines of his face, as he said, "This where my world fell apart, you know." He stared down into the depths as if trying to see the bones of the *Global Kulik* lying on the bottom.

Asa's obvious distress moved Will. He tried to understand how the mechanic felt. There had never been a time in his life that he had not wanted to be or had worked to become a sailor. That other people lived their lives with a sense of honor or duty different from his was a difficult concept to absorb. "I know. I'm sorry. It may be too late, but I offer my apology nevertheless." He offered his hand to Asa.

Asa hesitated. Will wasn't sure if he would accept the peace gesture.

"Oh, for God's sake, Asa, shake his hand," Simon barked out. "It's too late to hold a grudge." He had watched the entire conversation from the cabin door. He smiled at Asa and hugged his chest. "It's too damn cold to fight."

Asa shook Will's hand. "Truce."

"That's better," Simon said. He walked over and slapped both men on the back. "I have a few sips of Scotch left, it you care for some?"

Will shook his head. "Too much to do." He looked at Asa. "We're sinking, you know."

Asa smiled. "I'll take a drop to fight the cold."

"Don't overdo it. This is still a Navy vessel."

"Aye, aye, Captain," both Asa and Simon said in unison.

This time, Will smiled.

* * * *

Asa's dread settled over him like a dark storm cloud. The nearer they had gotten to their destination, the more difficult it had become to breathe. The foul air brought back bitter memories but did not shorten his breath. That came from the weight of his guilt sitting heavy on his chest. His logical mind fought to remind him that he had not caused Ilsa's death or anyone else's death, but the vision of the megalodon circling his makeshift raft swept aside such thoughts. The intense fear he experienced extended as far back in his memory as his mind could reach, as if it had always been a part of him. Did his fear prevent him from saving her, or did the fear come later, after the event? He no longer knew. Which begat the other, the fear or her death?

He had no target upon which to vent his fear and his frustrations with the *Sunfish's* engine except her captain. He knew it was a useless gesture aimed at the wrong target, but it didn't matter. He had to strike out at something or explode. First, he had let Simon enlist him in his hopeless one-man crusade; then, the captain of the *Sunfish* had recruited him in his. He had no say so in the matter; therefore, he felt like flotsam swept inland before a tidal surge, or an engine running wide open with no shutoff switch. Neither event could end other than badly.

He had accepted Will's apology begrudgingly to placate Simon. He was sure the captain meant it, but an apology solved nothing as far as Asa was concerned. He was still in the middle of the Chukchi Sea on a sinking boat.

He threw back the shot of Scotch offered by Simon, letting the burn race down his throat. Months earlier, he could not have stopped with only one shot. Now, he must.

"Good stuff," he said.

Simon downed his shot, looked at the bottle with its single shot left inside, and frowned.

"Don't look at me, Simon. It's your Scotch."

"Yeah, you're right." He poured the dregs into his glass and downed it in one gulp. "I'm going to miss that," he said of the empty bottle of *Bunnahabhain*.

"Save the bottle," Asa told him. "We might need to put a note with an S.O.S. inside and send it riding the waves."

Simon cocked his head slightly to one side and stared at Asa. "You're getting cynical."

Asa chuckled. "Getting? Man, my cynicism is world renown."

"Help will come," Simon pronounced, slapping the tabletop, and then glanced around to see if he had woken Haig and Levitt, who were trying to catch some shuteye. Neither man stirred.

"Yeah?" Asa asked, speaking more softly. "Which will come first, the Navy or that big bruiser of a megalodon?"

"Get a grip," Simon growled. "You sound like an old man waiting for the Grim Reaper."

Asa shook his head. "I would like to become an old man, but the future looks damn bleak right now."

"When I'm baking a cake, I always look at the batter and think, 'This isn't going to come out right. It's too thin or too thick.' It's always something, but the cake comes out perfect—light and moist."

Asa cocked his head to one side and stared at Simon. "Are you trying to teach me how to bake, or is there a point to your anecdote?"

"I'm trying to say you can't let first appearances fool you. Don't let the ghosts of the past drag you down with them."

"You're one to talk."

Simon nodded. "You're right. I let my vendetta rule my life for a long time. I still want to kill the megalodon, but it's not so burning anymore." He looked at Asa. "Maybe you put Ilsa's ghost to rest for me."

"It's …" Asa hesitated, unsure how to explain. "I've come full circle. I'm in the very spot I almost died, where everyone but me died. I didn't choose to come back here; yet, here I am. That … this can't be a coincidence."

"You think fate brought you back here?"

Asa shrugged. He wasn't sure what forces were in play. "I can't discount it."

Simon shook his head. "No, that's too philosophical for me. We're here because that great beast of a megalodon is here. Our lives and it entwine somehow. I don't believe in fate, but I think we're being offered a chance at redemption."

"Redemption? Now who's waxing philosophical? We're here, all right, but we may just be here to drown. It may be as simple as that."

Simon sat back, rolling the empty Scotch bottle in his hands. "Maybe so."

Asa rose from his seat. "It's all moot if we sink. I'm going to see if I can do something about the worst leaks."

Simon shot Asa a quizzical look. "How can you use the welder with no power?"

"There's a small handheld torch." He shrugged. "It's better than nothing."

Simon set the empty bottle on the table. "No Scotch left. I guess I'll come with you. I can't fit through the bilge hatch, but I can lend moral support."

Asa smiled. Simon had changed. He liked this Simon better. He seemed more the man he probably had been before the death of his sister. *Now, if only I can become more of the man I was.*

18

December 28, 2018, 6:00 p.m.   Russian Icebreaker *Prilagat' Usiliya*, Chukchi Sea–

The Russian nuclear icebreaker *Prilagat' Usiliya* was far from her normal waters. The maritime ministry had ordered the ship deep into the Chukchi Sea, ostensibly to observe changes in the sea due to the algae incursion and expansion of primeval sea life. Anastasiy Berezhnoy suspected his mission had more to do with the American Fleet than megalodon sharks. His ship was a target, sent to test the Americans' will. He did not like his ship or his crew used in such a manner.

Her captain stood at the helm of his ship, wheel gripped firmly in his rough, weathered hands. He and the well-worn mahogany wheel, polished smooth by so many hands at the helm over the decades of her life, felt as one, as if the wood and his flesh were part of the same entity, the *Usiliya*. He felt the vibrations of the grinding ice crushed by the ship's prow through the wooden wheel, using it to judge his path through the white expanse. It was possible he was wrong about the ministry. The warmer water flowing from the undersea cavern had reduced the winter sea ice. From the Kara Sea, the Laptev, to the East Siberian Sea, the waterways were free of ice. His icebreaker had no function in an iceless sea. Perhaps his mission was simply good Russian pragmatism at work—utilizing scarce resources. The region north of the Chukchi Sea remained ice covered, pushed southward from the colder north. His vessel was the ideal choice for the task.

He had much rather be at home with his wife for the holidays, the last before his retirement, but here he was a thousand miles from home in unknown waters searching for giant sharks.

Something had occurred in the Beaufort Sea, something the Americans did not wish known. Their U.S. Arctic Fleet was now steaming in his direction. He did not want to be here when they arrived.

"Evgeni, check with the lookouts. See if they have sighted anything?"

Evgeni Aleyev, his first officer, scratched his head. "What, Anastasiy?"

"I don't know," Anastasiy snapped. "Anything."

Aleyev recoiled from Anastasiy's harsh tone, and he immediately regretted showing his frustration. More gently, he added, "Ask them if they see any of the gray algae. I wish to avoid it if possible."

Aleyev nodded and left the bridge. Anastasiy loosened his grip for a moment and worked his hands to reduce the ache in his muscles. He had been at the helm for twelve hours, taking young Dimi's watch; else, he would be pacing in his cabin worrying about the future. They had seen no megalodon since his encounter months earlier. So far, the coastal waters of Russia had remained free of the creatures. Not so for the Americans. The megalodon seemed to congregate in American waters. Many in the Kremlin saw a sort of justice in that. The recent storm had driven the sharks eastward. Perhaps that was the reason for the presence of the American Fleet, to intercept the creatures' migration.

He did not understand the Americans' need for secrecy, but then his own countrymen were very sparse with news of the creatures as well. Very few Russians knew about the strange occurrences in the Arctic Ocean. *What's good for the goose is good for the gander.*

"Captain," Leonid Antonov called out through the open door between the radio room and the bridge. "I'm picking up a weak radio signal."

Were they straying too close to the American Fleet? If so, should he continue on course or defy his orders and return to Russian waters? "What language?"

"English."

Anastasiy sighed. So near retirement, he did not wish his last voyage to end in disgrace. He had no choice but continue. "Is it a military frequency?"

"Yes, but it is odd. It is a Mayday call. They report they are damaged and are sinking."

Anastasiy perked up. "A distress call from an American Naval vessel. That is indeed news. Are they being answered?"

"No. Their signal is very weak. I do not think anyone can hear it but us."

Anastasiy rubbed his chin as he thought. "Hmm. What vessel is it?"

"The USS Sunfish."

"Sunfish? I am not familiar with that vessel."

"I can Google it?"

Anastasiy shook his head. It amazed him that one could learn both the number and classification of military ships from the internet. The old KGB would be rolling over in its grave. He wondered if anyone was looking up the Usiliya on their computer at that very moment.

A few minutes later, Antonov replied, "It is a Mark VI fast attack patrol boat with a crew of eight."

A patrol boat in the Arctic Ocean? That seemed ludicrous. "Very well. Whoever it is, we cannot allow them to drown. How far away are they?"

Antonov frowned. "That is odd as well. The coordinates they give are just over a hundred miles away, but the signal seems to be coming from a source much closer."

"Is it a trick?" Why the Americans would attempt to lure an icebreaker into a trap defied logic, but he must err on the side of caution.

"Perhaps they are using a buoy or radio beacon on the ice floe as a relay. That might explain the low signal strength."

"Very well. Give Dimi the coordinates. We will investigate." He turned to Dimi. "The helm is yours. I must consider our options."

Aleyev entered the bridge. "Lookouts report nothing but ice."

Anastasiy nodded. "Very good. Mr. Aleyev, please accompany me to my quarters."

"Captain, should I respond to their distress call?"

Normally, he would have said yes. Men on a sinking ship needed hope, but these were trying times. "No, it is best if we slip in unannounced, just in case."

"What distress call?" Aleyev asked, his gaze moving between the two men.

"I will explain in my cabin."

* * * *

"I do not like it," Aleyev complained as he sipped his glass of vodka. He leaned on the tabletop across from Anastasiy, staring intently in his captain's eyes.

A slight sneer played on Anastasiy's lips, as he replied, "Nor do I, but what choices have I. I will not ignore a distress call, even from an American Naval vessel."

"Of course not," Aleyev snapped, slamming his glass on the table. "That would be …" he searched for the proper word, "barbaric. But we must be cautious."

"We will not go in blindly. Have Guryev arm the crew with the SKS 7.62mm carbines and the Bizon 9mm machineguns. They will be no match for an armed military vessel, but we will go in as tigers, not as sheep." He downed his glass of vodka in one gulp. "I do not think the Americans would send a distress call if they were not in trouble. They are very near the location of the undersea cavern. Perhaps they have encountered the giant sharks."

Aleyev shuddered. "I do not wish to meet them again." He rose from his seat. "I will inform Kalek Guryev to arm everyone. I will also uncrate more of the RAMs just in case."

Anastasiy nodded. The one-kilo C4 packages for ice floe demolition had worked once before on a megalodon. It increased their odds of survival. "Do so."

As Anastasiy sat in his chair, the full weight of his responsibility seemed to press him down into the fabric of the cushion. He was no military captain. He did not wish to lead men into battle. He wanted no one to die, especially his crew. Fate, however, had placed him in the middle of a crisis, and he could not shirk his duty, both to his crew and to Mother Russia.

He glanced at the bottle of vodka longingly, but replaced the cap. He must keep a clear head. Sleep deprivation was taking its toll on him. Adding alcohol to the mix would be dangerous.

He sighed heavily. *I am too old for such intrigues.*

19

December 28, 2018, 9:00 p.m.   *USS Sunfish*, Chukchi Sea–

At night on the ocean on a moonless night, the darkness becomes an ebony shroud enveloping you, muffling sounds, and tricking the ear. The ocean is a fuliginous, undulating carpet. You feel the effects of the waves, as the boat rides them up and down, but you cannot see it. From horizon to horizon, darkness prevails.

Will sat on the bow of the *Sunfish*, letting the night enfold him in its cool embrace. A breeze carried off the worst of the sulfur stench rising from the dark water. With just a little imagination, he could imagine he was anywhere in the world instead of in the Arctic on a sinking ship. So far, they had heard no reply to their Mayday. The drones, powered by solar cells, would soon lose power and drop into the ocean, ending their last chance at rescue. The *Utah* had not made an appearance, nor had the Arctic Fleet. They were alone.

He saw a flicker of light as a cigarette butt arced from amidships and disappeared into the water. He glanced back and saw Asa standing by the open door. His face, bathed by the dim emergency light inside the cabin, bore a dour expression.

"It's been six hours and nothing," he said. "I don't think anyone heard us."

Will sighed. His moment of solitude was gone, and the immediate problems of the real world were reasserting themselves. "It was worth a shot."

"Maybe, but without the pumps, we're doomed." He glanced back at the cabin as the emergency light flickered. "We're almost out of battery power. When it's gone ..."

He did not need to complete his thought. Will knew they would sink. The *Sunfish* already rode eight inches lower in the water than when they had arrived at the subsea cavern. The Zodiac was gone, destroyed in the shark attack. When the boat sank, they would be adrift in small rubber rafts. He did not want to consider that possibility.

"Don't give up hope," he advised, though hope was running thin for him as well.

"Oh, I still have hope," Asa said. "I hope I freeze to death in the water rather than end up in the belly of that megalodon."

He had not forgotten the giant shark, but Asa's remark brought it back clearly. They had seen no sign of it since the battle at the *Vanguard*. Had the *Utah* caught up with it and killed it? Where was the sub? He rose from his seat. Before they lost power entirely, he would make one last broadcast, a dying effort.

"Grayson, crank up the radio. See what's out there."

Grayson roused himself from his seat and yawned. "Juice is almost gone," he warned.

"Just do it."

The crackle of the radio sounded weak to him. He hoped the drones were still up there. After positioning them, Grayson had set them on autopilot and switched off the remote controls to conserve battery. A faint hiss, and then a series of taps erupted from the speaker. Grayson almost slid from his seat in his excitement.

"I've got something! I've got something!"

Will's heart pounded. He hoped Grayson had managed to contact someone with clear orders, relieve him of his responsibility. "Who is it?"

A wide grin creased Grayson's tired face. "It's the *Utah*. No voice, just Morse. The signal is very weak." He glanced down. "They must be directly below us."

Will grabbed the mic from Grayson's hand and in Morse, code typed out, "*Utah*. This is the *USS Sunfish*. What is your situation?" using the mic's talk button.

He listened to the faint reply, also in Morse using short sentences for clarity in case of signal loss. "*Sunfish*, this is Commander Prescott. Boat crippled after encountering giant megalodon. Seven-hundred-fifty feet down inside the cavern resting on a ledge. Engine room flooded. Reactor losing coolant. Sixty-six dead, twenty injured. Sixty-nine survivors. Can you relay a message to Fleet for a DSRV?"

Will swore off-mic, and then tapped, "Negative, Commander. We have no long-distance communication capability and zero contact with the fleet."

After a pause, Prescott replied, "Copy, *Sunfish*."

"Roger, *Utah*. Did you contact the fleet before following the megalodon?"

The reply faded in and out. Will had to strain to separate the dits and dashes from the static. "Negative. No communication with fleet. Repeat, negative on communication with fleet."

The cabin spun around Will. He gripped the console to stay on his feet, as he fought back the dark, dizzying fog threatening to consume him. He needed sleep, and the news from the *Utah* was the last thing he expected, the last thing his crew needed to hear. The fleet was not coming. They had no idea where the *Sunfish*, the *Utah*, or the last remaining megalodon were. A sunken sub and a crippled and sinking fast attack boat: hardly the armada he had hoped for to engage the megalodon.

"We'll be standing by, *Utah*. If we receive any word, I'll relay. *Sunfish* out."

He gripped the silent mic hard enough to imprint the grooves of the microphone body into his flesh. Both he and the sub's captain knew that was all he could do, stand by over the dying sub to shoo the flies away. He felt it served no purpose to inform the sub's commander that the *Sunfish* might soon join them in the briny deep.

"I don't know if they received that last, Skipper. The thermals are wreaking havoc with the signal."

"That tears it," Asa growled. "We're royally screwed now."

Simon had been listening from the galley table. "Those poor men," he said.

"Poor us," Asa replied.

Will needed to maintain contact with the *Utah*, if for no other reason than to keep them company. "Grayson, break out the SeaFox."

The SeaFox Mk-II was an unmanned underwater mine detection and disposal tool, a mini-ROV controlled by a fiber optic cable from a mobile modular console. After locating the sunken sub and positioning it near the sub's photonic mast, he could use the lights on the ROV as a signal lamp.

"Aye, sir," Grayson replied. "Haig, can you lend a hand?"

The DSV pilot nodded and joined Grayson. Fifteen minutes later, they came on deck bearing a four-foot-long cylinder with four smaller tubes attached. Each tube bore a thruster on the rear for propulsion. A fifth thruster at the nose controlled vertical movement. The entire device weighed less than ninety pounds. They also carried a reel containing three-thousand feet of fiber optic cable and a small laptop control unit. Haig set up the control panel, while Grayson attached one end of the thin fiber-optic the cable to the rear of the laptop and the other end into an input at the rear of the SeaFox. While they did this, Will removed the small explosive device used to detonate mines and replaced it with underwater lights and a High-Definition CCTV camera.

"Won't the sonar attract the megalodon?" Simon asked.

"We'll use it sparingly. Once we locate the sub, we'll fly by wire. If all the creatures down there are blind, the lights shouldn't attract them."

"Can we do anything for them?"

Will swallowed the lump in his throat to keep his emotions from his voice. "No. We're just keeping them company. If anyone arrives in time, we'll know where they are; however," he paused, "it's unlikely any ships that arrive will carry a DSRV. There's very little hope of saving them."

"That sucks," Simon said.

"Yes, it does," Will agreed. "Big time."

Will, Asa, Levitt, and Grayson lowered the ROV over the side, while Haig controlled it from the mobile unit sitting cross-legged on the rear deck. They all crowded around to watch the small screen on the laptop. At first, they saw nothing in the murky water; then, at the edge of the light field, they saw clouds of pastel gray plankton and small ribbon snails undulating like rippling leaves. Fish with bony plates on their heads darted in and out of the plankton cloud with open mouths.

Asa jerked back when a large gray shape passed by the ROV only a dozen yards away.

"It's okay," Simon told him. "It's not a megalodon. It's a *cetotheium*, an early whale. Watch." The twenty-foot long cetacean opened its mouth and glide along the edge of the plankton. "It's a plankton eater. It has baleen instead of teeth."

"How do you know so much about whales?" Asa asked.

"When I learned about the megalodon, I studied the Miocene Epoch."

Asa shook his head. "Wait. Aren't whales air breathers? Why haven't we seen any on the surface?"

"There must be air pockets down there produced by the kelp. Maybe the air on the surface tastes different to them. Or maybe they're afraid of the megalodon."

The ROV entered an area of empty darkness. Haig watched a small screen in the lower right corner of the main screen, the sonar screen. He pinged the sonar every so often. Finally, he located the sunken sub. He entered the coordinates into the computers and let the ROV follow the course. Fifteen minutes later, the dark hulk of the *Utah* appeared from the surrounding darkness, resting on a ledge just barely large enough to hold it.

Haig whistled. "If it hadn't found that ledge, the bottom is below the sub's crush depth. They got lucky."

"In a relative manner of speaking," Asa said. Haig shot him a dirty look.

Haig took the ROV on a tour of the submarine's exterior, at least the accessible port side. The sub had been through a battle. Streams of bubbles leaked from several ruptured seams just forward of the engine room. The crushed bow protruded at an odd angle. Several of the masts on the sail had sheared away.

"She's going nowhere," he whispered. He moved the ROV to the two photonic masts. One was a broken stub. He nudged the intact one several times with the ROV, producing a loud metallic clang. A few moments later, an exterior light flashed on, indicating the camera was operational. "They know we're here." He turned to Will. "Okay. What do you want me to tell them?"

Will took a deep breath. The captain of the *Utah* would know he was lying if he said help was on the way. He would not build their hopes that way. "Ask him his condition."

Haig toggled the control for the ROV lights and waited for an answer. "Stern section abandoned. C-and-C and crews quarters sealed off. Scrubbers nearing maximum. Batteries low."

Will shook his head. Once the carbon dioxide scrubbers went, the gas would build up to a lethal level. The future looked dark for the trapped crew. "Ask them if they know where the megalodon is."

"It disappeared after damaging them, but the captain thinks it went back into the next chamber."

"Can they use their rescue suits to buy some time?" he asked Haig. The Navy diver was more familiar with submarine rescue than he was.

Each submarine carried Mk11 Submarine Escape Immersion Ensemble suits, a full body garment designed to inflate and allow the wearer to reach the surface from a depth of six hundred feet, well above the Utah's current depth, but they had been tested, unmanned, to eight-hundred feet. Once on the surface, the thermal suit inflated into a small raft. Theoretically, they could reach the surface, but he had no room on the *Sunfish* for more than a dozen. In the frigid water, they would not survive long.

Haig shook his head. "Each SEIE suit only supplies a few minutes of air, enough to reach the surface. They could replenish them with air from divers' tanks, but I doubt he has enough suits."

"Ask anyway. Maybe the captain can come up with a solution."

The reply came, "Saving SEIEs for emergency. Divers' compartment flooded. Cannot reach rubber rafts."

"See if ... see if any of his crew would like to relay any messages to family."

Given their own situation, he couldn't guarantee they would ever reach their destinations, but it might offer the doomed crew some solace.

Haig looked up with a tear in his eye. He brushed it away. "He says thanks. He will relay to crew."

Will slammed his fist into the cabin bulkhead; then, rubbed his bloody knuckles. The pain helped him focus his thoughts on solutions rather than succumb to despair. "Damn it to hell! There has to be something we can do."

"Easy, Captain," Haig said. "He's trained for this situation. You're not. I'm sure he's aware of the odds. It's part of the job. He knows that if you could help, you would. All we can do is wait."

Will nodded. "If someone heard our distress call, they might stand a chance."

"If they arrive soon enough," Haig reminded him. "We don't know how badly damaged the *Utah* is. It sounds as if the damage is extensive. The pressure at that depth is over 325 PSI. Any weak seams will expand. If the reactor is leaking …" He shrugged. "Any help will have to show up soon."

Haig closed the lid on the laptop to conserve power. They all sat on the rear deck. The yellowish glow of the emergency lights in the cabin enhanced the looks of gloom and concern marking their faces. Each one knew their fate might soon be the same as that of the men trapped below them. Will knew it was his job to keep up their morale, convince them things weren't as dark as they seemed, but try as he might, sitting in the dark, he could not find the kind of courage it took in his despondent heart.

Slowly, one by one, they rose and drifted off, leaving him alone on the deck to contemplate his future.

* * * *

December 29, 2018, 1:45 a.m.   *USS Utah*, Chukchi Sea–

Captain Prescott appreciated the contact with the *Sunfish*. Trapped beneath the ocean, the presence of another human being, even one a tantalizing seven-hundred-fifty feet away made the waiting less daunting. He had come to terms with his mortality, but he regretted his actions had endangered his crew. Many were dead. All faced death.

He could save a few. The crew knew that, although no one had yet mentioned it. The SEIE suits would allow them to reach the surface, but only fifteen suits were accessible. The rest were stored in the aft cargo escape trunk, an impossible one-hundred-ten feet away through a flooded boat. Who could he choose to save—the officers, the injured, hold a lottery for the lucky few, charge for them, and die a rich man? That time had not yet arrived. He would not give up hope until he was gasping on his last breath of stale air.

Around him, the expressions on the crews' young faces ranged from pallid with fear to stoic acceptance. They were submariners. They knew the risks every time they left port. Odds were that one time they would not return. This was that time.

He chuckled, startling a few of them. "You know, back in Philly, I had a job for a while at a hotel as a valet. Some folks didn't like a young black boy with tattoos parking their shiny new automobiles. Now, I drive around in a 2.5 billion dollar submarine." He shook his head. "If they could only see me now. Of course, I did manage to ding it up a bit," he added.

He kept a close eye on the radiation level. So far, it remained below 100 Roentgen Equivalent Man units. Prolonged exposure of a dosage over 100 rems would cause vomiting, diarrhea, and lethargy. They would run out of oxygen or succumb to carbon dioxide poisoning before then, as soon as the lithium hydroxide scrubbers failed. If the levels rose any higher, he would move the men from the crews' quarters to the control room and seal the hatch. He did not want to do that. It would mean cutting off passage to food and water and reducing the amount of remaining air.

The injuries ranged from severe steam burns, broken bones, and concussions, to cuts and bruises. The overworked pharmacist's mate and a few of the crew who had first-aid training attended to the injured in their berths. He had cautioned the rest of the crew to limit their activity to conserve oxygen. Most lay in their berths in the habitat module aft of C-and-C or in the AMR module a deck below it or playing cards in the galley. Only the watch crew remained on duty.

When the sub suddenly lurched to starboard, Prescott grabbed a console and held on. The hull slid forward and ground against the rocks. He checked the camera monitor and saw the tail of the behemoth megalodon swim by. The shark was checking them out. The SeaFox ROV was still there. He flashed a message to the *Sunfish* telling them the megalodon had returned. Moments later, the shark rammed the sail. Metal groaned under the strain as the boat canted five more degrees to starboard. A broken high-pressure water pipe began spraying water across the control center. Two men rushed to shut off the closest valve feeding it.

The attack reinforced the danger they faced. Several of the crew began praying aloud. "Pray quietly," he said. "I need to think."

If the shark nudged them off the ledge, they would sink below crush depth and implode. If it opened up another seam, they would lose precious air. With the torpedo room flooded, they could not fire their last torpedoes at it. All they could do was sit and take it.

"Signal the *Sunfish* to hold off on communications. The clicking of the ROV's lights might attract the creature. They need not acknowledge."

The megalodon made another pass by the sub. Prescott marveled at its size. He had seen blue whales just shy of ninety-feet long, but the giant megalodon had it almost doubled. He estimated it weighed over two-hundred-fifty tons. That was a significant amount of mass when directed at his boat. He caught a flash of the upper lobe of the tail flash through the darkness.

"Brace yourselves!" he yelled.

The shark struck the top of the submarine just aft of the sail. Prescott heard metal shearing and men screaming and knew the damage was severe. The boat wobbled for a long moment before heaving over onto her port side. As she slid forward, Prescott held his breath for fear she was going over the lip of the ledge for her final death plunge. Water began pouring through the open hatch and flooding the control center. Only a handful of crewmen made it into the C-and-C module from the flooding habitat module. The water rose at an alarming rate. Soon, they would be unable to close the door. He made a hard decision.

"Seal the hatch," he ordered.

Men complied without question. His order had trapped men inside the crews' quarters, killing them, but he had saved the control center, the heart of the boat. He prayed that some of the trapped men made it down into the AMR module to Chief Petty Officer territory, but knew the most severely wounded would not have had time.

"Bring everyone up to C-and-C."

He waited as soaked seamen, trembling from the cold and from fear, straggled into the control center.

"Make a head count," he told the bosun's mate.

A few seconds later, he answered, "Nineteen, sir, including you."

Nineteen out of one-thirty-two. He had lost 6/7ths of his crew. The men stared at him with a sickening mixture of guilt at their joy in surviving and distress at the loss of their crewmates. As captain, they looked to him for a statement, words that might mitigate their misery. He had none. If he had, his words would mean very little if the shark attacked again.

"Keep an eye on that monster."

He helped pass out hot coffee and dry blankets to the shivering men. His own discomfort paled in comparison. In spite of everything that had happened over the past twenty-four hours, none of his crew complained. He felt honored to serve with such men, some barely more than boys. He spotted another black face, Electrical Technician Bobby Sewell from Mobile, Alabama. The two, a farmer's son from the Deep South and the son of a single mother who worked at a diner, had little in common except the color of their skin and their shared drive to better themselves in spite of some who objected. Sewell stared at him with pride that a fellow black man had risen through the ranks to become captain of a *Virginia*-class nuclear submarine. If his young life wasn't cut short, it offered him hope for his own future.

"It's coming back, sir."

Prescott tore his gaze from Sewell and the others and watched the monitor. The megalodon returned, but did not attack. It made several more passes along the length of the sub, but only scraped it with its fins, as if sensing it was no longer a threat. As he watched, the megalodon began acting strangely, darting in and out of the kelp forest. At first, Prescott thought it was hunting the giant crustaceans, but then it began contorting its body.

I hope the bastard's dying.

Curious about the creature's strange behavior, he risked attracting the shark by increasing the luminosity of the exterior floodlights. It paid no attention. A few minutes later, it floated in the water and began giving birth to the first baby megalodon. The newborn shark measured three feet in length and immediately dove for the safety of the kelp forest. More followed over the next half hour, hundreds more. Many instantly became prey to the giant crustaceans lurking in the kelp, but the smaller crabs and fish in turn became food for the babies.

Prescott knew Great Whites were ovoviviparous, giving birth to live babies, but he had never seen it happen, not even in nature films. The megalodon were ovoviviparous as well. That explained the gigantic shark's behavior. Pregnant, she had eaten everything she could, even members of her own species, returned to familiar waters to give birth, and defended her territory. It all made sense that, like Great Whites, female megalodon sharks were larger than the males and were more dominant than the opposite sex. He eyed the hundreds of three-foot megalodons and a hard lump formed in his gut. A sense of impending apocalypse swept over him. Many of the young would fall prey to other denizens of the deep, but most would survive, maturing quickly into giant monsters.

He had to stop them and he had very little time. He hoped the crew of the *Sunfish* was watching through the ROV camera. He would risk one last message to them. Then, he would take action.

"Send this message. Hundreds of baby sharks from the giant. They seem content to remain here for now. Nineteen survivors in crew. Air gone. I will take steps to end the megalodon threat. Standby to recover crew in SEIE suits. I will detonate a nuke," He checked his watch and estimated the time required to prepare everything, "in thirty minutes. Recover my crew and get the hell out of the area. Commander Charles Raeburn Prescott, Captain of the *USS Utah,* out."

His crew looked at him, some aghast, some shaking their heads in acceptance.

He addressed them. "You know what it means if those sharks make it out into the open ocean. Stopping them is the job we came to do. We still have a chance. We have fifteen SEIE suits. There are eighteen of you. I won't order anyone to go or to stay. It's over seven-hundred feet to the surface. You might not make it. It's a decision you alone can make. It will be a tight squeeze, but I think all of you will fit into the forward lockout trunk." He moved his gaze among them. "Some of you are pretty skinny. The trunk was designed for well-fed Navy SEALs." This elicited a few laughs. "I will use a breather, flood the sub, and make my way to the weapons module. Once inside, I will prep a *Tomahawk* with a nuclear payload and fire the missile with the tube sealed. Thirty seconds later, it will explode, and I will blow a 2.6 billion dollar submarine to hell. Talk about Black Power."

"You'll need help, sir," weapons officer Tim Caruthers said. "I'm staying."

He nodded. "Three of you will have to remain here in any case. I can use some help. The rest of you, get into the SEIE suits just as in training and abandon ship."

The words almost stuck in his throat. He was abandoning his ship and firing a nuclear weapon without specific orders. His name might go down in history alongside Benedict Arnold's. *I guess I won't be spoken of during Black History Month.*

"Good luck to all of you. It's been a pleasure serving with you." He threw them a crisp salute. They responded, some with tears in their eyes. He was glad his wet face disguised the tears streaming down his face. They were not tears of fear or sadness. They came from a deep respect for his crew and from his duty as a submarine commander.

He left the compartment as CPO McNair and Bosun Chambers urged the crew to make ready to depart. He had a job to do.

20

December 29, 2018, 3:10 a.m.   *USS Sunfish*, Chukchi Sea–

"He's doing what?" Asa yelled. He stood up and walked around the table to confront Will, leaning into the table to stare into Will's eyes.

Although Asa seemed on the verge of panic, Will didn't back down. He met Asa's aggressive stance with a solid posture and an unflinching gaze. "You saw the vid. That damned mama shark just had babies, hundreds of fucking little megalodon monsters. If they get out of the cavern, everything we've done is for nothing. We lose. Period. Commander Prescott knows his ship is doomed. Most of his crew is already dead. He assessed the situation and is doing what he has to do to get the job done."

"Situation! It's madness! Things had gone from unreal to stark raving, dipshit insane. "

Will lowered the tone of his voice. He didn't need a confrontation, not now. He didn't have time. "He gave us thirty minutes. It will take the crew at least five minutes to evacuate the lockout hatch and reach the surface. Add another ten to get them aboard. That leaves us fifteen minutes to place as much distance as we can between that nuke and us. I suggest you get on the engines and make sure they're ready to go."

Asa wasn't through. His jaw clenched and unclenched from anger. "This boat is sinking. Loaded down, she won't make twenty knots, twenty-two if I burn out the engines."

"Burn them out. Let's concentrate on getting the hell away from here. Then we worry about sinking."

"Christ! Can it get much worse?"

"Don't even think that," Will warned. "Don't jinx us."

Asa shook his head in disgust and backed away from the table.

"I'll help," Grayson offered.

"No," Will replied before Asa could say anything. "I need all hands pulling survivors aboard. Levitt, you drive. I need not remind you what a ten or twenty-kilo nuke can do. It's going to get very unpleasant around here very soon. Gentlemen, let's get moving."

"I'll make coffee," Simon chimed in.

At first, Will couldn't follow the incongruity of the suggestion, but then decided the chef was trying to insert a bit of normalcy into the situation. "Good idea. Then, find blankets, sheets, towels, extra clothing—anything to dry them off and keep them warm. They're going to be cold and wet, and we have no heat. I have extra uniforms in my locker, use them."

Will noticed the look of concern in the chef's face, as he said, "Seven-hundred-fifty feet is a long ascent without rest stops to equalize the pressure. What if some of them get the bends?"

That thought had crossed his mind, along with a dozen others just as dark. "We have no decompression chamber. They'll die in agony. It's that simple. Some might not make it anyway. As you said, seven-hundred-fifty feet is a long way for free ascent. They might drift beneath the cavern roof in the dark and lose their way. There are creatures down there that might eat them. They're pushing their luck to the max, and they've already used up more luck than most people are dealt. If some of them pop up too far away to reach in time, we may have to leave them. There's nothing in the manual about this situation. I'm winging it."

His admission to Simon of his lack of viable options drove home to him how dire the situation had become. They could all die in the next half hour. *Now I know how Asa feels.* He left Simon in the galley and went outside to Haig sitting on the deck with the controls for the SeaFox on his lap.

"Anything?" he asked.

"They popped the hatch a minute or two ago. I counted twelve suits rising."

"Only twelve?"

He glanced up with a hint of sadness in his eyes. "Some of them must have stayed behind to help Prescott. Good men. Maybe others figured a quick death was better than freezing. I panned the camera on the ROV. I can't find big mama megalodon. She left her brood."

"Bring up the ROV. Follow the crew if you can. They can follow the light, and it may help us locate them more quickly."

Finding a dozen red SEIE suits in the dark would not be easy, especially scattered over a wide area. Each suit had a flashing beacon attached, but the chop of the waves could hide them from view unless they were right on top of them. He helped Grayson drape a cargo net over the side and mount battery lanterns on the stern, bow, and both sides of the *Sunfish* to light up the boat. The suits were too bulky for swimming or pulling them aboard. He hoped Prescott had suggested ditching them when they surfaced.

Three minutes later, Haig announced, "They're a hundred feet from the surface about eighty yards to starboard, about four o'clock. I'm following three suits. I lost the rest when they spread out."

"Levitt, take us 120-degrees to starboard, five knots."

The boat began moving toward the rising survivors. Will spotted the lights of the ROV before he saw the first blinking emergency lights of the suits. He quickly counted six in a group and directed Levitt to position the boat among them. Four unzipped their suits when they saw the *Sunfish* and swam to meet them, clambering aboard on their own power using the nets. Two kept their suits on. He and Grayson snagged them with boat hooks, pulled them within reach, and with Apone's help, dragged them onto the deck like sacks of flour. More men popped up and began calling to them. Simon came out to escort the survivors to the galley.

"Ditch the ROV," he told Haig. "We need your help."

Haig pulled out his knife and sliced the fiber optic cable controlling the SeaFox. The lights dimmed as it began sinking to join the *Utah*. Altogether, they rescued eight men.

"Where are the others?" he asked of one young ensign gasping for breath.

"I saw the shark get one man. I think it was Glisson." He shook his head. "I don't know."

Will patted him on the shoulder. "Get out of those wet clothes, son. Join the others below for some hot coffee. We'll take it from here."

"The captain, he ..."

"I know. He did his duty."

The ensign nodded and went below. Will checked his watch. They were taking too long. He waited three precious extra minutes drifting and looking, but saw no emergency beacons or heard no cries for help. They had all the survivors aboard they were going to find. It had taken sixteen minutes. They had nine minutes until all hell broke loose. "Levitt, tell Asa to give us all she's got. We're cutting it close." They would still be less than four miles from ground zero when the nuke went off. The bottom was less than two-hundred feet deep outside the cavern, shallow enough to roll up a dangerous tsunami wave that could crush them.

"Wait! Wait!" someone cried from the darkness.

Will scanned the water and saw a flashing light two hundred yards away in the opposite direction. The crewman was frantic, waving his arms as he bobbed on the waves. Apone glanced at him with a question on his face. Will shook his head.

"We'll never reach him and get away in time."

The boat jumped as the engines kicked to full throttle. Will turned away from the man he was abandoning to die alone in the dark.

Asa didn't spare the engines any wear and tear. The boat felt slightly sluggish with the extra weight of the rescued crew and the water in the bilge, but Will was confident twenty-two knots was not demanding too much from her. His chest burned as if he had held his breath the entire nine minutes. *Fifteen seconds to detonation.* It felt as if they were sitting still on the ocean instead of fleeing for their lives.

"Close all watertight hatches. Everyone find a spot on the deck and stay away from the windows. Levitt, strap yourself in tight."

Fifteen seconds later, the sky behind them erupted in a new dawn, as the nuclear sun rose from the bowels of the cavern, illuminating a square mile of ocean from beneath. After the initial flash, he trained his binoculars on the explosion. The spherical cloud of the blast became a columnar chimney of superheated steam that rose half a mile into the air. He followed the leading edge of the shock wave as it raced across the surface toward them, making the surface dance like water in a hot frying pan.

He had tightened his harness as tight as he could get it, but he held onto the console with both hands. "Hold on!" he warned the others.

He felt a deep rumbling in his chest just before the shockwave slammed into the stern, lifting it four feet out of the water. The bow submerged to the forward gun mount, and the engines screamed as they pushed air instead of water. Every unbroken window shattered. Glass sprayed across the cabin. One large shard embedded itself in his headrest. Several smaller ones peppered his arms. He heard a groan and saw Levitt pluck a shard of glass from his right hand. Blood streamed over the controls, but he held on, fighting the boat back onto a straight course.

The thunderous roar reached them moments later, the sound of a thousand artillery pieces firing simultaneously in an underground tunnel. A mile closer and the noise would have struck them deaf. He waited for the wave he knew would follow. Because of the darkness, the tsunami was almost invisible. At first, it appeared as a barely discernible ripple with the lava-lamp glow of the blast behind it. As it rushed at them at nearly two-hundred mph, it climbed slowly from the depths of the ocean until it reached a crest height of thirty feet. The sloping wall of the wave on the open ocean allowed them to ride up its face like a surfer catching a big curl, but as it passed through the lip at the wave's peak, the boat dropped like a rock down its steep backside. They hit the water stern first and went under. Water poured in through the shattered windows. Just when he thought they were going to the bottom, the *Sunfish* popped to the surface.

The engines had died. They were dead in the water, but they were still afloat. *Not for long,* he thought, as water sloshed around his feet. "Everybody grab something and form a bailing line before we sink."

Men fought to throw off their shock and scrambled to keep the *Sunfish* afloat.

That's not something I would want to do every day.

He didn't worry about radiation. Most of the deadly cloud would pass south of them, dropping radioactive dust on Inuit towns, oil fields, caribou herds, and northern Canada. The U.S.'s northern neighbor would not be happy about that. The radioactive water that drenched the *Sunfish* might make them glow at night, but wouldn't kill them, or at least he hoped not. That was one more thing beyond his control. He reached out and patted the console in front of him.

"Good boat," he said and meant it.

* * * *

December 29, 2018, 4:30 a.m.   *USS Sunfish*, Chukchi Sea–

Asa was shaking as he sat in the drenched main cabin of the *Sunfish* with its pitiful crew and the double handful of hapless survivors of the *Utah*, and not all of it was from the wet clothes he wore. A battle with giant megalodon sharks, sinking boats, shanghaiing him and Simon, a battle with giant crabs who wanted them for lunch, sunken submarines, baby megalodon, underwater nuclear explosions, a tsunami——what was Captain Cobb going to offer next on the entertainment menu?

When he had survived the sinking of the *Global Kulik*, the event that had set in motion the slow tidal wave of events (He laughed at his unintentional metaphor), his life had gone into a downward spiral that might have driven others to suicide. Perhaps he was too stupid to take what the uninformed or the heartless call the easy way out. Maybe he was just too stubborn. Events beyond his control had rolled him up and smoked him like a bad doobie. The fine line between reality and fantasy blurred so often, he sometimes wasn't sure what day it was, or even what month.

Lack of sleep and the accumulative effects of life shoving him along like a cop rousting a protestor had made him irritable and short-tempered. Add to the mix that he was now more frightened than he had ever been, up to and including the last half hour. Every muscle ached and he had so many bruises from the tsunami's passing, he couldn't tell where one ended and another began. He was in no mood to listen to another of Will's lectures on duty. He was a civilian, and a pissed off civilian to boot. Nevertheless, he listened as Will's speech as intently as the others. He wanted to know what the captain of the *Sunfish* intended to subject him to next, not that he could do anything about it. He was trapped like the others on a sinking boat in the middle of the Arctic Ocean surrounded by 34-degree water that would kill him in ten minutes. He paused in his mental tirade a moment to take stock of his morbid thoughts. *Yeah, that about sums it up.*

Simon leaned back in his seat with his eyes closed, but Asa knew he was not sleeping. Finally, Simon had realized his main goal—the last of the megalodon were dead. He finally had his revenge. It might not have been as hands on as he wanted, but the deed was done. His sister's shade could now rest in peace.

Asa turned his attention back to Will, who paced the cabin like a brush arbor preacher working up to a hell and damnation sermon. Soaked like everyone else, Will wore a damp blanket thrown around his shoulders. His cap was missing, and light brown fuzz covered his normally shaven scalp. It matched the three-day stubble of beard on his cheeks. His green eyes looked sunken into his pallid face, but they flashed with an animated brightness that spoke of an inner strength Asa wished he could match. Looking at Will's disheveled appearance, Asa wondered if they all looked like scarecrows.

"We're alive," Will said as preface.

Asa bit his tongue to curb the acerbic rejoinder on his lips. *I'll let him have his General George S. Patton moment.*

"To the crew of the *Utah*, I say, 'Welcome aboard, and I offer my condolences for the loss of your captain, your crewmates, and your ship.' Unfortunately, you might have jumped from the fire into the frying pan. The engines are flooded," He nodded to Asa, who glanced away, "and we're sinking. We can't contact anyone, and no one knows where we are. It's been a harrowing two days, but we can't quit. I, for one, am not ready to give up."

Everyone's gaze followed him around the room in his pacing circuit, even Asa's, who had unwittingly let Will's words and sincerity draw him in.

"We will: 1. Get the engines running; 2. Bail by hand if necessary to remain afloat; and 3. Make contact with someone and await rescue. We will not despair. We will not sit on our asses and wait on death. We will get out of this."

Asa was almost ready to believe him, but he could see the water lapping at the edge of the step-down cut out, and the reality of the sea trumped his faith in the captain's bold boasts.

"Ideas, anyone?"

Grayson spoke up. "If you let me use a little juice, I can check if any drones are still flying. It's unlikely, but it's worth a shot."

"Okay, but don't take too long. Send a signal if you can."

"I'll start a conga line," Apone said, meaning a line of men passing water buckets. "We'll bail with the fire buckets and pots and pans."

An idea had been rattling around in Asa's mind about the inoperative bilge pumps. He raised his hand; then, felt foolish for acting like a schoolboy in class.

"Yes, Asa."

"I noticed several compressed air tanks in the hold. If I can find the material, I might be able to build a single-stage pneumatic vacuum pump."

Will nodded. "Will that work?"

Asa shrugged. "If I can make a drop-pressure valve or two, we can use the compressed air in the tanks to create a vacuum and use the Venturi effect to exhaust the bilge water off the boat. Since I'll have to work with small tubing, it won't be fast, but it will be faster than bailing by hand and certainly not as tiring."

"Good. Show Apone what you need. Once the pumps are ready, see what you can do about the engines." He looked at the *Utah* survivors. "Any engineers or mechanics here?"

Two men raised hands. One, a boy who looked barely out of his teens said, "I'm a mechanic. I can help." An older man said, "Yo, I can use tools and a torch."

"Good, you two go with Asa and Mr. Apone. Simon, I know it's asking a lot, but do you think you could whip up something warm to eat and more coffee? We need something to combat the cold."

Simon roused from his stupor. "Can do, coach. How are you fixed for propane?"

Will scratched his head. "We filled them in Barrow, uh, four days ago. We should have plenty. Why?"

"If we cover the windows and doors with tarps, we can use the stove's burners to heat this cabin and dry out our clothes. It will keep us from freezing." His gaze scanned the wet crew of the *Utah*. "These boys need to dry out."

"Good thinking. I should have thought of that." Will tossed his blanket on the table. "Here, start with this one."

Asa glanced at Simon, who grinned at him. For the first time since he had met him, the chef looked at peace with himself. Asa envied him.

Using odds and end from the spare parts bins, Asa cobbled together a pair of crude valves. One of the men from the *Utah*, Chief Petty Officer Pulaski, welded the pieces together, while he showed the young mechanic how to rig the tubing. As Asa watched him work, he wondered how Settlemires, his apprentice, was faring. Was he back on the mainland? Did he know the fate of the *Vanguard*? Did he wonder if Asa was alive or dead? Probably not. Young men quickly moved on with their lives. The past became yesterday's news. Asa wished he could move on. In spite of the end of the megalodon threat, a sense of gloom crowded into his thoughts, a dread beyond the fear of drowning that pushed him to work quickly. Somehow, he knew it wasn't over. Mother Nature still waited around, lurking somewhere in the background with a rod to shove up his ass. The bitch liked that. It kept men standing on their toes, like a worn-out ballet dancer.

21

December 29, 2018, 6:20 a.m.   *USS Sunfish*, Chukchi Sea–

They were still afloat thanks to Asa's ingenuity. Will was not above giving credit where credit was due. However, Asa shrugged off his attempted compliment with a snide remark and went to work on the engines. Maybe it was his heightened sense of self-preservation, but the mechanic had worked miracles twice for the *Sunfish*, if not for her captain, and he owed him a debt of gratitude. More, considering he had conscripted him into service. Asa's jury-rigged vacuum pumps worked. The process was slow, but with six SCUBA air tanks, and the oxygen tank and two acetylene tanks for the gas welder, they could keep the water level manageable.

The luck on the communication front was not as rosy. Grayson had made no contact with anyone and battery power was almost gone. It was unlikely the solar-powered drones had remained aloft throughout the night. They could expect no help from that quarter.

As if they did not face enough problems, packs of sea ice driven south by the wind began to converge on the boat. East of the underwater cavern system with its magma-warmed water, the water temperature dropped drastically, nearer to normal winter temperatures. Once the engines were operational, he would turn the boat southward and hope for the best, although the fleet's last known position was northeast of the cavern. If they encountered no more problems, they could reach Barrow in thirty hours. After that, it didn't matter. He did not think the Navy would wish to continue its professional relationship with a boat captain that lost half his crew and participated in the first non-test nuclear weapon explosion since WWII. He was so exhausted that the threat of court martial did not alarm him. Time in the brig with some peace and quiet might be worth it.

At dawn, they had moored the *Sunfish* to the edge of a small ice floe to keep her from drifting with the current, but he did not like the rapidity with which the ice was building up around the boat. If it accumulated too quickly, they might not break free. He scanned the area with his binoculars, but the glare from the rising sun made seeing the full floe too difficult. He decided to risk what power remained in the batteries to run quick sonar and radar scans to discover the extent of the ice pack.

"Apone, crank up the radar. Levitt, get a depth reading on the ice. We need to find out which way to go."

Both men, eager to do anything to take their minds off their problems, quickly complied. Will felt sorrier for the men of the *Utah*. Except for the mechanic helping Asa, they had nothing to do but sit and dwell on their close escape and on dead friends.

"Ice is building to the north and to the west," Apone reported. "Scattered fields to the east." He sighed. "No ship contact."

Neither was good news. West or southwest would put them beneath the radioactive fallout. No ships meant they were on their own.

"Grayson?"

Grayson yawned, covering his mouth with his bandaged hand. Will had almost forgotten his own cuts and abrasions. They didn't bother him enough to treat them. "The ice within visual range is between eight-inches and sixteen-inches thick. To the west and the north, it builds to eight feet as far as I can range out."

Eight feet could easily crush his boat. They had to get out of the area soon. He heard one engine crank, run for a moment, and then cut out. He swore, but at least Asa was getting close. Removing the plugs and drying them, as well as draining the condensate from the fuel lines and blowing out the lines, took time. Working while lying in a foot of water did not help. He considered going below to check on Asa's progress, but feared antagonizing him further would not be a wise idea. Best to let him have time to vent his frustration on the engines.

"Picking up something on sonar, Skipper," Grayson announced.

"A sub?" he asked. Two more U.S. subs were patrolling the Arctic Ocean. He was certain of at least one Russian sub as well. He would welcome anyone's help.

Grayson paused; then, his face paled. "It's big, but it's definitely not metallic."

As if Grayson's words were an arrow made of ice, a sharp pain struck Will's heart, impaling him to the moment, an interminable, agonizing few seconds that sucked away his breath and with it, all hope. Only one thing would leave a sonar signature that large—big mama megalodon. She had escaped the cavern, escaped the nuclear blast, and was following them. If the megalodon possessed even the limited intelligence their behavior suggested, she would connect the fleeing *Sunfish* with the blast that had killed her brood. Now, she was the one bent on revenge. Even likely dying from radiation exposure, she would be capable of sinking them with little effort.

"Skipper?" Grayson stared at him with the headphones half off his head, concern marring his face.

"Kill the sonar. Now!" If the shark was not aware of exactly where they were, he did not want to offer her a signal to home in on. They could not escape her wrath. Even with both engines operating at peak efficiency, they could not outrun her. Less than a thousand rounds remained for the .50 calibers. Those and a few rifles would not be enough to bring her down. She was twice the size of the *Sunfish* and weighed two-hundred tons to the Sunfish's seventy-five tons. At eighteen feet high and twenty-two feet wide, her jaws could almost encompass the entire boat in her mouth. He had born witness to her attack on the *Amberjack*. He did not want his crew to go out in that ignoble and gruesome manner.

They had one chance, albeit a slim one at best. If they abandoned the *Sunfish* and struck out on foot across the ice, she might satisfy her rage on the boat and ignore the puny humans. On the other hand, she might assume they were walruses and eat them for a snack. It would be a cold run. Only the crew of the *Sunfish*, Asa, and Simon had cold weather gear of any kind, and that was parkas and hats. That left four extra sets to share among nine men, plus assorted blankets. Their clothing was only half-dry from the propane heat Simon had rigged in the galley. With temperatures barely above freezing midday and dropping well below zero at night, if rescue did not come soon, they would surely die of exposure. The nearest land was Wrangel Island over three-hundred miles to the west-northwest, a long hike under any circumstances. He felt a bit like Ernest Shackelford leaving the *Endurance* behind.

He did not ask for opinions or discussions. He was the officer in charge. The responsibility for success or failure fell on him. He would have no man share the blame if things went south.

To Grayson, he asked, "How long do we have?"

"At the speed it was making, I'd say half an hour or less."

"Apone, go get Asa. Tell him to get one engine running. Forget the other one."

"What's the plan, Skipper?" he asked.

"We're taking a hike on the ice. Get everyone prepared. Bring a .50 cal and all the ammo we can round up. Make sure everyone carries a weapon or survival gear."

"Aye, Skipper." He paused. "Then why the single engine?"

"To buy us some time. We'll set the rudder amidships and shove her off. Maybe the shark will follow the *Fish*."

Apone nodded. "I hate to see her go that way. She's a good boat."

"She'll be joining some good men."

A slight spasm rippled Apone's face. "Aye, there's that."

A few minutes later, everyone stood on deck. Apone had spread the word. Mismatched layers of clothing clung like scarecrow rags on the men, anything to stave off the bitter cold. Apone had handed out every pistol, each SCAR 5.56mm and MK58 7.62mm machinegun, and a 12-gauge shotgun Will kept aboard for sharks. Grayson shouldered the .50 caliber, and one of the ensigns from the *Utah* carried two ammo cans. Those without weapons carried boathooks, battle lanterns, or bags of food and water.

"Where's Apone?"

"Below deck with the engine," Asa answered. "The throttle keeps shutting down. He's wiring it open." The engine cranked, raced for a moment, and then settled down to a slow idle. Asa smiled. "I think he's got it."

"Everyone onto the ice. Keep moving northeast."

They all scrambled from the *Sunfish* onto the ice, slipping and sliding as they headed away from the edge. Everyone knew what was coming and wanted to place as much distance between them and the angry big mama megalodon as possible. Will waited for Apone, as Apone jumped down from the boat and grabbed the mooring line.

"I'll shove her off," he said.

As Will turned away to join the others, Apone took the mooring line, shoved the boat away from the floe, and leaped aboard as she drifted away.

"What the hell are you doing, Apone?" Will demanded. "Get your ass back here."

"I can't get her to idle faster unless I hold in the throttle by hand. At slow rev, she won't make a mile by the time the shark gets here. You said it yourself. It's a slim chance. I'll try to even the odds a bit."

"How?"

His face turned grim. "I'll ram the bitch if I get the chance." He held out a belt with four hand grenades. "When I do, I'll shove these babies down her fucking throat." He smiled. "Boom!"

"Don't do it, Apone," Will pleaded, but he knew it was useless.

"Sorry, Skipper. It's my life, my choice." He nodded to Grayson and Levitt, who both stood staring aghast at him. "Keep them safe."

He turned and disappeared below deck. A few seconds later, the single engine revved up, and the *Sunfish* began pulling away from the ice floe. Will stood there staring after her. He should have been the one to do the job, not Apone.

Grayson clasped his shoulder and squeezed. "Come on, Skipper," he said. "We need you."

Will nodded and fell in line behind the others. The sound of the engine gradually faded, leaving them walking in silence but for the steady crunch of boots on ice and the panting of exhaled breath. He was surprised when Asa stepped up beside him and walked with him. For a couple of minutes, he said nothing, but then he spoke, quietly so the others wouldn't hear him. What he had to say was for Will's ears alone.

"I didn't know. Apone said he could fix the throttle while I changed out of my wet clothes. I wouldn't have ... I would have ... told you." He groaned. "I should have been the one."

"No. No," Will replied. "My job, my responsibility. I'm the captain."

Asa looked at him with remorse in his eyes. "I've been a dick. I'm sorry. I focused my ire on you because you were an easy target. The megalodon didn't care if I was angry or not. You tried to make amends, but I shut you down. I'm not sure what I want. Part of me wants to survive, to get back at least part of the life I once had. I've wanted that for fifteen months. Another part, the one that seems to be becoming dominant, knows that's impossible. You're military, so you know. It's like PTSD. I can't control it; it controls me. Some days I make it through with no problem. Others, anything reminds me of what happened. All this," he jerked his head around to encompass everything around him, not just the ice upon which they trod, "just puts the icing on the cake." He paused, as if gathering courage for what he had to say next. "I don't expect to make it. If it comes down to a choice between saving someone, like Simon, or me, make it Simon. I'm a burned-out shell. I can't go on."

"Yes, you can," Will snapped. "You will. No more people die on my watch. No one."

He brushed past Asa and walked quickly to move ahead of the group. He was the leader. He would meet whatever they encountered head on. *No more people on my watch. Damn you, Apone.*

22

December 29, 2018, 7:10 a.m. *USS Sunfish–*
Apone had lied to his captain. Not a big lie, at least not in the grand scheme of things, but a lie nevertheless. He had managed to fix the throttle in a fashion. It was the first lie he could remember telling Will. He regretted his act of insubordination, but too many lives were at stake. Too many friends had died already. He didn't want to see more die. The crew of the *Utah* had suffered enough. Someone had to survive to tell their story; someone had to tell all the stories of heroism and foolishness, of terror and inspiration. Such tales were the lives of sailors, the litany of dead ships, dead crews, and captains—*Titanic, Lusitania, Arizona, Lexington, Thresher, Utah,* and countless others.

The one thing he had not lied about was his determination to kill the damn megalodon that had killed his friends. He stood at the throttle, pushing the single engine for every horsepower it could churn out heading directly for the shark. He had powered up the sonar and the blip aimed for the *Sunfish* like a giant gray arrow fired from a bow straight from the heart of hell. Four M67 fragmentation grenades lay on the console in front of him, duct taped around a box of magnesium signal flares. When the time came, he would pull all four pins and shove the package down the bitch's throat like a red hot, high-explosive cocktail, chasing it with a seventy-five-ton, cold steel aperitif.

The *Sunfish* limped along at fifteen knots; the megalodon raced toward her at thirty-five. One thing he had learned growing up on the streets in Secaucus, New Jersey—in a boxing match, size, weight, and reach went to the opponent. Heart played a role, but it was hard to trump physics. That's why he didn't fight by the rules.

His style was more WWE wrestling meets MMA cage fighting: kick, punch, slam, bite, and use anything handy to batter his opponent into submission. Anger helped, and he was mad enough at the shark to take the fight to her with righteous retribution.

He checked the sonar. She was rising from the depths to meet him, *spy-hopping*. He had read a book about sharks once on shore leave on a rainy day with nothing to do. Sharks fascinated him. He had dived around sharks many times—Makos, White tips, Tigers, Bulls, Hammerheads, even Great Whites—without fear. However, the megalodon racing to meet him was like a Great White on steroids with an attitude. He knew that sharks detected electrical impulses of their prey using a row of sensory organs called the Ampullae of Lorenzini. The sonar was blasting out an invitation to come take a bite.

"Eat this, bitch," he muttered, as he pushed the throttles forward and held them there, hoping for a few extra revolutions, a few more pounds of force to throw at the creature.

He saw the gray first dorsal fin break the surface three hundred yards out; then, the second smaller dorsal fin behind it. Both fins rose into the sky until he thought they would scrape the clouds. Then the head appeared, a conical snout and a jaw the size of a cargo bay door below it. The upper lobe of the caudal tail fin swished back and forth like a curious cat's tail, as it propelled the megalodon forward at great speed. He imagined its giant pectoral fins spread out just below the surface, acting like the diving planes of a WWII submarine, keeping it level and true.

If it had any fear of the *Sunfish*, the shark did not show it. Its course did not vary, nor its speed. He was close enough to see the creature's dead white eyes, sightless but still menacing. He raced to the bow of the boat with his deadly package, waiting. His gaze focused on a spot between the shark's eyes, painting an imaginary target on its forehead. Channeling all his rage and frustration at the shark, he willed it into her brain.

"If you can read my mind, bitch, you'll love this." He pulled the pins and clasped the package to his chest, counting down silently to his and the megalodon's deaths.

Then, to his horror, at twenty yards, the megalodon stopped swimming and dove beneath the surface. The tip of the dorsal fin looked like a ski ramp as he rammed it. With a bone-jarring thud, the *Sunfish* left the water, sailing like a flying fish for thirty feet. Apone fell backwards and slid into the bridge forward bulkhead. As it flew, the *Sunfish* rolled to port. Apone rolled with it. He tried to grab onto the 22mm minigun, but he would not release his package. One arm wasn't enough to stop his momentum. He disappeared over the side and came up sputtering seawater. The *Sunfish* landed on her port side, powered into the water, and sank from sight.

Without looking, Apone knew the megalodon was coming up from below for him. It wasn't the boat she was after; it was human flesh. He could do nothing. He waited, still counting down silently in his head. He felt the water rush up around him, smelled the stench of sulfur and decaying meat, just as his bomb exploded.

"Fuck you," was his last coherent thought.

23

December 29, 2018, 7:25 a.m.   An ice flow, Chukchi Sea, Antarctic Ocean–

Everyone stopped walking, and all heads turned toward the sound of the faraway explosion. Its echo reverberated across the surface for a dozen heartbeats before dying away.

"Do you think he killed it?" Asa asked. His heart vacillated between delight and despair. His nerves, raw from so many days of living on the edge with little sleep and no hope, tingled like high-voltage power lines singing in his head. He wanted to dance, to run, to laugh, or cry, anything to prove he was whole and alive, but uncertainty prevented him from such release.

Simon continued to stare toward the distant explosion. Asa could not read his expression, but he seemed subdued, perhaps reflective. After all, Apone had struck the blow he had wanted to deliver. "I don't know," he answered quietly. "I hope to God he did. It was a brave thing he did."

"It was foolish," Asa countered, but in his heart, he knew it had not been a fool's errand, at least not to Apone.

Simon nodded. "Maybe, but brave nonetheless."

One by one, they continued their march across the ice. Only the Sunfish's captain, remained standing, gazing back the way they had come. Asa understood Will's anguish. He considered it his duty to save his crew, not his crew's duty to save him. Apone had died for them all. Asa hoped it had not been for nothing.

They trudged in silence. No one spoke, but by their posture and the will with which they moved forward in spite of the cold and their misery, Asa knew they did not believe Apone had succeeded. They had all seen the gargantuan megalodon and did not believe a man with a small bomb could prevail against a thing that torpedoes, mines, missiles, and a nuclear bomb had failed to vanquish. Asa was of their mind. He could feel the megalodon's presence like a giant specter looming over the fifteen months of his life. The shark was still out there, and it was coming for them. *For me*, he thought, *to finish the job it started.*

An hour later, the shark still had not arrived. Asa began to believe he was wrong. Maybe Apone had delivered a lethal bellyache to the creature. He grasped at the thin sliver of hope like the shiny brass ring of a merry-go-round.

"I see something, Skipper," Levitt called out.

Asa's stomach clenched. "No," he moaned. "Is it the megalodon?"

Levitt laughed aloud. "No, it's a ship."

Asa followed the direction of Levitt's gaze. Sure enough, a large ship, an icebreaker approached from the northwest. It was too far away to see any markings or flag, but to Asa, it didn't matter. They were saved. Without a word, they all turned and trekked toward the ship, too eager to meet it to wait for it to come to them. The low rumble of steel grinding the thick ice to rubble reverberated through the ice, up through the soles of his boots, directly into his soul. If he had not been so exhausted, he would have laughed with joy.

At first, occupied with the approaching ship, now clearly a Russian icebreaker, he failed to notice the other sound, the high-pitched squeals from beneath the ice. Then, a hundred yards away the ice bowed and heaved, a ripple moving toward them. Shards of ice and a frozen cloud of ice dust rose above it. All eyes fixed on the movement.

"Scatter!" Will yelled out.

Limbs frozen with fear finally moved. Men ran in all directions. Asa dropped the bag of food he carried and grasped the boathook tightly. He glanced at the slim rod and felt a sense of impending doom. The boathook was too flimsy to fight off a hungry stray dog, much less a two-hundred-ton mega-shark. His speech to Will about believing he would not survive haunted him. He found he very much wanted to live, but the bitch shark was not making it easy. He turned away from the shark and faced the ship.

Simon did not run. He dropped the SCAR Mk 12 and began pulling something from the bag he carried slung over his shoulder. Asa shuddered in dumbfounded astonishment when he withdrew the injector arm assembly for the *Vanguard's* ROV. Asa had brought it aboard the *Sunfish* on a whim and had promptly forgotten about it. He had no idea Simon had added it to his load when they fled the *Sunfish*. The chef stood like a pudgy Pillsbury Doughboy, legs splayed slightly apart, with the injector aimed toward the shark, its deadly load of *saxitoxin* ready for delivery.

"My God, Simon," Asa yelled. "It's not enough. We estimated the dosage for a megalodon half this one's size."

Simon shook his head. "It doesn't matter."

Simon's acquiescence troubled Asa. He had thought the chef over his vendetta against the megalodon. "Don't be a hard-headed fool, Simon." He waved toward the Russian icebreaker, now just a hundred yards away. Men scrambled over her deck, many with weapons. Someone was lowering the ship's boarding gangway. Others threw ropes over the side. "Let's run for safety. We've both been through enough."

"You go, Asa. I'm too fat to run and too tired to care. It has to end here, now."

Asa pleaded. "No, Simon. Come with me. We'll do a bottle of *Bunnahabhain* together. I'll buy." He did not want to be a coward and leave his friend behind to face death alone—he had lost too many friends and acquaintances—but he found it difficult to summon the same kind of courage or rage that Simon had discovered within him. Asa's legs ached to run away. Only his friendship with Simon kept him from bolting blindly toward the Russian ship.

Others of the group had decided to make a stand as well. Grayson held the .50 caliber in both hands and peppered the ice ahead of the advancing ripple. With clenched jaw and deeply furrowed forehead, he held down the trigger, ignoring the danger. The bullets did not penetrate the four feet of solid ice, but he did not care. His intentions were not to kill the creature. Drawn by the sound, the vibrations in the ice, the rippled veered slightly toward him.

The three-foot-high wall of ice slammed into Grayson's leg and bowled him over. He spun one complete rotation and landed on his knees still holding the .50 cal. He reversed direction and continued to fire at the megalodon.

The icebreaker blew its horn, as the captain of the icebreaker attempted to draw the shark to him. The deep rumbling blast rolled across the ice like a clap of thunder. The megalodon did not take the bait. It turned and circled back toward the group of men on the ice. The ripple disappeared. Asa held his breath for what he knew was coming. The ice beneath Grayson bulged upward, and then erupted around him in an explosion of ice shards, as the megalodon broke through the floe. A shower of ice chunks and powdery ice dust sprayed Asa and Simon. Massive jaws closed around Grayson while he poured lead into its open mouth. Then the jaws snapped shut and the .50 caliber went silent. The shark landed on the ice with a thunderous thud, its massive body barely supported by it. Asa noticed the scars on its snout and that several of its two-foot-long teeth were missing, leaving blackened gaps in its pale gums. It still had enough teeth to slice through steel, and given time would replace the missing teeth from the rows of teeth beneath the missing ones. One blind eye dangled from its right socket. Apone's bomb had injured it, but had not stopped it.

The thin ice could not support the creature's massive weight. The ice cracked beneath it, sending cracks racing outward it like the rays of a star. One passed directly between Asa's legs, sending him scrambling to keep his footing. Will walked calmly past him toward the shark firing his 9mm pistol, his face a twisted mask of wrath. It would have been funny for the absurdity if not for the dire consequences the captain of the *Sunfish* faced.

"Asa!"

Asa looked to Simon. The plate of ice upon which he stood tilted upward with the shark on the low end and him perched on the upper end. His eyes went wide with panic, but as Asa watched, a change came over the chef. He squared his shoulders and held the injector arm ramrod stiff in front of him, as he slid inexorably toward the shark. Asa ran at the creature with the boathook, but couldn't reach it for the open water around it. Simon picked up speed, propelling himself forward to meet his fate. As he reached the megalodon's waiting open mouth, he jammed the injector into its snout and held on with both hands, as he held down the pressure valve, releasing the full supply of neurotoxin into the creature's bloodstream. Then, the shark swung him like a pendulum. Its jaws closed around Simon's upper torso and jerked its head, ripping Simon in half like a ripsaw through a board. Dead, he released his grip on the injector, and his upper body fell onto the ice amid a shower of blood.

"No!" Asa screamed and ran forward.

Will grabbed him and pulled him away from the edge of the ice as the megalodon thrashed around sending cracks all around it. He didn't know if the dosage was sufficient to kill such a behemoth, but the saxitoxin had begun to affect it. Asa relished its suffering as the potent neurotoxin rushed through the creature's bloodstream, the *saxitoxin dihydrochloride* binding with the sodium in the axon nerve cell membranes, paralyzing the creature.

Asa wanted to stand and watch its death throes, but Will shoved him toward the icebreaker, now stopped less than a hundred feet from them. Some of their group was already scrambling aboard up the gangway. Others clung to ropes as members of the Russian crew pulled them aboard. Voices in English and in Russian urged them to run to the icebreaker. Four Russians in heavy parkas rushed passed them. Each carried two harpoons with bundles attached. They surrounded the last megalodon and hurled their harpoons into its flesh; then rushed back to help him and Will up the gangway. He tried to protest. Harpoons would not kill it. They needed to hack it to pieces, burn the pieces, and scatter the ashes to the winds so that even its ghost could not return to haunt them.

As soon as they were on the gangway, the icebreaker reversed engines and began backing away from the shark.

"No!" he yelled, but no one paid him any heed.

He reached the deck and joined the crew of the icebreaker and the group they had rescued in watching the megalodon's death throes. The ship's captain stepped to the forward rail with a remote control switch in his hand. He pushed the button. Simultaneously, eight explosions blew holes in the megalodon's body. Sprays of blood turned the ice red. The shark did not stop thrashing, but its movements became sluggish as the neurotoxin took effect.

Mortally wounded by the explosions and paralyzed by the saxitoxin, it slipped into the water and sank out of sight, leaving a pool of blood on the surface that quickly began congealing in the cold, a telltale stain on the otherwise pristine white surface.

"It's over," Will said. His rage had left him with the shark's death. He stared at the spot where the megalodon had rested with clinical interest. "Simon's concoction worked. If it can't move, it can't breathe. If its wounds don't kill it, it will soon suffocate."

Asa stared at him, unable to say anything. The churn of emotions, a mixture of grief and relief, threatened to overwhelm him. He knew the creature was dead, but the vacuum its passing had left had yet to heal. It would take time for him to separate his emotions and deal with them. This time, he would not shove them away and try to forget them. He nodded.

The Russian captain approached them, a broad-shouldered elderly man with a graying beard and intense sea-blue eyes. He shoved a well-worn *Nagant* M1898 revolver into the waistband of his pants. "I am Captain Anastasiy Berezhnoy," he said in heavily accented English. "This is my ship, the *Prilagat' Usiliya*. Welcome aboard."

Will saluted him, and then reached out to shake his hand. "Captain Will Cobb, U.S. Navy, of the *USS Sunfish*. Your arrival was timely, sir."

Anastasiy frowned. "We intercepted your distress call. I did not reply because, frankly, I was not sure what to make of it." He rubbed his fingers along his cheek, scratching it lightly with the backs of his fingertips, and nodded. "Tensions are very high between our two countries at present. You have a fleet very near Russian territory. When we detected the nuclear explosion, my trepidation increased. However, in good conscience, I could not ignore a ship in distress. I proceeded cautiously." He glanced at the receding gap in the ice where the megalodon had died. "I hope that beast is the last one."

"The captain of the *Utah* gave his life and the lives of most of his crew to see to it. He wiped out that monster's brood. God willing, it is the last."

"Good. I have encountered these creatures before." He paused. "I wish to see them all dead."

Asa saw a hard glint in the Russian captain's eyes similar to the one in Simon's eye when he spoke about the megalodon. The creatures seemed to touch the lives of everyone who encountered them.

Russians sailors emerged from the superstructure bearing trays of coffee and bottles of vodka.

"My crewmen will escort your men below to change into warm clothing and provide something to warm their bellies."

Asa eyed the vodka, but didn't feel much like drinking. His heart was too heavy with grief to celebrate, and his mind had not yet fully grasped the fact that it was all over. He still stood at the edge of a precipice, staring into the black abyss of his life, but now he had the strength to take a step back.

Anastasiy handed glasses of vodka to Will and Asa and kept one for himself. Asa tried to refuse, but Will stopped him with a shake of his head. "Please join me in a toast to lost comrades. I saw what your men did. It was very brave. Your Navy trains its men well."

The words caught in Asa's throat, as he said, "One of them wasn't Navy. He was a chef."

Anastasiy arched an eyebrow and raised his glass. "Indeed. Then to comrades and chefs."

Asa could not refuse. He lifted his glass to his lips. "To Simon," he said as he sipped the liquor. The unfamiliar burn of the strong vodka almost choked him. He caught the Russian captain's quick grin.

Anastasiy downed his glass in one gulp and smacked his lips. "I will not interrogate you. You are my guests, but I would very much like to know what has happened. Your Navy helicopters will arrive in the area soon, and I will deliver you to them. I fear the story about what has happened here will not reach the public without many layers of truth and half-truths muddling the facts. It would be good to know."

"It's a long story," Will said. "Another round of vodka and some coffee, and I'll fill you in as best I can."

Anastasiy smiled. "Come then. I have a better brand of vodka in my quarters. Do either of you play Vint? No? Too bad. It is any easy game. I will teach you as we talk and drink." He turned to another officer. "Evgeni, please see to the Americans. We owe them much."

Evgeni Aleyev grinned and handed both Will and Asa cigarettes. "Real American tobacco," he said. To Asa's surprise, it was a Pall Mall. He returned the Russian's smile as he lit their cigarettes. Asa did not join them in the captain's quarters. The single shot of vodka had warmed his insides, and he did not want to hear the tale told again for their Russian host. He had lived it. He could add nothing of interest. The rest was personal, and he wasn't quite sure how to deal with that. He leaned against the rail to look back at the ice floe. He could no longer see the hole in the ice or the bloodstains, but he knew they were there, would always be there in his mind. He took a long drag off the cigarette, allowing the familiar taste to fill his mouth and lungs and the nicotine to calm his nerves. He felt like an addict after main-lining heroin. For a moment, he was simply a mechanic taking a break.

24

January 12, 2019, 11:00 a.m.   Bachelor Quarters, San Diego Naval Base–

To his surprise, Will did not face a court martial. Instead, the Navy gave him the command of a recently re-commissioned *Cyclone*-class patrol boat, the *USS Haboob*. The *Haboob* was twice the size as the *Sunfish* with a crew of twenty-four. Levitt joined him as his navigation chief, as did one of the older ensigns from the *Utah*. He wanted another Mark VI, but the Navy had studied his report and had decided to incorporate a few design changes. Another Mark VI wouldn't be available for a year.

He had escaped any blame in the nuclear explosion, but the country needed a scapegoat. The Russians demanded one. Captain Prescott offered the obvious choice. He was dead and could not tell his side of the story, and he had been the one to detonate the nuke. The Russians protested, but in the end, accepted the straw villain offered them. Will detested the Navy brass and the politicians for sullying a good man's name and honor, especially a black man's, but in the ranks, the real story made the rounds. Prescott would not be forgotten. The conflict created the opportunity for a new era of cooperation between Russia and the United States. Will hoped the politicians didn't screw it up but suspected they would find a way.

A hastily convened international expedition to the cavern site discovered that the *Utah's* blast had resealed the cavern by collapsing the tunnel. Any creatures surviving in the dark depths would remain there. The scientists, crypto-zoologists, marine biologists, and paleo-biologists had only a few hours of video from the SeaFox ROV's camera to witness the wonders now forever

hidden from them and sigh in regret. Will had no such regrets. He hoped the creatures never again saw the light of day.

The scientists did have the algal mat to study, with its mixed habitat of ancient creatures and newcomers. They would make their careful studies, take samples, and eventually find a way to destroy it, thereby erasing all traces of the primeval world impinging on the present.

He had heard from Asa once a few weeks after their rescue. Determined to get his life back on track, he had immediately taken a job on a drill boat in the South Pacific seeking warmer climates. Will doubted he would ever hear from the mechanic again, but he was glad Asa had survived relatively intact. He hoped everything worked out for him. Asa was obstinate, acerbic, and could be an ass at times, but he had kept the *Sunfish* going. That made him almost crew.

Will awoke some nights in a cold sweat from a nightmare he could thankfully barely recall. He hoped with time, they would fade. Already, it seemed like a bad dream. His mind could barely grasp the reality of giant megalodon. It instead wanted to shunt them into an area of his mind related to fairy tales and make believe. However, they would never completely fade. He would not allow that. He owed it to his dead crew to remember the megalodon feeding frenzy and the part they played in ending it. He prayed they had ended it.

CHECK OUT OTHER GREAT DEEP SEA THRILLERS

MEGA
by Jake Bible

There is something in the deep. Something large. Something hungry. Something prehistoric.
And Team Grendel must find it, fight it, and kill it.
Kinsey Thorne, the first female US Navy SEAL candidate has hit rock bottom. Having washed out of the Navy, she turned to every drink and drug she could get her hands on. Until her father and cousins, all ex-Navy SEALS themselves, offer her a way back into the life: as part of a private, elite combat Team being put together to find and hunt down an impossible monster in the Indian Ocean. Kinsey has a second chance, but can she live through it?

THE BLACK
by Paul E Cooley

Under 30,000 feet of water, the exploration rig Leaguer has discovered an oil field larger than Saudi Arabia, with oil so sweet and pure, nations would go to war for the rights to it. But as the team starts drilling exploration well after exploration well in their race to claim the sweet crude, a deep rumbling beneath the ocean floor shakes them all to their core. Something has been living in the oil and it's about to give birth to the greatest threat humanity has ever seen.

"The Black" is a techno/horror-thriller that puts the horror and action of movies such as Leviathan and The Thing right into readers' hands. Ocean exploration will never be the same."

CHECK OUT OTHER GREAT
DEEP SEA THRILLERS

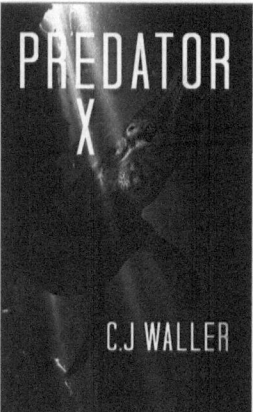

PREDATOR X
by C.J Waller

When deep level oil fracking uncovers a vast subterranean sea, a crack team of cavers and scientists are sent down to investigate. Upon their arrival, they disappear without a trace. A second team, including sedimentologist Dr Megan Stoker, are ordered to seek out Alpha Team and report back their findings. But Alpha team are nowhere to be found – instead, they are faced with something unexpected in the depths. Something ancient. Something huge. Something dangerous. Predator X

DEAD BAIT
by Tim Curran

A husband hell-bent on revenge hunts a Wereshark...A Russian mail order bride with a fishy secret...Crabs with a collective consciousness...A vampire who transforms into a Candiru...Zombie piranha...Bait that will have you crawling out of your skin and more. Drawing on horror, humor with a helping of dark fantasy and a touch of deviance, these 19 contemporary stories pay homage to the monsters that lurk in the murky waters of our imaginations. If you thought it was safe to go back in the water...Think Again!

CHECK OUT OTHER GREAT DEEP SEA THRILLERS

LAMPREYS
by Alan Spencer

A secret government tactical team is sent to perform a clean sweep of a private research installation. Horrible atrocities lurk within the abandoned corridors. Mutated sea creatures with insane killing abilities are waiting to suck the blood and meat from their prey.

Unemployed college professor Conrad Garfield is forced to assist and is soon separated from the team. Alone and afraid, Conrad must use his wits to battle mutated lampreys, infected scientists and go head-to-head with the biggest monstrosity of all.

Can Conrad survive, or will the deadly monsters suck the very life from his body?

DEEP DEVOTION
by M.C. Norris

Rising from the depths, a mind-bending monster unleashes a wave of terror across the American heartland. Kate Browning, a Kansas City EMT confronts her paralyzing fear of water when she traces the source of a deadly parasitic affliction to the Gulf of Mexico. Cooperating with a marine biologist, she travels to Florida in an effort to save the life of one very special patient, but the source of the epidemic happens to be the nest of a terrifying monster, one that last rose from the depths to annihilate the lost continent of Atlantis.

Leviathan, destroyer, devoted lifemate and parent, the abomination is not going to take the extermination of its brood well.

CHECK OUT OTHER GREAT
DEEP SEA THRILLERS

MEGATOOTH
by Viktor Zarkov

When the death rate of sperm whales rises dramatically, a well-respected environmental activist puts together a ragtag team to hit the high seas to investigate the matter. They suspect that the deaths are due to poachers and they are all driven by a need for justice.

Elsewhere, an experimental government vessel is enhancing deep sea mining equipment. They see one of these dead whales up close and personal...and are fairly certain that it wasn't poachers that killed it.

Both of these teams are about to discover that poachers are the least of their worries. There is something hunting the whales...

Something big
Something prehistoric.
Something terrifying.
MEGATOOTH!

BLOOD CRUISE
by Jake Bible

Ben Clow's plans are set. Drop off kids, pick up girlfriend, head to the marina, and hop on best friend's cruiser for a weekend of fun at sea. But Ben's happy plans are about to be changed by a tentacled horror that lurks beneath the waves.

International crime lords! Deep cover black ops agents! A ravenous, bloodsucking monster! A storm of evil and danger conspire to turn Ben Clow's vacation from a fun ocean getaway into a nightmare of a Blood Cruise!

www.ingramcontent.com/pod-product-compliance
Lightning Source LLC
Chambersburg PA
CBHW031954170626
46807CB00006B/2487